WHITE SPIDER

A BREED THRILLER

CAMERON CURTIS

INKUBATOR
BOOKS

Published by Inkubator Books
www.inkubatorbooks.com

ISBN (eBook): 978-1-83756-170-4
ISBN (Paperback): 978-1-83756-171-1

For Noa

Fire and Ice
By Robert Frost

Some say the world will end in fire,
Some say in ice
From what I've tasted of desire
I hold with those who favor fire

But if it had to perish twice,
I think I know enough of hate
To say that for destruction ice
Is also great
And would suffice

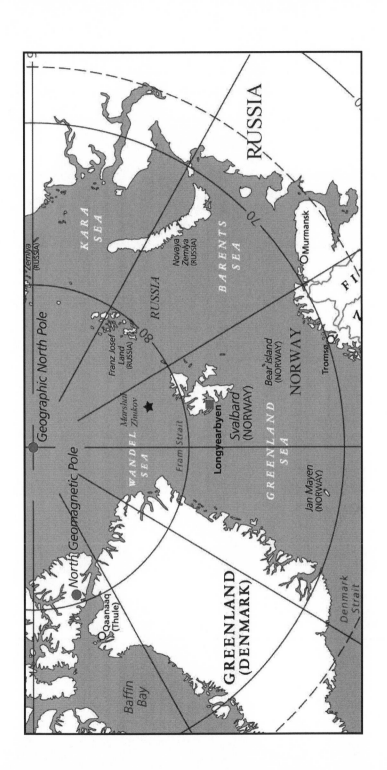

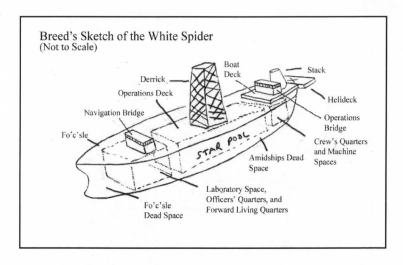

Breed's Sketch of the White Spider
(Not to Scale)

Boat Deck

Derrick

Stack

Operations Deck

Navigation Bridge

Helideck

Fo'c'sle

Operations Bridge

STAR POOL

Crew's Quarters and Machine Spaces

Amidships Dead Space

Laboratory Space, Officers' Quarters, and Forward Living Quarters

Fo'c'sle Dead Space

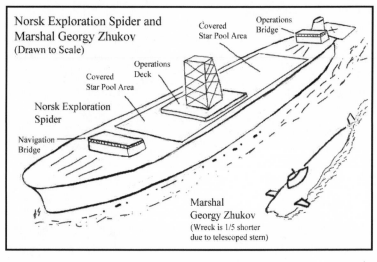

Norsk Exploration Spider and Marshal Georgy Zhukov
(Drawn to Scale)

Covered Star Pool Area

Operations Bridge

Operations Deck

Covered Star Pool Area

Norsk Exploration Spider

Navigation Bridge

Marshal Georgy Zhukov
(Wreck is 1/5 shorter due to telescoped stern)

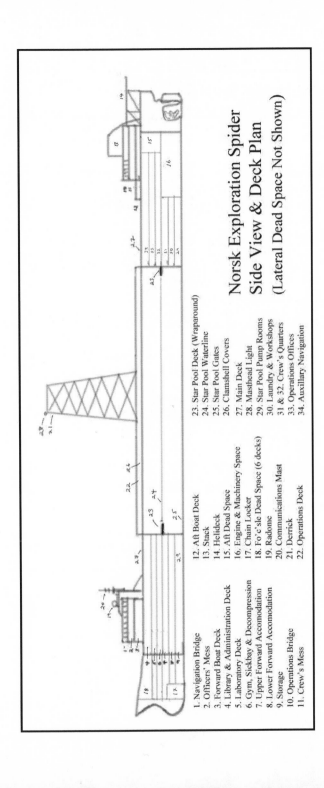

Norsk Exploration Spider
Side View & Deck Plan
(Lateral Dead Space Not Shown)

1. Navigation Bridge
2. Officers' Mess
3. Forward Boat Deck
4. Library & Administration Deck
5. Laboratory Deck
6. Gym, Sickbay & Decompression
7. Upper Forward Accomodation
8. Lower Forward Accomodation
9. Storage
10. Operations Bridge
11. Crew's Mess

12. Aft Boat Deck
13. Stack
14. Helideck
15. Aft Dead Space
16. Engine & Machinery Space
17. Chain Locker
18. Fo'c'sle Dead Space (6 decks)
19. Radome
20. Communications Mast
21. Derrick
22. Operations Deck

23. Star Pool Deck (Wraparound)
24. Star Pool Waterline
25. Star Pool Gates
26. Clamshell Covers
27. Main Deck
28. Masthead Light
29. Star Pool Pump Rooms
30. Laundry & Workshops
31. & 32. Crew's Quarters
33. Operations Offices
34. Auxillary Navigation

1

BURKINA FASO, SEVEN YEARS AGO - 2015

I tried to talk Paul Butler out of the mission. In the end,
the Green Beret captain talked me into helping him.
That's why I'm crawling on my belly across the
Burkina Faso desert. Slow is fast. Our progress is measured
in minutes per yard rather than yards per minute.

The new moon helps. The sky above is a blanket of stars,
but there is little light on the ground. Butler crawls along six
feet behind me. We've covered our belt buckles, sling
swivels, and anything that might rattle with black duct tape.

I squint through my NODs—Night Optical Devices—
and study the jihadi camp. Three pickup trucks stand
parked a quarter mile away. Their high silhouettes make
them easy to spot. I know from satellite photographs they
are arranged in a loose triangle. A tarp was spread between
their roofs during the day, a makeshift awning. It's been
rolled up and stowed.

Within the triangle are six men. Three Boko Haram
fighters and three hostages. The hostages are American jour-

nalist Benjamin Kagen, his son, and a third Caucasian yet to be identified. Four more insurgents stand watch in the desert, a hundred yards from the trucks. They form a square around the vehicles. During the day, they can see for over a mile in every direction. On a moonless night, they can see the vehicles and each other. They can see approaching vehicles and men on foot.

There's no way to take out the sentries without attracting attention. Our suppressed HK-416 rifles fire supersonic ammunition. You can't mask the supersonic crack of a bullet.

I stop, flip up my NODs, and scan the ground with thermal binoculars. Black-hot or white-hot. I thumb the selector into white-hot mode. The sky and desert are black and shades of gray. The sentries glow white from their body heat. I mark one man's position, and another guard two hundred yards behind him. Panning slowly right, I pick up the vehicles. Their metal skin retains heat more effectively than the ground. The trucks glow bright. Further to the right are two more sentries.

Butler and his team sergeant have joined on either side of me. I hand the thermals to Butler and lower my NODs.

Without a word, I crawl forward, and Butler follows me. The team sergeant and three men remain at Phase Line Bravo.

I'm America's only Tier I asset in West Africa. A former Delta Force operator, I'm on contract to the CIA's Ground Branch. A-Teams like Butler's are not specialists in hostage rescue or capture-kill missions. This mission is their unicorn moment. I can help them succeed.

The ground is flat, littered with short, scruffy bushes. I crawl through the scrub, the 416 cradled in my arms. The sandy earth, inches from my nose, smells of dust. I'm patient... Slow is fast.

Boko Haram fighters know their business. The camp was arranged to make it difficult for anyone to approach undetected. It's impossible during the day. You can't kill one sentry without the other three becoming immediately aware. My plan is to bypass the lookouts. Butler and I will slip *between* them and free the hostages. Only then will the team sergeant and our remaining men kill the sentries.

I stick my head up, peer left and right. Using binocular NODs is like looking through a pair of drinking straws. You have no peripheral vision. You have to turn your head to see one hundred eighty degrees. A monocular NOD fouls up your depth perception. Quad tubes offer a better view, but they're heavy and I hate them. We make do.

The sentries are behind us. The vehicles are less than a hundred yards away. I resist the temptation to hurry. Force myself to tuck my head and advance at a measured, deliberate pace.

Chins on the ground, Butler and I look underneath the vehicles. We can see the forms of sleeping men. They lie inside the triangle, covered with thin blankets. One man sleeps behind the wheel of a Land Cruiser.

I'm nervous because Butler and I have never worked together. The strength of a Tier I unit lies in its continuity. In Afghanistan, my team and I knew each other's thoughts. We moved like one animal because we had worked together so long. Butler is a competent Green Beret, but he remains an unknown quantity.

I point to the man in the Land Cruiser. Butler nods. He will leave the two jihadis sleeping inside the triangle to me. I still cannot distinguish them from the three hostages. Five men, two targets. A discrimination problem.

The targets will be armed, and they will lie apart from the hostages. I rise to my feet, present my rifle. My left thumb and forefinger "C-clamp" the foregrip. In CQB—Close Quarters Battle—my thumb is my favorite gunsight. When I hold a handgun in an isosceles grip, I point my thumbs at the target and blaze away. I treat a rifle the same. Butt to my shoulder, left thumb over the forestock, controlling the muzzle. My thumb drives the rifle onto the target before I line up my sights.

I step through the perimeter of vehicles. Pass between the Land Cruiser and a Hilux. The man in the Land Cruiser is oblivious.

When I was lying prone, the sleeping forms looked jumbled up. Looking down on them, I see three are sleeping in a row. The other two lie ten feet away, next to the third vehicle. Through the green glow of night vision, I see two AK-47s. One is leaning against the pickup. The other is on the ground next to a sleeping jihadi. His hand is on the pistol grip.

Speed, surprise and violence of action.

I take a breath and punch the clock.

The man sleeping with his hand on the rifle is the first to go. I shoot him three times in the head. Turn thirty degrees in one motion. The second man sits up, reaches for his weapon. I shoot him twice in the chest. Blood sprays from the exit wounds and splatters the side of the vehicle. It looks black in the night vision. The man slumps against the driver's door.

Supersonic rounds crack behind me and punch through the windshield of the Land Cruiser. Butler has executed the third man. I take a step closer to my own target, point the 416 at his face, shoot him in the bridge of the nose. His head bounces once against the side of the pickup and he slumps to the ground.

More shooting outside the camp. Butler's team is dispatching the sentries. I keep my weapon on the men I've killed. Bend down, separate them from their weapon systems. Check again. They're dead.

Turn to Butler. He jerks the Land Cruiser door open. Reaches in, grabs the dead man by the arm, drags the corpse from the vehicle.

Only seconds have passed. The hostages are sitting up. They're staring at me, eyes wide in my night vision. "Kagen," I say. "Stay down."

There is still shooting outside the vehicular triangle. I hear 416s firing, followed by the hammer of an AK-47. A stray round could kill a hostage, upset the mission.

I recognize the older Kagen in my NODs. Push him in the chest, knock him down. I kneel on him, turn to his son. Grab the boy by the shoulders, push him flat next to his father. "Stay there."

The third hostage, an older man of about sixty, needs no urging. He flattens himself on the ground, stares at me with frightened eyes.

"Who are you?" I ask. *"Qui etes vous?"*

"Reynaud," the man says. "Michel Reynaud. I speak English."

"Stay down."

The shooting has stopped. Butler's squad radio crackles. "Two-two Actual, this is Two-two Zulu."

"Go ahead, Two-two Zulu."

Butler's team sergeant's voice is clipped. "Sentries neutralized."

"Leave two men outside. Get Echo in here."

"Roger that."

I straighten, look down at the hostages. "Stay where you are. We'll have you out of here in no time."

The team sergeant and 18-Echo join us inside the triangle of pickups. The Echo is Butler's communications sergeant. He's carrying the team's ManPack, a portable High Frequency transmitter.

"Contact C2," Butler says. "Get the bird in here."

C2 is Butler's command and control. The B-Team in Ouagadougou. The United States doesn't have enough resources in West Africa to mount our own exfil. We're relying on the French Army in Mali to provide helo extraction.

We've done well so far, but nothing about this mission is right. In fact, nothing about Butler's deployment is right. That's why I tried to talk him out of it.

To the United States, Burkina Faso is a backwater. West Africa is France's backyard. America wants to keep its finger on the pulse, so it scatters a few Special Forces A-Teams across the region. They call it a light footprint. That means no dedicated aviation support, no Tier I assets, and nothing heavier than small arms. The vehicles supplied to the A-Teams are lightweight. Butler's team roll around in Toyota Hilux pickups, the same kind Boko Haram use. In this part of the world, the vehicles all look alike. Except Boko Haram units also have M113 armored personnel carriers captured from the military. In many respects, Boko Haram is better equipped than we are.

Reliance on the French for aviation assets is a major

problem. Butler's 18-Delta medical sergeant told me CASEVAC from field to hospital would take three hours. From what I've seen, it'll take six. Both figures are way outside the Magic Hour we worked to in Afghanistan. Simply put, if you can get a wounded man from the field to a modern hospital in one hour, his chances of survival go up exponentially.

That's why I told Butler he should let the SEALs have the mission. He wouldn't hear of it. Paul Butler wanted the hostage rescue for his A-Team. He wanted to give them this chance to do the very thing they had joined the Army to do.

In the six months I've known him, I've grown to like Paul Butler. He's badass and aggressive, but he's not too proud to ask for help. I couldn't let him go on the mission when I could contribute my experience. We looked through the intel together, and I helped formulate the plan.

The kidnappers moved Kagen and his son around every day. I rallied the intelligence sergeants from every A-Team in the region. Got them working their sources, following all their leads. I got mobile service providers to set up their equipment so Kagen's phone could only call his wife's number. We had a hostage negotiator waiting. The kidnappers asked for forty-five million dollars. Our negotiator stalled while we tracked the phone.

The kidnappers were moving the Kagens north-by-east toward the tri-border with Mali and Niger. They were moving deeper into the Sahel. The Sahel is a wide band of land that stretches from coast to coast. It's a belt that separates the Sahara Desert from Central Africa. Most of it is an arid, dusty wilderness. It would not be long before we lost the ability to track them.

Yesterday, we tracked the group to a location east of

Silgadji, just inside the tri-border. Satellite intel suggested they were about to cross into Niger. There, they would rendezvous with a large Boko Haram unit. The kind with armor and .50-caliber machine guns. We had to move fast.

Butler and I decided to split his A-Team. He and I would take the team sergeant and three men. The remaining seven would wait in Silgadji under his warrant officer. We'd go in three Toyota Hilux pickups, take three Burkina Faso commandos along as drivers. They would drive us to Phase Line Alpha, two miles from the insurgent camp. They would remain with the vehicles while our six Americans proceeded on foot. At Phase Line Bravo, we'd leave the team sergeant and three shooters. Butler and I would enter the camp together.

Before we mounted up, I heard Butler telephone his wife. He got voicemail. "Hi, hon," he said. "I just wanted to hear your voice. I'll call you tonight, hon. Love you."

THE SUN IS low in the sky. Flies are buzzing around the bodies of the dead insurgents. The Echo keys the HF microphone. "Six-four Echo from Two-two Echo. What's the word on our ride, over."

"Two-two Echo, the French have a TIC across the Mali border. They're in heavy contact and their gunships have been diverted."

"Six-four, we are not in contact. Get them to send our bus."

"Negative, Two-two. The French will not send your bird without gunship escort."

"Roger that, Six-four. Keep us informed. Two-two, out."

Butler and I exchange glances. The French have a TIC—

Troops In Contact—in Mali. A heavy engagement, and they have diverted their helo gunships to support the infantry. It's standard procedure to send gunships to escort troop-carrying helos. The French are refusing to send our extraction helo without escort.

Without dedicated aviation resources, we're stuck. In Afghanistan, we had the 160th Special Operations Aviation Regiment—the Nightstalkers—to support us. Those pilots were badass. They would go anywhere. In a gunfight, when no one else raised their hands, the Nightstalkers would go. With or without gunship support.

"Two-two Echo from Six-four Fox," the radio crackles.

"Two-two Echo. Go ahead."

"Let me speak with your Actual, over."

Six-four Fox is the B-Team's intelligence officer. The hairs stand on the back of my neck.

Butler takes the microphone. "Two-two Actual. Go ahead."

"We have eyes on a large force moving your way from the east. Technicals and an APC. Estimate strength fifty."

He's referring to drone intelligence. Technicals are pickup trucks with heavy weapons mounted on their cargo beds. Everything from machine guns to 20mm cannon or recoilless rifles. They are usually unarmored, or fitted with makeshift plates. The APC—Armored Personnel Carrier—is bad news. Probably an American-built M113 captured from the Army. Fifty men is a large force for Boko Haram to field.

"How far?"

"Fifteen clicks. Recommend you exfil by truck."

"Understood. Two-two Actual, out."

Butler hands the microphone back to the communications sergeant. "Okay, bring in the trucks."

Our Burkina Faso commandos are waiting with the pickups at Phase Line Alpha. They were meant to return to Silgadji once the French helicopters extracted us. Now, they have to take us home.

"Those dicks were meant to rendezvous further east," Butler says. "What happened?"

I scan the horizon for signs of a dust cloud. Squinting into the rising sun, I see nothing. "We've been sitting here for hours. These guys we schwacked missed the RV, missed a radio check."

"So we drive home," Butler says. "No factor."

No factor. A radio operator's dismissive expression for *not a concern.* Butler is putting on a brave face, but the problems with the mission are mounting.

"What's the word on our SEAL backup?" I ask.

"They arrived in Silgadji after we left. Their orders were to establish blocking positions south and west."

Another result of rushed execution. If I had my way, Butler's team and the SEALs would have sat down with the Burkina Faso commandos and French pilots ahead of time. You always want everybody to know everybody else on sight. AFRICOM made us go, drop of a hat. The briefing didn't happen.

"We might need them for cover. Best get in touch, tell them we're going to exfil by truck."

"Is anyone coming for us?" Kagen asks.

The journalist looks gaunt, much older than his fifty-five years. Mussed hair, unshaven jaw, dirty clothes. His son looks like any other sixteen-year-old would in this situation. Skinny, confused, and twice as scared as his old man.

"Our trucks will be here in a few minutes," I tell him. "We'll drive back to Silgadji."

Reynaud, who we've learned is a French doctor for *Medicines Sans Frontiers*, stares at one of the dead bodies. It's already going ripe in the mounting heat. The Frenchman has been held captive longer than the Kagens. He looks numb, like he's ready to accept whatever happens to him.

The comms sergeant looks up from the radio. "Can't raise the SEALs, sir."

Butler plants his hands on his hips. "What the fuck is this, Robin Sage?"

Robin Sage is a Special Forces war game. Special Forces teams conduct simulated missions. The exercise is a massive event tree where one can never make a perfect decision. The training cadre always have a curve ball to throw at you.

Like comms going down.

The team sergeant walks into the triangle. "Trucks are here."

Butler turns to the comms sergeant. "Advise C2 we are exfiling. Have them inform the SEALs."

We climb into our Toyotas. Butler and I get in the middle vehicle with the Kagens. Butler rides in front. I sit behind him, and Kagen sits behind the driver. The boy sits between us. I jam my rifle between my right knee and the door. If I leave the vehicle, my rifle goes with me.

The team sergeant rides in the front of the lead vehicle with two of our men in back. The comms sergeant and Reynaud get in the third pickup.

Butler speaks into his squad radio. "Let's go."

The Toyotas race across the desert. The road is distinguishable from the barren landscape only by the absence of scrub. In the distance, I see a line of low hills to the south. I remember passing this way. To our right is a shallow wadi—a dry riverbed. We're roasting along at fifty miles an hour. With any luck, we'll get to Silgadji in time for lunch.

I reach forward, tap Butler on the shoulder. "Let's increase separation."

"Why?"

"We're eating too much dust."

We aren't, as a matter of fact, but wider separation makes us harder targets. I'm reluctant to voice my misgivings. Butler gives the order. The lead vehicle maintains speed, and we drop back. The trailing vehicle allows space to open up between us.

I don't like the look of the hills. To a soldier, they're the only elevated position for miles. The only road to Silgadji passes between them and the wadi. That makes those hills the perfect place to stage an ambush. Last night, before leaving, I had C2 overfly them with a drone to make certain they were unoccupied.

Butler keys his squad radio. "Two-two Echo, this is Actual. Any word on those SEALs?"

"Negative, Actual. Have advised C2 our exfil."

"Okay. Keep trying."

What a clusterfuck. Can't wait for this to be over. If we get the Kagens to Silgadji, everything will be fine. Mission accomplished, beers and cheers. I lay my hand on the grip of my 416.

From a couple of miles away, the hills looked motionless. As we approach, they appear to grow larger in the windshield, then sweep to our left as we drive by. They're about six hundred yards south. I look to my right. The desert stretches for almost twenty miles in the direction of Mali. The bank of the wadi is fifteen yards away.

Out of the corner of my eye, I see a flash of light. Painful, it's like the sun glaring off chrome. I jerk my head in time to see the lead vehicle explode. The interior of the cab blazes with orange fire. Jets of thick black smoke squirt from the windows on either side. The pickup fishtails, flips over, and rolls on the road, scattering metal debris.

"Around," Butler yells. "Go around!"

Our driver instinctively steps on the brakes. Wrong move. Butler's not wearing a seat belt and he's thrown against the dash. My lap belt holds, but I'm not wearing a shoulder belt. I slam into the back of Butler's seat.

The side windows on the driver's side explode. Blood sprays from the driver and Kagen. Splatters Butler and Kagen's son. The driver and Kagen jerk in their seats. My ears ring with metallic hammer blows as bullets penetrate the doors and side panels. The driver slumps and the truck slows to a stop.

I release my lap belt and throw my door open. Spill out, fall on my rifle. Rise to one knee, grab the boy by his arm. He's sobbing. I haul him across the bench seat and throw him to the ground.

The air is filled with the sound of rifle and machine gun fire. I reach in, grab Kagen. Drag his inert body out of the truck. Brain matter is spilling out the side of his head. Fragments of his skull are held together by skin and connective tissue. One round hit him in the neck and there's blood on his shirt. He was drilled in the torso by bullets slashing through the passenger door.

Butler's out of the truck. He slams his passenger door shut, crawls behind the engine. The block is the only truly bulletproof part of an unarmored vehicle. Bullets rake the Toyota, punch right through one side and out the other. I haul the boy over his father's lifeless body, shove him up against the right rear wheel and lean against him. Axles are bulletproof too, but they're skinny. The wheel rims are better.

Cool, calm and collected, Butler speaks into his squad radio. "Two-two Echo, this is Actual."

The trailing vehicle has stopped thirty feet behind us. Incredibly, its three occupants are alive, huddled behind the vehicle on the passenger side. "Go ahead, Actual."

"Get away from the vehicle," Butler says. "Into the wadi."

The comms sergeant grabs Reynaud, drags him to the bank of the wadi, and they roll behind cover. The driver follows them. I look past Butler. The lead pickup, a blazing inferno, lies on its side. None of its occupants survived.

"Go," Butler says.

The boy won't leave his father's body. He screams, "Dad!" I push him ahead of me.

You *know* when someone is shooting at you. One hundred percent. It's not something you learn, it's something you *experience*. You hear a bullet going one way, a bullet going the other way. They sound different, you ignore them. When a round comes right at you, it *snaps*. That *snap* stays with you forever.

Butler keeps his head down. He raises his 416 above his head, over the hood, and unloads in the general direction of the hills. Without aiming, he moves the muzzle in a circle, spraying rounds. It's a futile gesture. The effective range of 416 ammunition is four hundred yards. The enemy is out of reach.

I shove the kid over the bank of the wadi and roll on top of him. He's still sobbing. There's another flash and the trailing vehicle explodes. I risk a glance over the berm. All I can see are muzzle flashes winking from the hills. Fireflies here, fireflies there. Bullets rake the vehicle and smack the ground inches from my face. I duck, hold my rifle over my head, open fire.

Butler scrambles into the wadi next to us.

Only two or three minutes have passed since the first rocket struck. I fight to orient myself. Butler grabs his squad radio. "Two-two Echo," he says. "Report TIC, call for air support. I want those hills *wasted*."

The French are hours away. Good luck with that.

The sound weapons make is distinctive. AK-47s pound like hammers. The cracks of M-4s and HK-416s are high-pitched. You can always tell them apart.

Butler changes out his mags, sticks his rifle up, dumps another thirty rounds. I do the same, force myself to think.

The rounds fired at us are more powerful than those of HK-416s and AK-47s. They're not assault rifle rounds. They're like .308s from rifles and machine guns firing the same ammunition. The bullets are falling all around us.

From an elevated position, at this range, the machine guns shoot in arcs. They're dropping the rounds on us from almost directly above. We're in the beaten ground—the berm offers no cover from plunging fire. I watch bullets fall into the stream bed around me. *Splat...* three feet away. *Splat...* two feet away. *Splat...* six inches from my boot. The fuckers have us dialed in.

Please God, I don't want to die.

Butler screams, drops his rifle. A bullet has hit his right hand. It looks like he's lost one finger, and another is dangling by a strip of skin. I empty my third mag over the top of the berm. Butler picks up his rifle, tries to fire it one-handed.

Splat.

Blood spurts from Butler's collar. A machine gun round fell on him from above, drilled him between his front and back plates. He slumps onto his face.

I crawl to Butler and roll him over. His eyes are sightless. I've seen that look too many times. It's the look that remains when the soul leaves a once animated body. The look of an empty shell.

We're all going to die.

Protect the objective. I drag Butler's body, use it to cover the boy. "Stay there."

I lie flat on my belly. There's a *smack* and the breath explodes from my chest with an awful grunt. I feel like someone has brought a sledgehammer down between my shoulder blades. A round has struck my back plate.

Splat. Another round buries itself in the dirt inches from my nose. I blink dust from my eyes. Fight for breath and spit. I cradle my rifle, crawl to the comms sergeant.

The driver of the trailing pickup is firing his rifle over his head. The comms sergeant is yelling into the HF radio's microphone. "They're engaging us! Check fire! Check fire!"

The sergeant's words are a shock. "Tell me."

"C2 says the SEALs are in contact with an enemy column."

The Boko Haram column is twelve miles away. The SEALs are firing on us. We are sitting on the X, victims of a blue-on-blue clusterfuck.

"Son of a bitch." I reach across the sergeant, slap the commando's shoulder. "Cease fire."

The shooting stops as quickly as it began.

"C2, C2. We have taken heavy casualties. Five... no, seven KIA."

The radio crackles. "SEALs withdrawing to the south. Are your vehicles drivable?"

I look around. The engagement couldn't have lasted more than five minutes. Gunfights are like that. Once one person shoots, everybody unloads. People die all over the place before you can say *cease fire*.

The Boko Haram unit is coming fast. We can't afford to wait for help. The SEALs should come down, but they know there's going to be an investigation. The last thing they want to do is join us for a chat. No, they'll hightail it home, huddle and get their stories straight.

I get to my feet and step back onto the road. What a devastated piece of territory. The lead and trailing pickups are burning fiercely. Thick plumes of oily black smoke curl into the sky. Boko Haram will know exactly where we are.

Our remaining vehicle has been riddled with rifle and machine gun fire, but looks drivable. Kagen's body lies next to it. The commando is slumped in the driver's compartment. I haul his body from behind the wheel and climb in. The cab is an abattoir. The rear passenger bench is stained with Kagen's blood. Shattered glass, brain tissue and bits of skull litter the upholstery. One piece, like cracked ceramic covered by scalp, still has hair on it. I toss it out the window.

I get the engine running and climb out. The comms sergeant, the remaining commando, and Reynaud are on their feet. The Kagen boy is catatonic.

We'll lay the bodies of Kagen and Butler on the cargo bed. Carry them back to Silgadji.

Rage will come later. Right now, I'm happy to be alive.

. . .

THE CIA STATION chief glares at me from behind his desk.
We're in his air-conditioned office in Ouagadougou. It's on
the third floor of the American Mission. The offices of the
US Military Assistance Group are on the second floor.
Civilian aid occupies the first. The station chief's back
windows overlook the city streets, while the interior wall is
glassed-in. The people in the bull pen are trying to look
busy, but they're straining to hear.

"Breed, you were *not* there."

"The hell I *wasn't*."

The air conditioner is an old unit, mounted in a window.
Its fan clatters like the machine is on life support. The office
is cool, but the station chief is sweating. His salt-and-pepper
hair looks damp and drops are running down the sides of his
face. The collar of his white, short-sleeved dress shirt has
gone two-toned. White, and an ugly wet gray.

"Paul Butler's detachment was ambushed by Boko
Haram. It's a tragedy, but that's what happened."

"Bullshit. Ben Kagen is dead, along with four Green
Berets. You can't sweep that under the rug."

"We're doing nothing of the sort. None of you saw your
attackers. The engagement lasted seven minutes. Lieutenant
Stefan Knauss's SEALs pursued your ambushers, but lost
track of them in the desert."

"Knauss."

I remember Navy Lieutenant Stefan Knauss from
Afghanistan. In the mountains and valleys of the Hindu
Kush, he had a nickname. Robo-SEAL. A reference to the
movie about a cyborg cop who lit up anything that moved.
Knauss had one interest—body count. I think he just
enjoyed killing. He once led a raid to capture a High Value
Target. Beat the man to death with a brick.

Knauss's victim was not a loss to humanity, but the information he carried was.

"That's *Lieutenant* Knauss to you, Breed."

"Kagen's boy was there. So was Butler's 18-Echo."

"The boy's so fucked up he barely remembers his name." The station chief rises to his feet and plants his fists on his desk. "The Echo will be decorated. He'll say whatever we want him to say."

"To Butler's wife?"

I remember Paul Butler's last phone call, the message he left on his wife's voicemail.

"To whomever we tell him. You think America is ready to watch this incident dissected on prime time news? Nobody wants to hear about a friendly fire incident that cost us four Green Berets *and* an American hostage."

"Knauss fucked up. The Boko Haram unit was fifty men in technicals and APCs. The trigger-happy son of a bitch lit up three Toyotas full of Americans."

"That's what *you* think. *We* think Paul Butler neglected to exercise due caution around a high risk terrain feature."

I suck a breath. "You're going to hang this on Butler."

"*Someone's* got to wear it, Breed. Like I said, you're a ghost. *You* weren't there."

"A dead man. You're going to blame a dead man. Stick his family with it the rest of their lives. How do you people live with yourselves?"

"Get off your high horse, Breed. Paul Butler's nothing to you." The station chief takes a breath, sits down. "AFRICOM and the Company want you out of this. Consider yourself lucky."

There's nothing left to say. I leave the station chief's office, cross the bull pen, and go downstairs.

Was Paul Butler nothing to me? I'd known him six months. Long enough to know he was a good guy, with the kind of life I often wish I had.

I'll call you tonight, hon. Love you.

The elevator doors suck open. I cross the lobby, push through the front doors, and step into hundred-degree heat. Ouagadougou tries to look modern, but it's constrained by the arid Sahel. The downtown avenue is broad, with a wide concrete divider. The divider has been adorned with what pass for graceful streetlamps, alternating with tired, stunted trees. The buildings on either side are adobe-colored or whitewashed. Few are taller than ten stories, most top out at four.

Butler's warrant officer and two sergeants are sitting in a Humvee, waiting to take me back to the barracks.

"Breed," the warrant officer says.

"You're not supposed to talk to me."

The man shrugs. "We've been told not to speak with anyone while the incident is under investigation. What's said between us stays between us."

I prop my rifle against the Humvee's bench seat. The upholstery is scorching hot from the sun. The vehicle smells of hot oil and synthetic upholstery. I shrug off my body armor, spread the plate carrier to sit on. There's a cavity where my back plate stopped a bullet. I'll carry the bruise for a week. "Not much to say. The head shed wants me out of the country. You'll be given a story to tell."

"Everyone knows what happened."

Bitterness rises from my stomach. I can control rage, but there are times it feels good to let go. It can be a treat to feed off your emotions.

"Everyone's memory is faulty," I say. "Repairs will be necessary for career progression."

I look over the warrant officer's shoulder and my jaw tightens. Across the parking lot, half a dozen SEALs are lounging around a Humvee. Chocolate chip camouflage, plate carriers, baseball caps. They're all bearded, burned dark by the sun. They look like they just got off a plane from Kandahar.

The SEALs carry 7.62mm SCAR-Heavy battle rifles and M-240 general purpose machine guns. Those weapons have an effective range of a thousand yards. They were adopted specifically for desert combat. Those are the weapons the SEALs turned on us in the wadi.

"What the fuck are they doing here?"

The warrant officer is as unhappy as I am. "Same thing we are. Getting orders from the head shed."

One of the SEALs stands out. A giant, he's six-five, maybe two-thirty. He wears his ball cap backwards over shoulder-length red hair. That broad shovel of a beard almost reaches his chest. Sleeves rolled up, his brawny forearms and thick wrists are covered with tattoos. He carries a SIG P226 in a drop-leg holster and a SCAR-H on a one-point sling.

Robo-SEAL.

Blood pounds in my temples. I clench my jaw and stride across the parking lot.

"Breed," the warrant officer calls. "Wait."

Knauss raises his SCAR-H. Points it at my belly. With my right hand, I sweep the muzzle aside. Chop him under the nose with the edge of my left. Blood spurts from his nostrils. I throw an arm bar on him, lock his elbow, bear him to the ground. Our combined weight pins his weapon. I kneel on his tricep and heave. Knauss's arm snaps like a tree branch. The detonation can be heard across the parking lot.

Knauss shrieks.

The warrant officer grabs me from behind and hauls me away. Knauss's men are on their feet, weapons leveled. Butler's two sergeants have their 416s pointed at the SEALs.

"Motherfucker," Knauss groans. "You're dead."

"Not before you."

2

PRESENT DAY - THURSDAY, 1900 HOURS - NARVIK

The interior of the Scandic Hotel in Narvik, on the north coast of Norway, is impressive. The exterior, less so. It's October, and the sun is setting early. The days will only get shorter from here, and the old iron ore port lies hushed under a carpet of snow.

Stein booked me one of the best suites in the hotel. The Scandic looks like a cylindrical telecom tower, and I'm on the top floor, with a view of the port. I'm sure it's not as fancy as the rooms she's used to sleeping in, but it beats the heck out of wooden cots in Afghanistan. This room has a bathroom and everything. In Kunar, we used to piss in empty Coke and Bourbon bottles so we wouldn't have to get up and go to the john.

I drop my duffel next to the closet and hang up my winter jacket. Underneath, I'm wearing jeans, a long-sleeved sport shirt, and a wool sweater. It's a couple of degrees above freezing outside, but the temperature will drop quickly during the night.

Stein is expecting me downstairs in half an hour.

Boosted by a tailwind, a C-17 Globemaster flew me from Joint Base Andrews to Evenes Air Station in record time. Two airmen met me in a Royal Norwegian Air Force sedan and drove me into town. They spoke English and told me they had instructions to escort me to my hotel.

Five minutes early is on time. I step outside, lock the door behind me, go downstairs.

The restaurant looks like it caters to monied executives. The waiter leads me to a corridor on the other side of the floor. The boy ushers me into a plush conference room. Modern, with a wall-sized audiovisual display. The paneling is modern, light-colored wood, the table a shade darker. The leather chairs are deep and comfortable. They swivel and recline. There's a well-stocked bar at the back.

"May I offer you a drink, sir?"

"Bourbon, neat. Thank you."

The waiter pours me two fingers in a whisky glass. Raises an eyebrow. I nod and he pours one finger more, sets the glass in front of me. "You're early, sir. Ms Stein will be along shortly."

I lower myself into a chair and stretch. C-17s are great for sleeping, and I'm well rested. Throw your inflatable mattress on top of a well-secured crate, pull a wide cargo strap around yourself, and close your eyes. Wake up seven hours later fresh as a daisy.

The door opens and Stein steps into the room. The CIA's Deputy Director of Special Situations is exactly as I remember her. Mid-thirties, tall and slender, with straight dark hair. She's wearing her signature knee-length black skirt and black suit jacket. Her shoes are low-heeled and sensible. An expensive leather briefcase dangles from two fingers of her elegant left hand.

Stein's suit jacket has been tailored to conceal a SIG P226 Legion clipped in a cross-draw holster. Always a field operative at heart, she's risen quickly at the agency.

"Breed." She smiles when she sees me.

I'm not prepared for the man who enters behind her. I thought Stein was coming alone. He's older, in his fifties. Five-eleven, wearing an expensive dark suit and a blue dress shirt open at the collar. Cupid lips set in a craggy face framed by a five-hundred-dollar haircut.

"It's good to see you, Stein."

Stein shakes my hand and introduces me to her companion. "This is Nathan Conrad."

The man's grip is firm, but his hand is soft. "Breed, Anya's told me a great deal about you."

I say nothing.

"I thought we might have a working dinner," Stein says briskly. "Breed, I've ordered for us. Are you still good with steak?"

"Steak works for me."

Stein sits at the head of the conference table. Conrad and I sit across from each other on either side. With swift, economical movements, Stein unzips her briefcase and takes out a compact laptop and an inch-thick folder. She boots up the laptop, frowns at the screen, and hooks up an agency VPN. Satisfied, she connects the machine to a USB bank in the table.

"Direct connection to AV," Stein explains. "Tougher to hack."

The audiovisual screen against the far wall comes to life. Displays an image of Stein's wallpaper, an artsy soft-focus photo of ballerinas.

There's a knock on the door. "Enter," Stein calls.

The waiter wheels a trolley into the room. Sets plates, cloth napkins and cutlery before us. Steak and potatoes for myself and Conrad. Salad for Stein. He takes bottles of red and white wine and pops the corks. Stein sniffs the white, delegates the red to Conrad. Like the meals, the wines have been preselected.

"Red or white, sir?" The waiter holds a bottle in each hand and smiles.

"Bourbon," I tell him.

"Very good, sir."

The boy pours me another three fingers. "Leave the bottle," Stein says, "and see that we're not disturbed for the remainder of the evening."

The waiter nods and leaves us alone.

It's good steak. The last time I was in Norway, I bunked with Royal Norwegian Special Forces at Ramsund. We were testing sniper rifles for arctic performance. Temperature, atmospheric pressure, and humidity all affect ballistics. We ate whale meat.

"Breed, this briefing is classified. I need you to sign this."

She slides two sheets of paper toward me. Hands me a gold Montblanc.

The non-disclosure agreement is standard. I sign the papers, slide one copy back to her, keep the other for myself. I've gotten used to these where Stein is concerned. The ritual has lost its drama.

Stein and I go back a ways. She's an intriguing woman, the granddaughter of a wealthy Russian Jew who fled the Soviet Union. The old man made his home in Boston and built on his mysterious fortune. Gifted the Stein Center to Harvard. His son became a private equity legend on Wall Street.

The young girl was the very image of a winner. Went to the best schools and Harvard Law. From there, she followed an unusual path. She joined the FBI. Two years as a field agent, and she transitioned to the CIA. She climbed quickly, taking on assignments no one else would take. Each was a gamble that might have ruined her career. She dodged the bullets and kept climbing. She joined operators in the field. Ukraine, Afghanistan, South America. The stories are true. I've seen her in action.

Stein slips the NDA into her briefcase. "Now that's out of the way, I have a story to tell you."

I sip my Bourbon. Conrad is enjoying his steak. He's heard this story before. The man's role in this play remains a mystery.

The picture of a nuclear submarine flashes on the wall panel. The vessel's cigar-shaped lines are distinctly Russian.

"That's the *Marshal Zhukov*," Stein says. "It's the first of the new Oscar III class. Two-thirds the size of the Oscar II, and fast as an Alpha. The *Zhukov* is designed to carry small hypersonic cruise missiles. She can make forty-five knots and runs quieter than the Yasen class."

"It must be a nightmare for our carriers."

"Not only our carriers," Stein says. "The *Zhukov* was designed to launch the Russians' new missile, the Kestrel. The Kestrel is hypersonic. It flies at Mach 10 at an altitude between 30 and 150 feet. It sprints to Mach 12 or faster upon closure. It's impossible to stop and carries either a 1,100 pound conventional or a half-megaton nuclear warhead. From the coasts, it can strike targets anywhere in the United States."

"Are the Kestrels on the *Zhukov* nuclear armed?" I ask.

"They are nuclear-capable, but not routinely nuclear-armed. On patrol, the boat carries nuclear warheads in a secure armory. If instructed, the crew installs the nuclear payloads."

A photograph of the submarine traveling on the surface appears on the panel. The image has been shot from above. The resolution is startling.

"That's a satellite photograph of the *Zhukov* putting out to sea, two years ago. This was shot in the Polyarny Inlet off the Kola Peninsula. It submerged and headed toward the Greenland-Iceland-UK Gap. Its mission was to break out of the GIUK Gap into the North Atlantic. There, it would conduct tests of capability."

Two years ago is a while and a half.

Stein throws a map of the Arctic and North Atlantic Oceans up on the screen. The land masses line up, left to right. North America, Greenland, Iceland, Europe. Norway sits at the top, with Sweden, Finland, and Russia's Kola Peninsula. To the south, the northern islands of Scotland.

A white skullcap, the Arctic Ocean crowns the globe. Between Greenland and Norway lies an expanse of ocean labeled Greenland Sea to the west and the Norwegian Sea to the east. High in that ocean lies Svalbard. The island stands like a mute sentinel, guarding access to the Arctic Ocean and the Barents Sea. During World War II, convoys had to sail past it to reach the Soviet Union's northern port in Murmansk.

Stein taps keys and a red dashed line curves from Russia through the Barents Sea, and down toward the Norwegian Sea, east of Svalbard.

"This was the *Marshal Zhukov's* course," Stein says. "Headed directly for the GIUK-Gap. The submarine never reached it."

The dashed line ends in an X, east of Bear Island, at the southern edge of Svalbard.

"At this point," Stein continues, "the Zhukov started to behave erratically. It continued at high speed south of Svalbard, then abruptly changed course. It maneuvered through the Greenland Sea and headed toward the Arctic Ocean. The submarine sank here, at the northern edge of the Greenland Sea, 230 miles north of Svalbard."

The dashed line traces a path around the southern tip of Svalbard, up through the Greenland Sea, and terminates in a second X.

"We don't know what caused the casualty, but there is no question the submarine sank there."

"You're certain?"

Stein meets my eyes. "One hundred percent. The *Zhukov* must have missed a couple of radio checks. Miss one radio check, no big deal. Miss two, and it means trouble. The Russians sortied their entire Northern Fleet. They swept through the Barents, down the Norwegian Sea, and out the GIUK-Gap. The movement was so massive, we put our Atlantic Fleet on high alert. They were obviously searching for something. Frankly, they got in their own way. After two months, they gave up."

"Did they search north and west of Svalbard?"

"Not even close."

"How do *you* know where the *Zhukov* sank?"

"We've upgraded the cold war SOSUS network. A series of deep-sea hydrophones that listen to everything that moves. We have databanks of acoustic signatures. We can identify any vessel by the sounds it makes."

I shut my eyes, rub my forehead. "Baloney."

"Why?"

"The Oscar III is a new class. Its signature wouldn't have been in your data bank."

"Does anything get by you?"

"Of course. So far, nothing important enough to get me killed."

Stein smiles. "You're right. We had no prior intel on the Oscar III. One of our *Los Angeles* class attack boats picked up the *Zhukov* in the Barents. We were tracking it and recording the Russian's signature."

"The *Zkukov* took evasive action."

"Yes. It went deep and accelerated to maximum speed."

"That's why the *Zhukov* didn't turn back to Kola. Its mission would have been a failure."

"The *Zhukov* went around Svalbard. The *Los Angeles* couldn't catch it. Then our hydrophones picked up an explosion. The *Zhukov* went dead in the water. The *Los Angeles* caught up, heard a second sound—the *Zhukov* imploding."

"What do you think happened?"

"The *Zhukov* was a brand-new boat. The Navy thinks that, at a sustained forty-five knots, a pipe burst and flooded an aft compartment. The water tripped enough circuit breakers to scram both reactors. The sub blew its ballast, achieved a positive up-angle. Normally, when you get in trouble at that depth, you crank it up and drive your way to the surface. But battery power wasn't enough. The boat slipped back, deeper and deeper. When it passed crush depth, the water pressure finished it."

There is a long moment of silence.

"The Russians have no idea where it went down?" I ask.

Stein shakes her head. "None whatsoever."

I finish my steak, wash it down with Bourbon. Conrad pours himself and Stein another glass of wine.

"The *Zhukov*," Stein continues, "is reasonably intact. The hull cracked a quarter of the way from the stern, and the rear of the submarine telescoped into the forward three-quarters. Most of the pressure hull remained undamaged."

Another photograph flashes onscreen. It was shot underwater, with the hull of the *Zhukov* bathed in floodlights. The long black whale lies upright on the bottom. Its tail seems foreshortened. The tail cone, with its twin propellers, has been forcibly jammed into the rest of the submarine.

"Were the reactors crushed?" I ask. "Is the wreck contaminated?"

"That's a legitimate concern," Stein says. "Our Advance Team took water samples at various locations around the *Zhukov's* hull. Radiation levels are normal."

"That's lucky, but I would still exercise caution while poking around there. Especially if you are going to be cutting into things."

"We are." Stein's tone is crisp. The tone of an executive who has a situation under perfect control. "Cutting, *and* exercising caution. We take regular water samples, and our divers wear dosimeters, which are monitored."

"You have *divers* on the wreck?"

"The *Marshal Zhukov* carries the latest in Russian submarine technology. Fast, quiet, heavily armed. The *Zhukov* carries twenty-four Kestrel cruise missiles in two banks of twelve each." Stein pauses for dramatic effect. "We intend to salvage it."

Another photograph flashes onscreen. This photo is of a supertanker on the open sea. It's a beautiful, sunny day. The ocean is calm and there is not a cloud in the sky.

"This," Stein says, "is the *Spider*. It's a converted Very

Large Crude Carrier—a VLCC. Look closely, and you'll notice a few unusual features."

I squint at the photo. "It has a bridge forward," I say. "Just aft of the fo'c'sle. That's unusual."

"Yes, that's the navigation bridge. What else?"

"Can't miss the derrick."

Rising from the main deck, amidships, is a tall derrick. It makes the *Spider* look like a cross between a supertanker and an oil well.

"And," I say, "it has a helideck just aft of the screws. There's a lot of space—this ship has hardly any pipes on the main deck."

"Is that everything?"

I squint. "It looks like it has another bridge aft. The usual cranes. These metal tubes folded along the sides look like collapsible struts of some sort."

"Very good. You caught all the external features." She leans back in her chair, glances at Nathan Conrad, and winks. "This is where Nathan comes in. The *Spider* is his ship."

Conrad beams. "It's a hobby, nothing more. Anya has provided the *Spider* with a truly significant mission."

Stein's wink annoys me. She and Conrad are acting too familiar.

"Nathan's holding company, Conrad International, owns Marine Dynamics International." Stein puts a flowchart of corporate ownership on-screen. "Marine Dynamics International, in turn, owns 51 percent of Norsk Exploration, a Norwegian company. Norsk Exploration owns the *Spider*. The VLCC was purchased for $250 million and converted to a research ship at a cost of a further $500 million. Its mission is to create a geological map of the ocean bottom and gather evidence to support national claims."

"Explain."

"Nations with Arctic ambitions argue over territorial boundaries. Look where the *Zhukov* went down. It's between Greenland, Svalbard, and Franz Josef Land. Greenland is Danish, Svalbard is Norwegian, and Franz Josef Land is Russian. Russia is aggressively expanding its claims. There are ethnic Russian settlements on Svalbard and military bases on Franz Josef Land. The Kola Peninsula is an armed camp. That entire region is disputed. By analyzing sediment and core samples, our scientists will cement the case for Norway's claim. Those claims are worth trillions of dollars."

"That's your cover story."

"Yes. Nathan was involved in deep sea exploration long before the Zhukov went down. But his project was less ambitious. We provided the financing."

"This isn't unusual," Conrad says. "The Woods Hole oceanographers who found the *Titanic* were financed by the US Navy. Years later, it was revealed their true mission was to find and document the wrecks of two sunken US nuclear submarines. The *USS Thresher*, and the *USS Scorpion*."

"Nathan was planning to build a special deep-sea research vessel. The *Zhukov's* sinking was serendipitous. The Company was prepared to augment his financing so he could build a bigger, more capable ship—the *Spider*."

Right. *Serendipitous.*

"I've loved building things since I was a kid." Conrad grins. "Bigger, better, faster. I made money to build things, not the other way around. The best thing about the engineering business is not having to grow up."

Stein taps a key and a cutaway side view of the *Spider*

appears on screen. Beneath the derrick, occupying two-thirds of the *Spider's* length amidships, is an open space that stretches from the keel to the main deck.

"That," Stein says, "is the Star Pool. It's 150 yards long. The *Spider* itself is 330 yards long. The Star Pool is long enough to accommodate the *Marshal Zhukov*. The derrick sits on the operations platform, which is gimbaled. The gimbals are computer-controlled from the operations bridge aft. The navigation bridge forward is used when the ship is underway. The operations bridge keeps the *Spider* on station for the recovery procedure."

Stein activates a digital pointer, which she manipulates with a stylus. "The gimbals keep the operations deck and the derrick perfectly flat regardless of pitch and roll. Those hydraulics are heave compensators. It's a lot like flying an airplane, except ships can move straight up and down as well. We have to keep the operations platform stationary in all sea conditions, or the pipe stream could break."

Conrad beams with pride. "This is the most advanced development of gimbal technology. The gimbals provide most of the stability, but there is more. Those struts you pointed to are mooring limbs. There are four on either side. They swing out and are used to lower miles of steel cables to anchor the *Spider* to the bottom. Eight in total, they give the *Spider* its arachnid appearance when deployed.

"Finally, there are thrusters on both sides of the ship. These fine adjustments provide engineers on the operations bridge the ability to keep the operations deck level. Coarse adjustments can be made by adjusting ballast in the ship's trim tanks."

I'm finding it hard not to be skeptical. "How deep is the wreck?"

"Six thousand feet," Stein says.

"That's over a mile."

"Give or take. We're the only ones with the technology to salvage that deep."

"Can divers operate at those depths?"

"And deeper, breathing mixed gasses. British commercial divers regularly operate at 1,000 feet with decompression of one day for every hundred feet. US commercial divers have operated at depths of over 2,000 feet for month long periods. They need weeks of decompression. A French team achieved 3,000 feet. Our military divers operate at 6,000 feet or more. They specialize in the recovery of warheads, tapping undersea communications cables, and the sabotage of undersea infrastructure. That information is classified, covered by your NDA."

"When do you start?"

"The operation has been ongoing since early summer." Stein flashes another chart on screen. It shows a timeline divided into three phases. "We spent the first two months shaking down the *Spider* and drilling at different locations. We tested the equipment and moved randomly to keep the opposition guessing."

"I thought the Russians didn't suspect you were after the sub."

"They don't know we are going after the sub. But they have territorial claims in all these waters. They are well aware of the *Spider's* stated mission, which is to document Norwegian claims. They have an interest."

"Where is the *Spider* now?"

"On-site," Stein says. "The area is covered with ice from early November to late May. As soon as the ice pack receded, we moved into position. We've organized three dive teams, one for each phase. In Phase I, an Advance Team of six divers evaluated the wreck and prepared it for later phases. They determined that it will be possible to recover the entire submarine in Phase III, but not without considerable risk."

"And Phase II?"

"In Phase II, we operated with a Gold Team of twelve divers. Their mission was to enter the hulk and recover as many Kestrels as possible in the time allowed."

"You've recovered missiles."

Stein smiles with satisfaction. "The mission is already a success. We are ready to take three Kestrels off the *Spider* for transport to the US. That is scheduled to take place within the next forty-eight hours."

"How are you going to do that?"

"A Navy destroyer will take them off the *Spider* by night." Stein waves the pointer at the screen. "Phase II is complete. The Blue Team of twelve divers was flown out to the *Spider* this morning from Evenes Air Station. In Phase III, those divers will rig the *Marshal Zhukov* for lifting. We will complete the work by the end of the month. Arctic night— 24/7 darkness—will descend upon us. And so will the ice pack. We will lift the *Zhukov* into the Star Pool and leave for home."

"We want to start right away," Conrad says. "Recovering the Kestrels was relatively straightforward. We used long lifting cables. The *Marshal Zhukov* weighs eight thousand tons. We'll have to use a special lifting device. It's as complex as the *Spider*."

People don't call me when everything is going according to plan. Breed gets a call when things go sideways. "Why am I here, Stein?"

Stein puts down the stylus.

"The *Spider* has a crew of two hundred," she says. "There are fifty research scientists and technicians aboard who do not know the *Spider's* true mission. The ship is equipped with all the laboratories it needs to analyze cores and samples drilled and brought up from the bottom. The scientific mission is one hundred percent legitimate. The rest of the ship's crew and divers know the true mission.

"I have two men aboard, riding shotgun. Frank Aron is the surface manager. He's a civilian... I needed someone who knew his way around a rig. He keeps me up on everything happening on the *Spider*. Sam Pruitt is an ex-SEAL, the Gold Team's dive leader. He keeps me up on matters down below at the wreck."

Stein hesitates. When she speaks, she sounds like she can't believe her own words. "Frank Aron disappeared yesterday."

Now everything is clear. Aron's disappearance explains Stein's phone call, and the rush to get me on a C-17 to Narvik. It explains Stein and Conrad flying from New York to meet me. "I assume they searched the ship."

"Thoroughly. The *Spider* is as big as an aircraft carrier. A carrier has a crew of six thousand. The *Spider* has a crew of two hundred. Compared to an aircraft carrier, the *Spider* looks and feels like a ghost town. There are a thousand places Aron could be."

"Assuming he's dead or injured."

"Yes. But the crew has searched the ship twice and found nothing. The captain and other managers think he was swept overboard."

"Freak wave?"

"That's the theory."

"You don't buy it."

"Breed, I don't believe in coincidences. Phase II is complete, we're getting ready to take off three Kestrels, and my surface manager disappears. That's a bit much."

"Yes, it is."

"I want you to go out to the *Spider* tomorrow to replace Aron."

"You think he was murdered."

"Yes."

"You have no idea who did it?"

"No, not really."

"You're sending me to play a tethered goat."

"Of course. You've squashed anyone who's ever tried to kill you." Stein smiles sweetly. "Like bugs."

Stein makes it sound so easy. But then, it's my job to make it look easy. "No way."

"I'll pay you double what I paid last time."

For some reason, I find myself offended. "It's not about the money."

"It never is, with you." Stein gives me a sly look. "If you go, I will throw in... *a bonus.*"

I groan. Stein is a mission-oriented patriot. Ambitious as hell, and too crafty by half. Sometimes, I think her heart beats twice a minute. I don't know why we get along so well. I actually *like* her.

"Are you *still* negotiating?"

"Do you want to hear it or not?"

"Can I stop you?"

Across the table from me, Conrad looks amused. Stein spreads her hands flat on either side of her laptop. Her fingers are long and sensitive. Her nails, without polish, have been neatly pruned.

"No, but you'll love it. The Dive Leader is... Stefan Knauss."

The woman's pale features flush with triumph.

Rage swells inside me. Stein sees it, but doesn't flinch.

"How do you know about Knauss?"

"We all have ghosts, Breed. You've been carrying Captain Paul Butler's with you for seven years. He and three other Green Berets were killed in a friendly fire ambush that Knauss initiated. But it wasn't only Butler's death, was it?"

"No, it wasn't."

"I'd like to hear it from you."

I remember the satisfaction I felt when I broke Knauss's arm. Wish I'd finished him then.

"Knauss didn't admit his mistake. I offered a statement, but the head shed wouldn't listen. They said Knauss was the hero of the hour, and Butler fucked up. He was disgraced. Reprimanded posthumously. His family were ostracized, pushed out of the community. Two years later, his wife overdosed on barbiturates. The whole business was a disgrace to the service."

"The word is, he's looking for a chance to sneak up behind you."

Stein knew I'd meet Knauss on the *Spider*. Figured he and I would sort out our differences. Held him back like a good negotiator. She's telling me she'll look the other way if he should have an accident. Anything can happen 230 miles north of Svalbard. She's giving me a chance to put a ghost to rest.

"Sneaking up behind is Knauss's style. I want to look into his eyes when I off him."

"Will you go?" Stein's eyes are moist.

"Yes, I'll go."

Stein slaps her laptop shut and disconnects the USB cable. She squeezes the machine and file into her briefcase. Takes a device out of a side pocket and hands it to me. "Nathan and I are flying back tonight. From New York, I will contact the destroyer picking up the Kestrels. Captain Abraham Cruik on the *USS Pressley Bannon* will relay our messages."

"What's this?"

The device is shaped like a black metal brick, the size of a mobile phone, but three times as thick. It has large plastic control buttons. The assembly is encased in clear laminated plastic.

"That," Stein says, "is a survival radio. Works like a satellite radio, but it's compact and one hundred percent waterproof down to a depth of three hundred feet."

I push the power button and the radio fires up. A pattern of twelve dots appears on the screen. It's a security screen like those on common mobile phones. More dots, more possible security patterns. "It's locked."

"Here." Stein takes the radio from me and draws a pattern among the dots with her index finger. "I've set them all up with my own pattern. You can change it later."

The security screen dissolves and the home screen appears. Stein waves her hand dismissively, like it's too easy. "The instruction manual is stored in memory, along with a directory of channels. The channel I'll be sharing with the *USS Pressley Bannon* is at the top. The keys are luminescent once activated, and there is default illumination you can switch off."

"You spooks always get the best gear."

"The technology has been around for a long time. All we did is have it packaged. As a survival radio, the battery is good for seventy-two hours steady discharge. There is a small ROM battery that allows you to boot the wireless charger even if the main battery is dry."

"Where's the charger?"

Stein hands me a thin, flat cardboard box not much thicker than the radio. "You shouldn't need it. It'll plug into any USB port."

"Thanks. When do I leave?"

"Tomorrow, first thing. There isn't much daylight this time of year, and an arctic storm is approaching from Siberia. You'll go out with a couple of research techs."

Conrad stands up. "Anya, I'll arrange our ride back to Evenes. Let the pilot know to get the plane ready. I'll leave you and Breed to catch up for a bit."

I shake Conrad's hand and watch him leave. Why did Stein bring him along?

Stein reads my mind. "I met Nathan when I was at college. He's friends with my father and he's helped the Company in the past."

If there is any doubt, there is no doubt. Stein's known Conrad a long time, and it's none of my business.

3

THURSDAY, 2200 HOURS - NARVIK, THE DJEVELKAFÉ

Mixed snow and sleet sting my face. It's early October, for heaven's sake. I slip and slide down the icy concrete walk and slam into the wooden door of the Djevelkafé bar. Music blares from the interior—the door throbs with the bass. The surface is splintery against my palm. The rustic effect. I jerk it open and dive inside.

I unzip my jacket, look around. The place is the same as I remember from my time in Ramsund. Narvik doesn't have a lot of choice in night life. Locals, sailors and servicemen from the Evenes and Ramsund military bases find their way to the Djevelkafé. It's attached to one of the cheaper hotels, a hundred yards down the road from mine. The place offers live music, gets tolerably rowdy. The soldiers and sailors don't raise too much hell. They don't want to kill their best hangout.

I belly up to the bar. They don't have Bourbon, so I order Scotch.

"You are American."

The stocky, crew-cut man next to me raises his glass. I acknowledge him with a clink and down my shot. "Yes, I am."

"Are you military?"

"No." I'm not lying. "I work for Norsk Exploration."

"Ah," the man says. "I fly helos out of Evenes."

"Do you fly for Norsk Exploration?"

The man shakes his head. "No, you have your own aircraft and crews. Your *special* corner."

The emphasis he places on the word "special" makes me leave the subject. It's pretty clear the Norsk Exploration crews keep to themselves.

"What kind of flying do you do?" I ask.

"Passengers and cargo. Whatever is required. I am based in Narvik, but I will move south soon."

"Why?"

"Flying the north pays well, but the money is to risk challenging conditions. There are many accidents. I am moving south to Oslo."

Sounds sensible. I know a lot of military helo pilots. Spec ops guys' balls tend to hang out of the aircraft. The ones who've crashed went down under fire. I knew aircrew on Extortion One and Redwings. The former had an RPG take out its tail rotor. The ship flipped out of control and disintegrated in seconds. The Redwings bird had an RPG fired straight up the ramp. The rocket hit the fuel bladders and turned the ship into a fireball.

"What kind of challenges?"

"Look outside. An arctic cyclone will be upon us by tomorrow afternoon." The man lifts his shoulders in a fatalistic shrug. "It may arrive early, it may arrive late. I am expected to make a delivery at Hammerfest before dark. No delivery, no money."

What is more malevolent? A Taliban with an RPG, or the hand of God sweeping you from the sky with an arctic storm. You can shoot the Taliban. The best you can do against a storm is go around it or stay home. I look at the man with new respect.

Do pilots believe in God?

I think back to that day in the wadi. Sitting in the beaten zone of two M-240 machine guns. There are no atheists under fire.

Order another whisky. Make it a double. The bar is getting noisier. The band has launched into a dance version of Alphaville's "Forever Young."

It's a vibrant crowd. No one over forty. Young and attractive.

I'm worried. Frank Aron was an experienced engineer. I have no experience relevant to the work on the *Spider*. Whoever killed Aron will know I'm there to troubleshoot for Stein. I may as well wear a bull's-eye on my shirt.

Stein's right, we have nothing to go on. All I can do is go to the *Spider* and see what happens. Offer myself as a target, draw out the enemy.

What did Stein say? *You've squashed anyone who's ever tried to kill you. Like bugs.*

Still offended, I push Stein from my mind.

A pretty blond girl is staring at me. Three guys have her standing with her back to the bar. Tall willowy girls grow like trees in Scandinavia. This girl is my height—she must be six foot. She is not willowy. She's broad-shouldered and fit. Long, toned legs under skintight jeans. Sweater's a bit thick, but God issued her two breasts. The body of a heptathlete. Bounce up and down on *her* all night.

The girl's looking at me like she's thinking much the same about me.

I lock eyes with the blond and we stare at each other. She's the first to look away.

The guys are trying hard, but she's unimpressed. That's a resting bitch face if I ever saw one. She looks pissed off at the world. Why did she bother to come out?

"No one is getting that one tonight." The pilot laughs.

I throw back the shot, signal the bartender for another. "What kind of helo do you fly?"

The pilot tells me about the hazards of flying helicopters in the north. The risk of ice degrading the efficiency of the rotors. The added weight turning the machine into a falling rock. I ask questions, learn all I can.

He stops, eyes fixed somewhere over my right shoulder. Tilts his chin to indicate something behind me.

"Buy me a drink."

A Lauren Bacall voice. The blond from across the crowded room is standing next to me. One elbow on the bartop, looking every bit as bitchy as she did ten minutes ago. A clipped accent. She's younger than I thought. Early twenties.

"No." I make it sound like *fuck off*.

"Why not?"

"You buy the first one. I'll buy the next."

"I don't buy men drinks."

This is surreal. "Excuse me. I'm speaking with my friend."

I turn back to the pilot. He laughs, finishes his drink, and slams the empty glass down. "I am flying tomorrow, my friend. Goodnight."

I watch the pilot leave and swear under my breath. The day has only gone downhill since Stein walked into the conference room. With that *rich* fucker.

"You must be American," the girl says.

"You must be Norwegian."

"You are half right. Only an American would be so rude."

I push off from the bar. "I'm rude, and you're frustrated. Go home and play with your *toys*."

She tries to slap me, but I block the blow.

Furious, she tries again. I block a second time, grab her around the waist, lift her off her feet. She punches my shoulders as hard as she can. I carry her to the door, body-checking people left and right. Damn, she's heavy.

She sinks her teeth into my shoulder. Gets a piece of my jacket.

"That taste good, hon? Like that?"

"Hei, hei." A bouncer steps in front of us. He doesn't like the disturbance.

"Relax," I tell him. "We're taking it outside."

The bouncer holds the door open and I stumble through. Icy wind blows snow into the Djevelkafé and he slams the door shut. I slip on the walk. Off-balance, I tip us toward a snow bank, fall on her. She gets the worst of it—grunts. She's swearing, and I can't understand a word.

The girl tries to butt me. I throw my head back. Teeth bared, she grabs the hair on the back of my head and pulls me to her. Tries to bite my lips. Draws blood.

Fucking hellion.

Wait.

This is a kiss. Kind of.

Teeth grinding, tongues probing. She's clutching me. We fight our way back to our feet and I shove her against the side of the building. The wind wails. Blasts sleet and wet snow over and around us.

We make out with shocking ferocity. Stop for breath, eyes locked. Hers are blue, all pupil. "Take me home," she gasps.

4

FRIDAY, 0800 HOURS - EVENES AIR STATION

The Air Force sedan pulls up in front of a heavy-lift helo. It's parked outside a hangar in a secluded corner of Evenes. The air station is blanketed with snow. A tanker truck is parked next to the aircraft, spraying it with de-icing fluid.

An airman wearing an olive drab parka over an orange survival suit comes out to meet us. My escorts don't bother to get out of the car. I throw open the passenger door and get out. Pull my duffel after me.

"Let me take that for you, sir."

The airman takes my duffel. I recognize his bearing, the way he speaks. Right away, I tag him as military. He leads me to the hangar. The sedan backs up and speeds away, its chains kicking up snow and ice.

"Where'd you get *that* bad boy?" I ask the airman.

"Sir?"

"Your helo. Can't be two dozen like it."

The helo sports the Norsk Exploration logo and markings. It's a CH-53K King Stallion, the most powerful helo in the world. The United States Marine Corps has ordered two hundred and only started taking deliveries. This is a Marine Corps Aviation unit, on loan to Stein.

"I don't know what you mean, sir. You can speak with the pilot if you like."

Ground crew bustle around the aircraft. The copilot is visible in the cockpit. He's running through his checks. The airman ushers me into the hangar and closes the door behind us.

Two more King Stallions occupy the hangar. "It takes three helos to supply the *White Spider,*" the airman says.

"I thought the ship's name is *Spider.*"

The young man flashes me a freckle-faced grin. "It is. *White Spider* is a bit catchier, don't you think? We call it that because when the weather's bad, the ship's all white. You'll see."

Another man in a survival suit walks up to us. He's in his thirties, sandy haired. Carries the bearing of an officer. "Mr Breed?"

"That's me."

"Dale McMaster. I'll be your pilot today. You'll need to wear a survival suit and take some safety instruction. Mandatory for flights over water."

"I wouldn't leave home without it. When do we get airborne?"

McMaster's face darkens. "Soon as possible. We have two more passengers, they should arrive soon. The storm's closing in, and this trip's going to get a little sporty."

Sporty. Aviators like to use words like that when they mean *dangerous.*

"Let me help you, sir." The airman holds an orange survival suit out to me.

The airman walks around me, studies my clothing with a critical eye. "No hoodies or high collars allowed. Your clothing should be okay under the suit, sir. We have to make sure the neck, wrist and ankle seals are tight."

I stuff the survival radio into my jacket pocket. Two minutes, and I'm encased in the survival suit.

The door opens and the pilot lets a man and woman into the hangar. My heart sinks. It's the blond girl from last night.

We don't even know each other's names. I took her back to my room and we fucked each other's brains out. After an hour and a half, the sex transitioned to tender lovemaking. I don't think we said more than two words to each other before falling asleep. There was nothing to say. All we knew was, this was the warm body we wanted to lie with. When I woke up, she was gone.

God, she's beautiful.

The girl recognizes me and drops her eyes. She's flustered. In a bar, she's the hot girl every dick wants to get with. This is a workplace. What is she, twenty-three? In many ways, she's very much a child.

McMaster introduces us.

"Mr Breed, this is Noa Larson. She's a sedimentology intern for Norsk Exploration. She'll be joining the research staff on the *White Spider*. This gentleman is Kevin Osborne, an oceanographer." The pilot gestures toward me. "Mr Breed will be the surface manager on the *Spider*."

Noa and I shake hands, and I squeeze gently. Turn my palm slightly upward and pull her toward me a fraction. She squeezes back, a reflex from last night. Catches herself, releases my hand.

. . .

SHE LAY ON HER BACK, hands on either side of her head, fingers interlaced with mine. Threw her head back, stared at the ceiling as she came. Her face and throat flushed scarlet.

"GOOD TO MEET YOU, MR BREED," Osborne says.

"There will be lots of time to get acquainted en route," McMaster says. "You have two minutes each to get into your suits. Our crew chief will give you the safety lecture in the helo. I want us out of here in half an hour."

The King Stallion is huge. There's room in the bay for thirty troops or a Humvee. Norsk Exploration must be using the Stallions to lift supplies and heavy equipment to the *Spider*.

We sit at the front, close to the pilots. Noa and Osborne sit together on the side with the door. I take a canvas seat behind McMaster, on the opposite side of the fuselage. The impossibly young crew chief sits between Noa and the door. He gives us the safety lecture.

The flight engineer, another Marine in an unmarked survival suit, hands us helmets. Wires dangle from the helmets, and the engineer plugs them into a bank of jacks on the cabin wall. "It'll be noisy when we lift off. You won't be able to talk unless you use the headsets and intercom."

"Belt yourselves in," the crew chief says. "It'll be rough."

The man hands us two plastic wrapped packages of paper bags. One for me, another for Noa and Osborne. Noa and Osborne look puzzled. I'm sure they've seen barf bags on airplanes before, but they've never been handed a year's supply.

A harsh whine pours from the Stallion's three engines and the airframe shudders. The flight engineer and crew chief belt themselves in. The flight engineer sits next to me. The pilot flips the radio select switch from R/T Radio Transmit to I/C Intercom. "Alright," he says, "show's on the road."

The Stallion lifts from the ground and claws for altitude. The windshield wipers beat a steady rhythm. Snow splatters against the glass and is whisked away. I lean back, look out the window next to me. The view of Evenes is slowly obscured by low cloud and drifting snow.

"We won't get this weather the whole way," the pilot says. "We're heading north-by-west and the storm is pushing in from the northeast. The weather should clear a bit over Svalbard, then close in again as we approach the *Spider*."

Noa avoids looking at me. I close my eyes and lean my helmet back against the fuselage. Listen to the pilot.

"Let me give you a run-down of our flight plan," the pilot says. "The *Spider* is 230 miles north of Svalbard, about 800 miles from Narvik. This is a long-range bird, but we can't do a round trip without refueling. To be safe, we usually make at least two pit stops, sometimes three. Depends on what we're carrying and how high we fly. The heavier the load and the lower we fly, the more gas we use. We figure we can make this trip with two stops. We'll meet our KC-130 Hercules tanker en route and on the way back."

Nothing new. I've seen mid-air refueling before.

"That's our refueling probe under this bird's chin," the pilot continues. "When we rendezvous with our tanker, the Hercules will lower a drogue and basket. The drogue's a long hose with a funnel on the end. We stick the probe into the funnel and fill our tanks. Easy peasy. Relax and enjoy the ride."

I release my belt, unplug my headset, and make my way

to the cockpit. I stand behind the pilots and plug the headset into a convenient jack.

"Stretching your legs, Mr Breed?" the pilot asks.

"I like to move around," I tell him. "How long before we reach *the Spider?*"

"We'll get you there before dark," McMaster says. "This time of year, that'll be about sixteen hundred hours. I'll get you there an hour before, turn around, and hightail it home. It's too bad you aren't making this trip in the summer."

"How come?"

"The *Spider* is only a few hundred miles from the North Pole. On a clear day, you can see the edge of the ice pack from this altitude. It's beautiful."

"How close is the *Spider* to the ice pack?"

"Fifty miles. That's why we have to finish before winter. *Spider* needs to pull up stakes before the site is covered by drift ice. It's possible the storm will blow scattered floes into the area."

"Will you have trouble putting us down in the storm?"

"I've landed in worse. The *White Spider* is big, and size helps. That ship was designed to be a stable platform." McMaster glances at me. "The challenge will be refueling. We've been able to pick our spots all summer, but bad weather can force us into a corner."

"When will you make your first stop?"

"The closer to the *Spider*, the better. There isn't any point refueling while we have full tanks. Of course, the longer we leave it, the closer we'll be to the storm. You see the problem?"

I see the problem. "If you refuel too early, you'll run dry earlier on the way home."

"Exactly. And the storm will be on us before we make

our second stop." McMaster frowns, weighing the odds. "I'll wait till we're past Svalbard."

McMaster knows what he's doing, we're in good hands. "Sounds like equal parts art and science."

"I won't lie," McMaster says. "We should have flown you over yesterday, with the dive team. You're a VIP, Breed. I don't know why they can't wait to get you to the *Spider*. They certainly could have waited for those other two."

"That's classified," I tell him.

"I know. This whole operation is classified. I'm sure you've guessed who we are. I know hard guys when I see them, Breed. Those divers yesterday, and now you. Whatever's going on, there will be trouble out there."

I say nothing.

"That's cool," McMaster continues. "My orders say I'm not supposed to know, so I don't. I'll put you down like a baby. Soon as, I'm taking this bird home."

What is there to say? I go back into the cargo compartment. My seat, next to the flight engineer, has a good view of the cockpit. Noa looks at me with doe eyes before turning away. She's conflicted, torn between what happened between us and the demands of her career.

An intern, this must be Noa's first job. It's obvious now. She's beautiful, all these guys in love with her, probably top of her class, never failed at anything in her life. She doesn't want complications on the *Spider*.

Neither do I. She doesn't need to worry, it was *meant* it to be a one night stand. But... by the time we fell asleep, we liked each other a lot.

"Lady and gentlemen," McMaster says, "we are now passing over Svalbard. You can see the island on your left. Svalbard falls under the jurisdiction of Norway, Greenland falls under Denmark. That's why we are formally leaving the Norwegian Sea behind us."

Noa and Osborne crane their necks to look out the windows. I look down, lean back. Before I close my eyes again, I see the crew chief and flight engineer exchange glances and smile. The crew chief is sitting between Noa and the main door. He points out features, explains the route. She's happy for the distraction.

Soldier's rules. Sleep when you can, eat when you can. You never know when you'll get your next meal, when you'll next be able to rest. I rest my helmet against the bulkhead, try to sleep.

I nod off, but I'm shaken awake by an air pocket that rattles the cabin. "Sorry about that, folks," McMaster says. "Things are going to get a bit bumpier from here on. The storm is coming our way."

"Look down there," Osborne says.

Below us, a warship is plying the waters of the Greenland Sea. It's a US Navy *Arleigh Burke* class destroyer, making its way north. It must be the *USS Pressley Bannon*, on its way to lift three Kestrels from the *Spider*.

Arleigh Burke class destroyers have a relatively low length-to-beam ratio compared to traditional destroyers. They are unusually wide. That makes the *Pressley Bannon* much more stable in the face of rough seas.

The ocean is getting rough. The wind whaling out of the northeast is Force 8 on the Beaufort Scale. Forty miles an hour, a fresh gale, whipping before it a growing swell. The waves are running 500 feet from crest to crest, and the destroyer is driving straight into a bow sea. This is only the beginning. Wind speed will exceed Force 10 by evening. Come midnight, the storm will maul the *Spider* and the

Pressley Bannon with Force 12 winds in excess of 75 miles per hour.

The waves seem to break regularly over the destroyer's fo'c'sle, washing over its deck and breaking against the forward five-inch gun mount.

Apart from that gun, the destroyer appears devoid of heavy weapons. It's an illusion. The ship's gray decks are flat and streamlined. They cover ranks of VLS—Vertical Launch System—missile tubes that hold the destroyer's array of anti-ship, anti-aircraft, anti-submarine, and land attack missiles. The superstructure aft of the stack serves as a helicopter hangar. Aft of that is a helideck.

"Looks rough," I say.

The flight engineer braces himself against increasing turbulence. "That destroyer's hardly rolling. It'll get worse."

It gets worse. We continue to forge our way north. The helo shudders and rocks constantly. One moment we're hurtling upward on a wave of air. The next, we're in freefall. Osborne's complexion turns a pasty green. Noa's fingers fumble at the package of barf bags. She rips it open and hands an inch of paper to the oceanographer. Keeps the rest for herself.

McMaster's voice crackles over the intercom. The pilot sounds bored. "Looks like that storm is going to hit us early, folks. We'll be hooking up with our tanker just in time."

There's a sharp clang like a sledgehammer striking the bottom of the helo. The King Stallion heaves, and we're thrown violently against our lap belts. Osborne loses the contents of his stomach before he can pull a bag open. The crew chief reaches behind the copilot's seat and hands the oceanographer a tin bucket.

The helo pitches nose down, then porpoises. For a

horrible instant, we're weightless. Anything not physically tied down goes airborne. The bucket and its contents literally float in the air. The next instant, the helo surges upward with such acceleration, we're crushed into our seats.

Terror-stricken, Noa stares at me.

5

FRIDAY, 1200 HOURS - GREENLAND SEA –
WAVES

The crew chief and Osborne are violently airsick. The young man recovers the tin pot and buries his face in it. When he's done, his face is the color of wet cement. He and the oceanographer pass the bucket back and forth across Noa. To her credit, she deposits her business in a paper bag. "Do you want to exchange seats?" she asks Osborne.

The oceanographer says nothing. Reaches for the bucket.

"Don't look," the flight engineer says. "It'll make you sick too. Watch the pilots."

Good advice. I watch McMaster and his copilot at work. I have a better view of the copilot, and he looks white. His cheek glistens with cold sweat. McMaster is giving him things to do. Keep him busy, keep him from getting sick. "Guide me to the tanker."

On a boat, I fix my eyes on the horizon. A stable reference point, it helps me fight off motion sickness. Today, I can't find the horizon. Ahead of us is a veil of cloud and sheets of blowing snow. Instead, I focus my attention on the pilots.

"Jumbo 54 from *Spider* 15," the copilot says. "We have you on radar, but no visual."

McMaster and the copilot strain to see through the veil of snow.

"Check altitude," the radio crackles. "We are at seven thousand."

"Roger that," McMaster says. "Seven thousand."

"There." The copilot points straight ahead. A shadow rears up ahead of us. A fat fuselage, long wings and roaring engines. "We have you, Jumbo 54. Let's go, we're thirsty."

"Deploying left drogue."

The Hercules tanker typically runs two drogues, one from the left wing, one from the right. The King Stallion's probe is under the chin of the helo, on the right side. Using the tanker's left drogue creates greater separation between the aircraft. In turbulence, it makes for safer refueling.

"Imagine doing this at night," the flight engineer mutters. "It'll be dark on the way back."

The drogue is a long hose that stretches from the tanker to the helo. At the end is the basket, a conical metal cage. Its weight helps stabilize the drogue. It looks impossible to miss.

"We need a long drogue," the flight engineer says. "You can see how long our rotor blades are. The drogue has to come in under the rotors so we can dock."

The rotors are a blurred, translucent disk. The edge of the blur reaches toward the drogue.

"What happens if the rotors hit the drogue?" I ask.

"Nothing good. Best case, we cut the drogue. Worst case, the blades snap and we disintegrate."

Noa stares at the engineer with horror. Buries her face in a paper bag.

When she comes up for air, the flight engineer manages a weak smile. "Sorry. If it happens, I promise you won't feel a thing."

McMaster closes on the drogue. The Stallion and the Hercules are bucking so violently it looks like the basket is jerking by the height of a man every few seconds. I find myself holding my breath.

"Damn." McMaster grunts as the Stallion overshoots the basket.

"Back." There's fear in the copilot's voice. The rotors are flashing dangerously close to the drogue. "Back, back."

McMaster withdraws to a safe distance. Pushes forward for a second attempt.

A gust lifts the Stallion and pitches it nose down at the same time. The basket, which had been directly in front of the probe, flies up and out of sight. The helo rights itself and the metal cone bangs its nose.

The copilot looks over at McMaster. "Want to try a different altitude?"

"It's worth a try."

First, we claw our way to ten thousand feet, then three thousand. Each time, we have to reestablish position with the Hercules. There is no improvement in the turbulence.

McMaster lines up the basket. "This is the money shot," he says. "I'm going to bust this cherry."

The basket is stationary, three feet from the probe. I suck a breath.

It's like watching a silent movie. The drogue, once a taut hose extending from the Hercules, snaps. The basket strikes the Stallion and smashes against the windshield in front of the copilot's face. For an instant, the hose ripples like the coils of a snake. Then it's gone, torn away into the slipstream.

The copilot is shaken. "I'm okay," he says. "The glass didn't break."

The windshield didn't break, but the copilot's side is a spiderweb of cracks. The refueling basket is heavy. We're lucky it didn't do more damage.

"*Spider* 15 from Jumbo 54," the radio crackles. "What happened?"

"This is *Spider* 15," the copilot says. "You've lost your drogue."

"We can see that. Did you cut it?"

"Negative. The drogue parted at the wing."

"We'll extend the right wing drogue."

Headwinds from the northeast slam into our Stallion. The airframe shudders and McMaster adds power to keep pace with the Hercules. It feels like an invisible giant is leaning against the helo.

McMaster shakes his head, gestures to the copilot to wait.

"Wait one, Jumbo 54. We'll be back."

"To hit the right wing drogue we'll have to belly up under their fuselage," McMaster says. "With this turbulence we're risking a midair."

"They're thinking the same," the copilot says. "They've got balls to let us try."

"I'm not going to kill two crews trying. How much gas do we have left?"

The copilot checks his gauges. "Including our reserve, twenty minutes."

"At this altitude," McMaster says, "it's less. Not enough to make the *Spider*, and too risky to tank up."

"Let's head back to the destroyer and ditch."

"Exactly what I'm thinking. They have helos that can pick us up."

I swallow hard. A ditching in the Arctic Ocean was not on our itinerary.

"Let's do it," the copilot says.

The pilots go into action. "Pilot to crew," McMaster says. "This isn't happening for us. Prepare to ditch."

"Jumbo 54 from *Spider* 15," the copilot says. "We are bingo fuel, preparing to ditch. We'll turn around, try to reach that destroyer."

"*Spider* 15 from Jumbo 54. Understood. We will follow and relay to all available. Good luck."

The flight engineer and crew chief get to their feet. The flight engineer checks the seals on my survival suit. The crew chief checks Noa and Osborne.

"What's happening?" Osborne looks lost.

"Everything's going to be alright," the crew chief says. "We're going to practice some of those safety lessons."

"I'm taking her down," McMaster tells the copilot.

"Mayday, mayday," the copilot calls. "This is *Spider* 15, CH-53 out of Narvik, preparing to ditch."

The radio crackles, a woman's voice. "*Spider* 15, this is *USS Pressley Bannon*. We have you on radar. Say fuel status."

"This is *Spider* 15. We have fifteen minutes fuel, descending from three thousand, heading your way. Can you render assistance?"

"Affirmative, *Spider* 15. Going to flight quarters. Say souls aboard."

"*Spider* 15. Seven souls aboard."

"Understood, *Spider* 15. Advise before you ditch."

"Can we reach them?" McMaster asks. "I'll set down on their helipad."

The copilot does a calculation, shakes his head. "Negative. Assuming they approach at 25 knots, even with this tailwind, we're five miles short."

"Can I help?" I ask the flight engineer.

"Sit tight," he says. "When we get in the water, do everything you can to keep people together."

The crew chief hauls out two inflatable life rafts, drags them to the side door, and prepares to deploy. The helo rocks and shudders, wallowing in the air currents. I sense a change in the sound of the engines above our heads. There may be less noise, but there is so much rattling and banging from the turbulence it's impossible to say.

"We're at two hundred feet, folks." McMaster's put on his best airline pilot drawl. "Follow the directions of the crew and everything will be fine."

"*Pressley Bannon* from *Spider* 15," the copilot says. "Mayday, mayday. Number three engine has flamed out. We have two plants on fumes. Position follows."

The copilot updates our position, relays it to the destroyer. All three engines should have flamed out at the same time. We could crash any second.

"Altitude," McMaster snaps.

"Oscillating," the copilot says. "Fifteen, forty-five feet."

Bad news. The altimeter is reading the distance from the belly of the helo to the waves. That means the waves are thirty feet, peak to trough. Our altitude is fifteen feet at the crest, forty-five at the trough.

If we jump and fall into a trough, it will be like falling out of a fourth floor window.

"Bail out," McMaster says.

The crew chief pushes a life raft out the door. It'll inflate automatically when it hits the water. He wrestles the second raft upright, kicks it over the side.

On my feet, I take Noa by the arm, jerk her close. Our faces are inches apart. Her eyes are wide and shocking blue.

"Listen," I tell her. "You have to *time* your jump. Jump into the *crest* of a wave, understand? If you miss, the fall can kill you."

Numb, Noa nods. Steps to the open door. The crew chief helps Osborne up, stands him next to her.

I look past them at the boiling ocean. Thank God, we still have daylight. The ocean is a mass of heaving black and gray water, frothing white at the crests.

Noa jumps.

"Go," the crew chief says.

Osborne freezes.

"Go!" For a minute, I fear the oceanographer will have to be pushed out. He squeezes his eyes shut and jumps.

I step to the door. No sign of the rafts. I see an orange survival suit bobbing below, can't tell who it is. The wave crests reach for us like they want to swallow the helo.

That's what I want.

A wave thrusts upward like it wants to devour me. I hurl myself at it. There's a smash and I'm engulfed. The shock of immersion in ice water is heart-stopping. The next instant, I'm tumbling, falling with the wave into the trough. One second I'm looking down, next I'm staring straight up at the belly of the helo, thirty-foot mountains of water on either side. Another body plunges from the helo, then another. Both from the side door.

I tread water, look around. Survival suits, sealed at the wrists, ankles and neck, provide some buoyancy. In addition, a CO_2 cartridge automatically inflated my life vest. We still have daylight. At the crests, it's like I can see for a mile around. The ocean is a frightening tableau of falling snow, gray ocean and whitecaps. In a trough, I'm at the bottom of a pitch-dark pit.

An object bumps into me. By sheer fluke, a wave has tossed me a life raft. Rubber, international orange. It's inverted, but there are nylon straps and lanyards along the sides. I grab one, pull the raft close.

There, fifteen feet away, a strobe flashes in the darkness of the trough. "Here," I yell. "Over here."

It's Noa. She's a strong swimmer, thrashes the water to reach me. She grabs one of the lanyards, pulls herself up to the raft. "Breed, are you alright?"

Noa's concern surprises me.

"Yes. Are you?"

"Yes. Where are the others? I thought I saw a light over there, but it is gone."

There's a screech from overhead. It's like the heavens are falling. I look up, watch the King Stallion disappear into a trough. Jagged pieces of metal fly high against the overcast. The rotors must have hit waves, snapped off and catapulted skyward.

McMaster's on that bird. The pilots stayed aboard to keep the helo from falling on us.

"Wait here," I tell Noa. "Stay with the raft."

I plunge into the waves, swim hard for the spot I saw the helo go down. A wave propels me skyward. At the crest, I look around. See Noa behind me, two more orange suits a hundred yards away, separated. There's the second raft, tossed by the waves like chefs tossing a pizza.

Below me, a dark well. At the bottom, the wreckage of

the helo. It's inverted and sinking. Another orange suit is splashing toward it. The wave collapses on itself and I fall with it toward the helo. I suck breath and fill my lungs before being submerged.

I claw back to the surface. Exhale, spit water. I'm next to the King Stallion.

"Breed!"

It's the flight engineer. He swims to me, grabs my shoulder. "The pilots are in there."

We tear off our flotation vests and dive together. Kick hard, grope toward the nose of the fuselage. It's dark, all I can see are shadows. A half-open door. The arm of an orange suit trying to force it open from inside.

I grab the edge of the door and pull. The flight engineer does the same, braces his feet against the side of the helo. The impact of the crash must have bent the airframe. With an almighty effort, the flight engineer wrenches the door open.

Forcing my eyes wide, I search the interior. McMaster is holding his breath, staring at me. He's supposed to have an oxygen bottle with three minutes breath strapped to his leg. I grab his survival suit, pull him toward me, look for the bottle. Damn, I can't find it. He grasps my shoulder, shakes his head. The oxygen bottle must have been torn off by the impact.

McMaster nods to me, gestures toward the surface. I withdraw from the helo's cockpit to make room. The flight engineer is straining to hold the door open. The pilot struggles clear of the wreck. He can't hold his breath much longer. I meet the flight engineer's eyes. Together, the three of us kick for the surface.

Chest on fire, I thrust my face above the ice water. My

first attempt at sucking breath is fruitless. My lungs are empty and unable to fill. I sink beneath the waves, fight off panic. Force myself to try again. This time, my lungs fill with air. I spit water, look around.

McMaster is treading water, dry heaving. "Gensler is still aboard," he gasps.

The helo is gone, completely submerged. The copilot is trapped in the cockpit. I suck three deep breaths. Hold the last one, dive a second time. I strain to reach the sinking wreckage. Can't get there. I cannot fucking get there. The Stallion is sinking faster than I can dive. I give up, turn for the surface.

I find McMaster and the flight engineer together. Disoriented, I look around. Walls of water tower on every side, I can't tell which direction to swim to reach Noa. My flotation vest is gone. So is the flight engineer's. We're relying on our suits to provide buoyancy.

There's a roar overhead. The Hercules circles, drops us a raft. The flight engineer grabs it. There's no use trying to right it, the waves flip it over. It's a serviceable flotation device, that's the best we can hope for. The Hercules drops a second raft. They're not going to drop it on empty water... they're dropping it to survivors. We swim in that direction.

Flares arc high into the sky from the Hercules. It's marking the crash site for the *Pressley Bannon*.

We crest another wave, slide down the other side, find ourselves on top of Noa. She's blue with cold, but had the presence of mind to tie herself to the raft with paracord.

I grab the line, hold it up to her. "Where did you get this stuff?"

Noa reaches for a flapped pouch in the raft. With fingers shaking from the cold, she tears at the Velcro. Digs inside,

takes out a survival pack and hands it to me. She's opened it
—coils of 550 paracord, a survival knife, flares.

I grab a handful of flares, hand them to McMaster and
the flight engineer. I cut two lengths of paracord, double
them, tie the rafts together.

The flight engineer swims hard in the direction of the
other raft dropped from the Hercules. Ten minutes later, he
reappears with the crew chief. They are dragging Osborne
behind them, lashed to the raft.

The oceanographer is delirious with pain. Right away, I
see that the only thing keeping him alive is his flotation vest
and the two men supporting him.

"What happened?" McMaster asks.

"Think he jumped into a trough, broke every bone in his
body."

I remember the altimeter readings before we jumped.
Osborne left the helo seconds after Noa. She hit the crest, *he*
went into the trough. Must have felt like hitting concrete.

The Hercules orbits our little group once more and fires
another set of flares. The flares fall to the sea, trailing
colored smoke. Jumbo 54 waggles his wings and flies off.
Clouds of snow swirl around us.

We're left with the moaning wind and the crashing
waves.

6

FRIDAY, 1300 HOURS - GREENLAND SEA –
SEA HAWK

The departure of the Hercules leaves me feeling alone. Now I know why they want groups of survivors to stick together. There's strength in numbers, if only for morale.

I'm exhausted. The water's 32^0F, but sea water freezes at 28.4^0F. There's no ice on the surface, but it's cold enough to kill you. Without the Mustang survival suits, we'd be dead by now.

McMaster's alert, taking stock. He's the senior officer in our little group, assessing our condition.

The flight engineer is a veteran. He splashes around our three rafts, cinches them together, collects survival gear. It won't help much if the *Pressley Bannon* doesn't arrive soon.

The crew chief is tending Osborne. Trying to keep the oceanographer from falling into a sleep from which he will never wake. The man's eyes keep closing. The crew chief speaks to him, prods him awake. Osborne groans with pain.

Noa clings to the raft with grim determination. When we're in the trough, she looks at the waves towering over us.

When we crest, she stares at the majestic violence of the ocean. Our eyes meet occasionally. I want to tell her we'll make it, there's a US destroyer five miles away. Then I see she's got her fear under control. Some fierce energy inside her wants to live.

An MH-60 Sea Hawk helo roars overhead. The flight engineer pops a flare, sends it arcing skyward. The helo executes a sharp turn, stands off fifty yards from us, settles into a hover.

Slowly, the pilot edges closer to our little band. He's cautious. Climbs higher to survey the situation. Eighty feet, well clear of the waves.

The Sea Hawk drops down to forty feet. The pilot stops when he is right over us. The waves are almost touching the belly of the aircraft. There are moments, if he came low enough, I could grab hold and pull myself up.

Not with these fingers. The pain from the cold is excruciating. I remind myself the pain is better than feeling nothing. The spray from the prop wash blinds me. I blink, my eyes burning from the salt water.

A rescue swimmer and flight engineer are at the door. They winch a rescue basket down to us.

They won't risk a rescue swimmer if they don't have to.

"Miss Larson first," McMaster says.

The pilot is holding the basket steady at the end of the cable. The wind howls around it, but the cable is thin, and the basket is framed with aluminum bars. I take the knife and cut Noa free of the raft. She slides an arm through a strap. The wave action is the problem. We lunge repeatedly for the basket, but the waves sweep us away. Finally, the flight engineer snags it when we're halfway up a crest. He reaches for Noa, but misses her hand.

Next thing, we're plunging into the trough, leaving the flight engineer to dangle from the basket.

"Go!" McMaster yells. "Take him!"

The rescue swimmer flashes a thumbs-up. The winch whines. Minutes later, they are pulling the flight engineer into the Sea Hawk. For all our good intentions, it was the first man to snag the basket who was rescued.

The pilot swings the helo around, hovers. The rescue swimmer adjusts his mask and snorkel. Dangles his legs over the side, times his move. He jumps and splashes down no more than thirty feet away. Swims to us with powerful strokes.

"I'm the officer in command," McMaster says. "That man's severely injured. I suggest he and the lady get priority."

The rescue swimmer examines Osborne, goes back to McMaster. "I don't think he'll make it, sir. But we can try. Let's get the lady up first."

Fighting the waves, the rescue swimmer snags the basket. The same thing happens. The wave collapses into a trough, leaving the swimmer dangling. He waits for the crest to reach him, rides the basket down. This time, he grabs Noa by the arm and hauls her into the basket. It's a difficult job. She's a strong girl, and she helps. Grabs the cable with her bare hands.

Noa's fair skin has gone pale blue. She looks like a ghost. The winch whines and she's lifted into the Sea Hawk. I feel a pang of relief.

Osborne's rescue won't be straightforward. The oceanographer was barely awake during Noa's rescue. We try to get him into the basket, and he shrieks with pain. The swimmer examines him more closely. Both his legs, an arm,

and God knows what else are broken. He's probably
bleeding inside.

I help the rescue swimmer get Osborne into the basket.
He's screaming and fighting us off with his good arm. I worry
he'll pitch himself out of the basket halfway up and take
another fall. We cram his limbs into the basket any which
way we can while the waves pitch us side to side, up and
down.

The swimmer and I let go of the basket and the winch
hauls it up. A wave propels us skyward, and we slam into the
basket from below. The wave catches the basket and carries
Osborne as far as the helo before receding. The wave
collapses. It looks like the helicopter and the basket are
shooting up an elevator shaft. In fact, we're falling with the
wave.

We splash back to the rafts. I'm staring at McMaster, the
crew chief, and the rescue swimmer. "It's no good," the
swimmer says.

McMaster grabs the straps. Hauls himself around the
rafts until he's nose-to-nose with the swimmer. "What are
you talking about?"

"The basket's too dangerous. The winch can't keep up
with the crests. If there's too much slack when the wave
collapses, whoever's in the basket will fall. The cable will
snap. If the passenger gets tangled in the cable, it's all over."

"What are we going to do?"

"Evacuate that injured man. The *Pressley Bannon* isn't far.
When it gets here, they'll pull the rest of us aboard."

The swimmer waves to the helo. His hand and arm
signals are unmistakable. The Sea Hawk turns in place,
pitches nose down, and flies south. "Don't worry," the
swimmer says. "They'll be back."

The crew chief vomits. He's swallowed so much ocean
his guts must be frozen. The waves are so violent it's impossible not to swallow or breathe water. A man can drown on
the surface. McMaster reaches over and grips the young
man's shoulder. "Hang in there. They know exactly where we
are, and there's a big destroyer with two helos coming."

I force myself to switch on. The helo headed south.
That's the direction from which salvation will arrive.

7

FRIDAY, 1400 HOURS - USS PRESSLEY BANNON

The *USS Pressley Bannon* shows us what an *Arleigh Burke* can do. She steams up at flank speed, shrugging off twenty degree rolls and thirty-foot seas. The Sea Hawk returns and hovers over us to mark our position.

"They'll use the ship as a windbreak," the rescue swimmer says.

Sure enough, the destroyer maneuvers between us and the wind. Chops speed, edges closer. Sailors on deck throw cargo nets over the side. The windbreak helps a little. Cuts the waves in half. In our condition, it's still a brutal swim.

"Make for the ship." The rescue swimmer pushes us in the direction of the destroyer.

We swim hard, digging deep for our last reserves. The swimmer hangs back with the crew chief. The young man's in the worst shape. This is like doing walls in Combat Dive School. The class is split in two, half on either side of a twenty-five meter pool. You swim underwater in relays until men drop like flies. Some pass out underwater. The survivors graduate.

It teaches you not to quit. It teaches you the limits of your body.

The wind actually helps. It pushes the *Pressley Bannon* closer. Keeps the waves from smashing us into the side of the destroyer. When we reach the ship, the wind practically pushes the ship and the nets into us.

Fingers numb with cold, we struggle to climb. McMaster and I make it halfway before our strength gives out. We have to stop. I cling to the net like I clung to the wall in Dive School. "*Get off my wall, mister,*" the instructor growled.

"Don't stop," the rescue swimmer screams at us. "If you stop, you die."

The sailors above—eighteen and nineteen-year-old kids —cheer us on. Strong hands help us aboard. I collapse on the deck like a drowned rat.

There's a cry. I look over the side in time to see the crew chief lose his grip. The rescue swimmer grabs a strap on the man's life vest with one hand and hangs on to the net with the other. That swimmer must be superhuman. "Get them up," I choke. "Get them up."

The sailors on deck put their backs to it and haul the net up the side of the ship. Willing hands grab the crew chief and take the load off the swimmer. I would not believe it had I not seen it with my own eyes.

We're all taken to sick bay. Noa and the flight engineer are there, wrapped in fresh clothes and blankets. Osborne is in the next compartment. The ship's doctor and corpsmen are working on him.

Corpsmen supply us with dark blue US Navy coveralls and nonskid shoes. We're given plastic bags for our wet clothes. Corpsmen take them away to throw in the ship's industrial laundry. They show us a small compartment in which to change. I surreptitiously pocket my survival radio in the new coveralls. The wireless charger is at the bottom of the Greenland Sea with the rest of my clothes.

We're cold, but none of us are seriously hypothermic. The Mustang survival suits did their job. Another hour in that water and the situation might have been very different. McMaster's decision to turn around and head for the destroyer saved our lives. I ask for a US Navy watch jacket.

A corpsman offers me coffee or hot chocolate.

"How about some Bourbon?"

"I'm sorry, sir. Liquor is not allowed on US Navy warships."

"I'm talking medicinal whisky, petty officer. We nearly died."

"I'll check with the doctor, sir."

The corpsman returns with a bottle. An adhesive label has been slapped on the green glass. With a black felt-tipped marker, the paper's been marked *POISON*. Fingers quivering, I pour three fingers into my coffee cup. Offer the bottle to Noa.

Fingers blue, knuckles bone-white, Noa takes it by the neck and swigs straight from the bottle. Her palm is raw from grabbing the hoist's steel cable.

McMaster and I exchange glances.

"WHICH ONE OF YOU IS BREED?"

The woman is dressed in Navy blue coveralls with silver oak leaves on her collars. Her dark hair is tied back in a severe bun. She's a fine-looking woman, with high cheekbones and dark eyes. Those functional coveralls, belted at the waist, would not be out of place on a fashion catwalk.

"I am."

"Commander Katie Palomas," the woman says. "I'm Executive Officer and Tactical Action Officer on the *Pressley Bannon*. Captain Cruik wants to see you."

I shrug on the Navy watch jacket and get up. Noa hands the bottle to McMaster, notices the glass is smeared red. "Oh no," she says.

"Let me bandage that," a corpsman says. He reaches for Noa's hand.

It's more of an abrasion than a cut. The girl must still be in shock not to have noticed.

Palomas opens the sickbay door. She steps into the passageway and leads me through the destroyer. The vessel is claustrophobic. Must be the Navy's determination to pack as much detection and killing power into the smallest possible package.

"Ton for ton, we're the deadliest ship afloat," Palomas tells me. "We have an integrated air defense. SPY-1 phased array radar. Standard 2 missiles for close-in anti-air, Standard 6 for long range anti-air, Standard 3 for terminal ballistic missile defense. If anything gets through, we have two Phalanx Gatling guns mounted fore and aft. Fully automatic CIWS—Close In Weapon Systems."

"What about anti-ship?"

"Harpoons and Tomahawk Anti-Ship missiles. We also carry TLAMs—Tomahawk Land Attack Missiles."

"Nuclear?"

"The TLAMs are nuclear capable, but at the moment they're armed with conventional warheads."

"Are there nuclear warheads aboard?"

"That's classified."

We've passed Marines with sidearms guarding compartments. I don't know where the armories on a destroyer are located, but I bet the *Pressley Bannon* carries nuclear warheads for the Tomahawks.

"I thought submarines were meat and potatoes for destroyers."

"They are. We carry active and towed array sonar. ASROC—Anti-Submarine Rockets. Basically rocket-boosted torpedoes. All of these weapons sit in our VLS tubes. The Vertical Launch System is like having a ship full of missile silos. Back in the day, we kept them in rotary magazines."

There are high-vis arrows painted at five-foot intervals on the floor of the passageway. The knee-knockers have been stenciled with labels.

"What are these marks on the floor?" I ask.

Palomas smiles. "There are no floors on a ship, Mr Breed. Only decks. Nor are there ceilings—only overheads. Doors permit movement along the length of the ship. Hatches allow you to move from one deck to another."

"Sorry, Commander. Remember, I am a landlubber you fished out of the Arctic Ocean."

"Corridors are called passageways," Palomas says. "If we're hit, these passageways will fill with smoke. You can follow those arrows and read those labels while crawling on your belly."

I follow the woman over a knee-knocker. The ship rolls, and I smash my elbow against the side of the door. "Damn."

"You'll find your sea legs." Palomas pats a bulkhead. "All steel construction. Not like the *Sheffield*, *Coventry* and *Stark*. If we're hit, we won't be sitting on a pile of beer cans. Aluminum ships will burn and melt right out from under you. The *Pressley Bannon* will take hits and keep on fighting."

As we progress through the destroyer, I notice the passageways, compartments and decks have been meticulously stripped of anything remotely flammable. There isn't a shred of flammable polyester in the crew's clothing. Like Commander Palomas, the crew—men and women—are stiff-lipped and one hundred percent professional.

That kind of professionalism filters from the top down. I am developing high expectations of Captain Abraham Cruik. What did John Paul Jones say? "All I desire is a fast ship, for I intend to go in harm's way." The *USS Pressley Bannon* is not a show vessel. It's rigged for combat.

"You're military," Palomas says. It's not a question.

"I was an Army warrant officer."

"Delta? Combat Applications Group? Whatever you call yourselves these days."

I say nothing.

"There are no indiscreet questions," Palomas says, "only indiscreet answers. Don't blame me. We have a SEAL team aboard."

I wonder how Palomas made rank with a little girl's name. I decide her first name must be *Commander*.

The red label on the floor says "CIC"—Combat Information Center. Palomas leads me into a large compartment decorated with wall-to-wall screens. Sailors sit at the consoles, monitoring the battlespace for hundreds of miles around the destroyer. Digital icons flicker on a large screen in the middle of the front bulkhead. The shape of the icon represents the type of platform, and the color whether it is hostile, friendly or neutral.

At the center of a raised dais is a deep leather armchair.

The man sitting in the chair can only be Captain Abraham Cruik. Early fifties, raw-boned and leathery. He looks like he would be as much at home on a Texas ranch as on the bridge of a man-o'-war.

"Captain Cruik," Palomas says, "this is Mr Breed."

We stand next to Cruik's chair. There's a whiff of cigarette tobacco and sweat about the man. Not offensive... masculine. There's a look in Palomas's eyes. She worships Cruik. As a man, and as her captain. I've seen it before. There's a line drawn, never crossed. That kind of tension can make a terrific team. If the line is crossed, the command can disintegrate.

Cruik takes a pack of cigarettes out of his breast pocket, taps one loose. He flicks a Ronson and lights up right there in *his* CIC. Of course. He's the Marlboro Man.

"Mr Breed. So you're Stein's operator. Speak freely. Commander Palomas and I have been read into your mission."

"Yes, Captain. We're keen to get aboard today. That landing was a bit premature."

"Bad luck, I'd say." Cruik looks thoughtful. "I just spoke with Stein. She wants to try again."

"So do I, Captain."

"Breed, people don't just fall overboard. What the hell are you supposed to be doing over there?"

"That should be obvious."

"Yes, to everybody, including Aron's killer. Did you dream this up, or did Stein?"

"I reckon great minds think alike."

"We've already lost one Marine. I don't like risking aircrew to help you get yourself killed."

"With all due respect, Captain, COMSURFLANT has

made that decision for you."

Cruik takes a deep drag on his cigarette. The Commander of Surface Forces Atlantic has impressed the importance of the mission upon him. The Captain stares at the center screen, exhales slowly. "See that red triangle blinking above the blue square?"

"Yes, sir."

"The blue square is the *Spider*. The red triangle is the *Lenin*, a Russian icebreaker frigate. The storm's on top of it right now, but it's still heading in our direction."

I say nothing.

"You're worried about getting on board the *Spider*," Cruik says. "I'm worried about the *Lenin*. You see, Mr Breed, military vessels are not subject to the international laws of salvage. Salvaging the *Marshal Zhukov* is an act of war. That frigate carries cruise missiles that constitute a threat to the *Pressley Bannon*. Stein tell you about that?"

"Stein told me the Russians have no idea where the *Marshal Zhukov* is."

Cruik draws on his cigarette. Fills his lungs, exhales like it's a luxury. "*That* is true, Mr Breed. But what if they find out?"

I say nothing.

Cruik straightens in his chair. Stubs his cigarette out in an ashtray labeled *CAPTAIN*. "Commander Palomas, a Sea Hawk should make the *Spider* before dark. There won't be time to get back before the storm hits. They'll have to stay over."

"That won't be a problem, Captain."

"Alright, Mr Breed." Cruik turns his attention back to the screen. The blinking red triangle that marks the Russian frigate. "It's your funeral."

8

FRIDAY, 1600 HOURS - THE SPIDER - THE ARRIVAL

McMaster guides our Sea Hawk toward the *Spider's* starboard quarter. He volunteered to fly me to the research ship. As one of the *Spider's* regular helo pilots, he's familiar with the nuances of landing on its helideck. He assured us he was fit to fly, and the *Pressley Bannon's* doctor signed him off.

"It's a big bastard." The photographs Stein showed me gave no impression of scale. This is my first look at Norsk Exploration's leviathan, and I'm stunned by its size.

"Bigger than an aircraft carrier," McMaster says. "I'll orbit once, approach the helideck from the port quarter. That will give us a better line on the bear trap."

"Bear trap?"

"It's a device that helps us land. It won't be hard. Look how stable the *Spider* is. The *Pressley Bannon's* rolling thirty degrees in these seas. The *Spider* is barely moving."

I'm sitting in the flight engineer's jump seat, behind and between the pilots. Noa and the flight engineer sit behind me. When she learned McMaster and I were flying out, Noa

insisted on joining us. It was hard to refuse. She's expected
on the *Spider*.

Osborne, on the other hand, won't be going anywhere for
a year. Not between orthopedic surgery and rehab.

The turbulence makes for a tooth-rattling white knuckle
ride. I'm gripping the metal frames of the pilots' seats. I'd
like to close my eyes until we're down, but can't. I'm fascinated by the ship below us.

Driven by a cold, merciless wind from the northeast,
snow and ice splatter against the windshield. It's the advance
guard of the approaching storm. With a giant's hand, the
wind leans against the Sea Hawk. Whips the ocean into a
gray carpet of rolling swells.

I can see why the vessel is nicknamed the *White Spider*.
Its decks have been dusted with snow. Driven by the wind,
flakes land on the deck, then tumble. They gather in piles
against solid structures. The anchor chains have become
ropes of white cotton candy. Winches have been cloaked in
white fur coats. The paint lockers are covered, their sides
encrusted in ice. Frozen daggers drip from their roofs toward
the deck.

McMaster is flying at three hundred feet. At that altitude,
it's possible to look down on the derrick amidships. A lattice
tower, it is mounted on two sturdy A-frames. The frames are
supported by four great pedestals that straddle the Star Pool.
The assembly is strong enough to lift an eight-thousand-ton
submarine and thirteen-hundred-ton pipe stream. The
metal structure is white to windward. The lee side is icy
black steel.

The derrick squats on the operations deck—the complex
gimbaled platform that covers the Star Pool. The platform
itself is equipped with steel shutters that provide a clamshell

cover. The touch of a button rolls them open. The shutters conceal the Star Pool and its contents from aircraft and satellites.

Satellites. These days, everybody has them. The Russians, the Chinese, the Europeans. From a thousand mile altitude, they can read the names on gravestones. They can pinpoint the location of any surface combatant 24/7. Drop of a hat, they can turn those coordinates into targeting data for precision strike weapons.

"It does look like a spider," Noa says. Hand on my shoulder, she's leaning forward as far as her lap belt will allow. "Look at its legs."

Noa's touch fills me with warmth. It's a distraction I enjoy. I lay my hand on hers and she doesn't withdraw. When I take my hand away, my fingers tingle with the ghost of sensation.

The legs give the ship an arachnid appearance. Eight tubular structures, each a hundred yards long. Four on each side, they telescope for stowage against the ship's gunwales. Extended, they provide runners to drop miles of cable to the sea floor. Those cables anchor the vessel. Once anchored to the bottom, winches apply tension to the cables to fix the vessel in place.

I strain to look into the windows of the navigation bridge, but the view is obscured by mist and snow. McMaster swings around the *Spider's* bow, flies out a quarter mile, and approaches the helideck from the port quarter.

"On a destroyer," McMaster says, "we worry about the relative motion of the ship *and* the helo. On seas like this, we don't like to have men come onto a destroyer's deck because of the risk."

I see two men in orange survival suits standing tethered on the helideck. "What are *they* doing out?"

"That's the point. The *Spider* is stable enough that we can risk having them help us. The pipe stream weighs thirteen hundred tons. It acts like a *massive* sea anchor that stretches a mile to the bottom. It gives the *Spider* an *extremely* low center of gravity. The problem is the wind. Our helo is swinging all over the place."

"Probe extended," the copilot says. "Lowering cable."

One of the men on deck carries two lighted paddles, one in each hand. He extends them to either side, uses them to adjust McMaster's orientation.

"There are optical guides on deck that help, but the snow makes them less reliable," McMaster says. "I'd rather have human eyes guiding me."

The wind forces the Sea Hawk to port. McMaster adjusts power, leans against the giant pushing us off the ship. "To land on a destroyer, I'd have to match the ship's speed," McMaster says. "The *Spider* isn't moving, so the job's easier."

I'll take his word for it.

With one sharp movement, the man on deck brings the paddles together and points them straight at us. The other man runs beneath the Sea Hawk. I lose sight of him, but feel a hard tug. The man has fastened our cable to a device on deck.

The man rushes out from under the Sea Hawk. McMaster applies power, matching the tension generated by a powerful winch below deck. The helo has been anchored to the *Spider*. All that remains is to reel us in.

McMaster lowers the Sea Hawk. He's still leaning against the wind. When he's satisfied with our position, he cuts power and the Sea Hawk bounces on its landing gear. We're down.

"There you go, folks." McMaster smiles with satisfaction. "Just like a baby."

The deck crewmen approach. One of them peers inside, nods to McMaster. "Which one's Breed?"

McMaster jerks a thumb in my direction. "We're not getting back tonight," he says. "You and the lady go ahead, we'll help the crew tie down the helo."

"Doesn't the *Spider* have a helo hangar?"

"No, they'd have to redesign the superstructure to install one."

Noa and I step onto the helipad. The *Spider* is pointed into the gale, and we stagger in the face of a forty-mile-an-hour wind. Squint against the driven sleet that slashes our faces.

The crew chief hands us our duffel bags. We lost ours in the ocean. Palomas provided us with US Navy-issued duffels for our clothes. They'd been dried and pressed in the *Pressley Bannon's* laundry.

A crewman leads us forward. The helipad is mounted aft of the *Spider's* stack. A big cantilever, the platform juts out to sea. It's supported by struts and secured to the hull by reinforcing steel bands. Without the reinforcement, the approaching storm would rip the helideck off the ship.

With sturdy cables, the deck crew and McMaster fasten the Sea Hawk to the helipad. Daylight is fading. We haven't seen more than a glimpse of the sun all day, and that was over Svalbard. The storm is closing in, and the world is going dark.

The ocean is more violent than when we ditched. The difference is—I can barely detect the *Spider's* roll. McMaster was right. Size matters, and the VLCC is far more stable than the *Pressley Bannon*.

Noa and I step through an opening and the crewman closes the door behind us. We wipe melted snow and sleet from our faces. Look around, find ourselves in a steel box. We're facing a two-man welcome party. One wears a black turtleneck sweater under gray coveralls, belted at the waist. The other is dressed in casual office clothes and a blue wool cardigan.

"Mr Breed, Ms Larson." The man in the turtleneck steps forward. "I'm Magnus Thorval, general manager. This is Dr Bertram Hansen, our laboratory manager."

Thorval is a small, slender man. Five-nine, wavy dark hair. Handsome and immaculately groomed. A trim mustache and pointy beard make him look like a nineteenth century stage magician. Dressed in a suit, he would cut a fine figure in a corporate boardroom. His hand is soft, his hand-shake delicate. When he releases my hand, he places his own back in his pocket. A cerebral man, not used to physical work.

Hansen, on the other hand, defines "average." A shade under six feet, he wears black plastic birth control glasses. His bland features have been cut from a cartoon.

"We heard about your mishap," Thorval says. "I must say you look none the worse for the experience. Dr Osborne's injuries are most unfortunate. In any case, we are happy you have arrived safely."

"The Navy was helpful," I say.

"Indeed. It would have been safer to allow the storm to pass." Thorval nods curtly to Noa. "Ms Larson, you will be working in Dr Hansen's department. He will take you to your quarters, orient you, and show you where to report tomorrow."

Hansen steps forward and picks up Noa's duffel. "I'm glad you arrived safely, Ms Larson. How is Dr Osborne?"

"He is lucky to be alive," Noa says. "They tell us he will require extensive orthopedic surgery and rehabilitation over coming months."

"That's terrible," Hansen says, "but he's lucky he wasn't killed. Please come with me."

Hansen and Noa descend a companionway to our left. As she follows the lab manager, Noa glances over her shoulder. She looks lost, like she wants to cling to me for security. Their footsteps echo as they disappear into the bowels of the ship.

They leave me alone with—Thorval.

9

Thorval and I appraise each other. He clasps his hands behind his back.

"There's no point beating around the bush," I say. "Frank Aron was murdered. I'm here to make sure the transfer of the Kestrels goes as planned."

Thorval furrows his brow, says nothing.

I prod him. "Any idea who did it?"

"None whatsoever. It's as though he was carried away by a freak wave."

"Phase I is complete and the Kestrels are about to be taken off for transport. There are no coincidences."

"Do *you* have any suspicions?"

Thorval's a careful man. He gathers what he can, gives away little. I get the sense he is like this with everybody. A control freak who dominates situations with intellectual superiority.

I stare at the little magician. "I suspect everyone."

Thorval blinks. "I see. You have my cooperation."

"Let's start at my quarters. Then I want to meet key personnel, speak with Sam Pruitt, and see the missiles."

"Very well."

"Show me the highlights of the ship. Send plans to my cabin, I'll study them."

"You've seen the helideck. This is the aft superstructure. In there, is the operations bridge."

Thorval tilts his head toward a doorway.

I step to the opening and look inside. The bridge is a large compartment with wide windows. One can look onto the operations deck and the towering derrick. A powerful white light atop the gantry warns any nearby aircraft of the *Spider's* presence. It also serves as the vessel's masthead light. Red and green navigation lights are positioned on the port and starboard sides of the ship.

"What functions are performed on the operations bridge?" I ask.

"From the operations bridge, we keep the *Spider* on station and manage drilling and lift operations. The position of the *Spider* relative to the bottom does not vary by more than a square meter. The legs hold us in place, and the thrusters are GPS guided. The crew do little more than monitor the computer's performance."

Thorval pauses for me to ask more questions. When I don't, he asks, "Would you like to go inside?"

"Not now."

Thorval turns on his heel and descends the companionway.

I take mental note of the operations bridge's position above the main deck. At least three decks high. We clatter down a series of steep companionways that fold on themselves in a series of dizzying switchbacks.

Thorval stops at a landing and leads me onto a catwalk. The deck is a broad metal grille that consists of flat steel bars an inch apart. We find ourselves looking down three stories into a vast machinery space. The catwalk shivers with the low frequency thrum of machines. The air is thick with the smell of hot machine oil.

Hands in his pockets, Thorval contemplates the machinery space.

"We're not underway," I say. "Why are the engines running?"

"Only one of three power plants is running. To provide electricity for the vessel. I would not advise wandering around unsupervised. Men have fallen into the machinery space before, with unfortunate results."

"Did you search the machinery space?"

"Of course. We searched the entire ship. *Twice.*"

"You have two hundred people on a ship the size of an aircraft carrier. There are thousands of places he could be."

Thorval squints. "Come now, Breed. You can do better than that."

The magician's patronizing attitude annoys me. "Tell me how."

"There are only a few places an injured man can fall. Most are accessible. If, indeed, Aron was murdered, the best place to conceal the body is the ocean."

Touché.

Thorval looks smug. "Shall we continue to your cabin?"

"Carry on."

Thorval steps to another door and hauls it open. We step through, and he dogs it shut behind us by turning a metal wheel. We find ourselves in a long passageway. The *Pressley Bannon* was battleship gray everywhere. So is the *Spider*. It must have been designed by a naval architect. Damn thing is all gray steel and rivets.

"There's so much space," I say. "It's like a ghost ship."

"The *Spider* is a modified Very Large Crude Carrier," Thorval says. "An enormous hull filled with tanks for millions of barrels of oil. Norsk Exploration gutted it. Removed the tanks and fitted a shoebox into the space. The center 150 yards of shoebox is the Star Pool. Norsk cut the bottom out of the ship to open the Star Pool to the sea. Installed pumps and hydraulically operated gates. Reinforced the sides."

"Why the reinforcement?"

Thorval extends his left hand, touches the passageway's steel bulkhead on the ocean side. He uses the tips of his fingers as though sensing the engine's vibrations through the steel. It's a surprisingly sensual gesture. He gives himself a few beats of silence to collect his thoughts.

"To build the Star Pool, they had to remove the keel. Without the keel, there is nothing to provide structural rigidity amidships. The sides are reinforced to provide that rigidity."

We've walked about a hundred and fifty yards down the passageway. I touch the inboard bulkhead. "The Star Pool is on the other side?"

"That's the machinery of the operations deck. Gimbals, heave compensator, what-have-you. The operations deck is on the main deck above us. The Star Pool extends six decks below those to the bottom of the ship. Think about the shoebox divided into thirds. The aft-most third is the crew's quarters and machinery space. The center is the Star Pool, beneath the operations deck and derrick. The forward third is quarters for officers, divers, and research staff."

I can imagine a three-dimensional image of the *Spider*. A hull surrounding a shoebox. A cavernous space in the middle, open to the sea below and the skies above. "It's like two ships connected by this passageway."

"Very good, Breed. There is a passageway like this on the other side of the ship. Together, they constitute the only climate-controlled ways for crew to travel from one end of the ship to the other."

"What about the passageways immediately below us?"

"Those are dead space," Thorval says. "The space between the climate-controlled shoebox and the outer hull. To save energy, those large spaces are not climate controlled."

"What's the dead space used for?"

"It houses ballast, fresh water, and trim tanks. General purpose storage. Under these climatic conditions, it's cold, but not freezing. The living spaces of the shoebox are kept at a constant 75 degrees Fahrenheit. They act like huge radiators that conduct warmth to the dead space. The temperature in the dead space falls between 37 and 42 degrees depending on location."

"Nowhere near freezing, but cold enough."

"Certainly not cold enough to store food. We have proper freezers for perishable goods. Remember, the *Spider* is also meant to operate at tropical latitudes."

We proceed on our way. On the left, a door opens. Three men in coveralls and hardhats step into the passageway. They have clearly finished work on the operations deck and are making their way aft. Two are roughnecks, the third is a manager. He wears a blue hardhat. The other two wear yellow. The manager nods to Thorval as we pass.

Thorval opens another door at the end of the passageway. Ushers me through. "We are now below the forward superstructure and the navigation bridge. This is the library space."

We walk further along the corridor, turn a corner, and find ourselves in another passageway that extends the beam of the ship. Halfway down the passageway are a companionway and an elevator. Thorval pushes a button and summons the lift.

"There are two decks of cabins. Your cabin is on the lower cabin deck."

The elevator door sucks open and we step inside. Thorval pushes another button and we plunge deep into the *Spider's* living space. The car descends so quickly, I feel like I'm falling out of the sky in McMaster's helo.

We jerk to a stop. The door opens, and we step into a corridor identical to the one we left four decks above. Thorval guides me along the port side. Stops at a metal door with the number 121 stenciled on it. He takes a plastic photo ID card from his pocket and waves it over a black sensor plate fixed to the bulkhead. A bolt slides aside with a loud click.

"Am I alone on this deck?"

"No, but there is much empty space. We have two hundred souls aboard. Fifty research staff and one hundred and fifty crew. All the crew, except for officers and divers, are aft. That leaves fifty forward. They occupy space built for a hundred and fifty."

"How privileged."

Thorval sniffs. "The arrangement facilitates security. All the crew are aware of the mission. None of the research staff know. Separating the two groups reduces the risk of an accidental slip."

I push the door open. It reveals a spacious cabin with wood paneling on the overhead and bulkheads.

The magician snaps the card between his index and middle fingers. Offers it to me with a precise flourish. "This is your electronic pass. It permits access to all compartments registered to your profile."

I take the card from Thorval and pocket it. Throw my duffel inside the cabin and pull the door shut. The bolt slides back into place.

"You'll find the cabin comfortable," Thorval says. "It was Aron's."

Thorval delivers the statement with a flat affect. I can't tell if he meant to shock me.

"How nice." I'll be sleeping in a dead man's bed.

"Come with me. I'll introduce you to the captain."

We turn back the way we came. Halfway down the passageway, a telephone handset and microphone are mounted to the bulkhead. A public address system and an interphone.

"These are installed all over the ship." Thorval picks up the handset. A row of plastic buttons sits in the handle. He presses one and lifts the handset to his ear. "Bridge, Thorval."

A voice responds. I can't make out the words.

"Inform the Captain I am bringing our guest to the bridge."

Thorval hangs up without waiting for a response. We walk together to the end of the passageway. There is a sealed door, but Thorval ignores it. He turns right and leads me back to the elevator.

"What's behind that door we passed?" I ask.

"The dead space in the fo'c'sle," Thorval says. "Remember, the only climate-controlled passageways that extend fore and aft are those immediately below the main deck."

Thorval summons a car and we step inside. He pushes a button marked *BRIDGE*.

The elevator whisks us up seven decks. When the doors suck open, we step into a central passageway with an open door at the far end. Between the elevator and the door are four compartments. The first two, left and right, are cabins. The one on the right has *CAPTAIN* stenciled on the door. The one on the left is unmarked.

At the end of the passageway are two large compartments. The one on the left is crammed with sophisticated radio equipment. I notice powerful HF and ELF—High Frequency and Extremely Low Frequency—radio sets. A radio operator sits at a desk, making notes on a pad.

"What's the ELF equipment for?" I ask. That sort of equipment is the only kind of radio equipment able to reach submarines.

"Are you familiar with radios?"

"Yes. What's the ELF for?"

Thorval shrugs. "Our divers live in submersibles at six thousand feet. The ELF is a tool we use to communicate."

The compartment on the right is packed with laptop computers and navigation equipment. At the center is a table, the surface of which is an illuminated map of the top of the world. At the back of the compartment is a cabinet stacked with paper charts. Hardcopy backup for digitized charts available on the laptops.

In the Greenland Sea, the *Spider* appears as a glowing blue dot. It sits below the white skullcap of the Arctic.

The magician continues to the end of the corridor and steps through the doorway. Beyond is a short companionway that leads to a mezzanine—the bridge area is raised above the navigation and radio deck.

I follow Thorval up the companionway. Impatient, he sprints up the steps. It's obvious why the bridge has been raised on a mezzanine. Wraparound windows make it look like an oblong airport control tower. The front overlooks the ocean and fo'c'sle. The back offers a view of the ship. Once again, I see the lonely masthead light at the top of the derrick, shining through the mist and snow. The aft super-structure is cloaked in darkness. I can barely make out the lights of the operations bridge.

My eyes sweep the compartment. The bulkheads are gray. Steel and rivets, it's all business. The wraparound windows are broad, but reinforced with steel ribs. A tradi-tional helm is front and center, facing the windows. The ship is not underway—no one is at the wheel. There are lookouts on either wing with binoculars. Other crewmen stand at radar and sonar consoles, checking for sea and air traffic in the *Spider's* immediate vicinity.

Behind the helm is a raised, leather-upholstered chair. The traditional captain's throne. On it sits a sturdy man of about sixty. Five-ten, lantern-jawed. He's a bit soft around the belly, but fit for a man his age. He's wearing slacks and a brown turtleneck pullover.

"Captain Angers," Thorval says, "this is Breed."

Angers rises from his chair and offers me his hand. The man's grip is rough and dry. The hand of a man who's spent a lifetime at physical work. I don't doubt he's the kind of captain who knows every rivet on his ship. Knows the job of every man.

"Stein did not waste time getting you here." Angers's eyes are unflinching.

"It's an inconvenient time for a key man like Aron to go missing," I say. "Are you sure he's dead?"

"Missing, presumed dead." Angers places his meaty hands on his hips. "We have searched everywhere. He is not on the ship. He can only have gone overboard."

"The question is, who helped him over the side."

Angers looks unhappy.

I press harder. "Where was he last seen?"

"I don't know who saw him last. The three of us were speaking here on the bridge. He left, and that's the last I saw of him. The crew reported him missing the next morning."

"Did you not question the crew?"

"No," Angers says. "We organized a search."

Two hundred people aboard. Of course they would organize a search before interviewing the crew. They aren't trained policemen.

"Have you notified the police?"

"No." Angers looks thoroughly miserable. "We discussed the matter with Stein. Agreed to report the disappearance when we return to port."

That sounds like Stein. Nothing can be gained by involving the police.

I turn on Thorval. "Didn't *you* question people?"

Thorval appraises me with studied calm. "I am not a policeman, Breed."

What did I expect him to say? The general manager flicks his eyes to the companionway behind me.

A massive figure steps onto the bridge. Six-foot-five, powerfully muscled. Shaggy red hair under a seaman's black watch cap. The man wears a shovel of a red beard. Despite his size, he moves like a cat.

Stefan Knauss.

10

Knauss looks me up and down.

"Stefan Knauss," Thorval says, "this is Breed. Stein sent him aboard to replace Frank Aron."

The SEAL is not surprised to see me. That means someone told him I was coming. Who? Thorval or Angers? I mustn't assume Knauss is involved in Aron's death, but I can't discount the possibility. If he *is* involved, there must be more than one killer aboard.

One *less* reason to feel guilty when I sort him out.

Knauss grunts. "I know Breed."

"It's been a while, Knauss. How's your tennis arm?"

"I can't fully extend it." Knauss balls his right fist and holds out his arm. Smiles like a Great White. "The Navy considers me disabled, but I'm still diving."

Thorval studies our exchange. "You gentlemen know each other. How convenient. Knauss led the Advance Team last spring and will lead the Blue Team through Phase III."

I address Knauss. "When did *you* last see Aron?"

Knauss scowls. "I don't remember."

"Bad case of amnesia?"

"Breed, you got no authority to bust my balls." Knauss turns to leave, Looks over his shoulder at Thorval and Angers. "I have work to do. See you around."

"One moment, Mr Knauss." Thorval's voice is soft, but it stops Knauss in his tracks. "When will Blue Team be ready to dive?"

Knauss stares at the general manager. "Soon as the storm clears. That's the work."

"Indeed. Make it so."

Knauss turns on his heel and leaves.

"Breed," Angers says, "you and Knauss deserve each other."

"A man's been killed, Captain. It's not my job to be pleasant. Are you in touch with the *Pressley Bannon*?"

"Yes. The destroyer will reach us this evening, but the storm will be upon us. Weather permitting, we will conduct the transfer tomorrow night."

I turn to Thorval. "Take me to Pruitt."

THE DECK IS unlike all the others I've seen. The steel and rivets have been painted white. It's the sickbay, with a fully equipped dental office and operating theatre. At the back is another metal door.

Black letters have been stenciled on the white paint. They identify the occupant as *LENA VOSS*.

Thorval raps on the door. His knuckles make a metallic sound, not a wooden one. A woman calls out, "Come."

"Dr Voss." Thorval pushes the door open.

The doctor is a small woman. No more than five-foot-two. Fiftyish, with cropped brown hair, stiff and colored. She has been reading a paperback novel, which she closes and sets on her desk. The cover shows a beautiful woman in a diaphanous shift leaning against a bare-chested swashbuckler who carries a naked cutlass in his free hand. The woman's fingers are flat against the man's rock-hard pectorals.

I smile.

"We're allowed our guilty pleasures," the woman says. "Alright, Thorval. Here's a man right out of a novel. Who is he?"

"Mr Breed is Frank Aron's replacement."

"I'm Lena Voss," the woman says. She shakes my hand. "I'm taking a bit of a holiday on this ship. What could possibly happen on a trip to the arctic circle?"

Right away, I like her. "Looks like your sickbay is outfitted to deal with anything."

"One man fell on the operations deck and broke a leg," Voss says. "Another developed an abscess in a tooth. It had to be extracted."

"Are you working up to an appendectomy?"

"I brought along my old surgical textbook. Will you hold it for me? I can do surgery by the numbers." Voss cackles.

I shudder.

The doctor winks. "Care to see my real passion, Breed?"

"You've got me hooked."

"I am interested in human performance," Voss says. "What better subjects than divers working six thousand feet below the surface? I manage their breathing mixture and monitor the decompression process. I am developing proprietary technology that will open the depths to mankind."

Now I understand the doctor's "hobby". She leads us to the bulkhead that separates us from the operations space.

Next to a black sensor pad stands a steel door, dogged with a wheel and lever. It looks like the entrance to a bank vault.

"Will my card open that?" I ask.

"Yes," Thorval says.

I take my pass from the pocket of my US Navy coveralls and wave it over the pad. There is the sound of bolts sliding aside. Voss turns a locking wheel and pulls the hatch open. We step into a vast compartment that houses three decompression chambers. It's the world of gray steel and rivets I've grown used to.

The decompression chambers are steel tanks thirty feet long by ten feet wide. They're painted a glossy white enamel and look like Airstream touring caravans. They even have shuttered windows. The occupants can open the shutters to see out, or slide them closed for privacy. A sophisticated airlock occupies one end of each chamber. A forest of colored pipes connects the chambers to pumps. A control panel has been bolted to a table, and the table has been secured to the floor.

"Each chamber sleeps eight men," Voss says proudly. "Each of our dive teams is twelve men, so we have capacity to accommodate two dive teams simultaneously."

"Have you had to do that?"

"No, but it's best to prepare for contingencies. The Gold Team is decompressing now, so only two chambers are in use. They're comfortable with six men to a chamber."

"Don't they decompress at waypoints as they surface?"

"Not exactly," Voss says. "You know something about diving, but let me explain further. On the surface, the weight of air on our bodies is one atmosphere. In deep space, atmospheric pressure is zero. The world record saturation dive is 1,000 yards or 100 atmospheres. Military divers have operated deeper, but their performance is classified. The *Zhukov* lies at 2,000 yards, or 200 atmospheres.

"The air we breathe consists of oxygen and nitrogen. At great depth, those gasses are compressed into our tissues. If we surface too quickly, the air expands rapidly, causing tissue damage. In our blood, joints, and in our nervous systems. The diver gets severe decompression sickness—the bends. If atmospheric pressure goes to zero, the diver's blood boils, like a carbonated soda shaken and opened.

"The solution is twofold. First, we give our divers mixed gas to breathe. A popular mixed gas is Heliox—helium and oxygen. We use a proprietary mixture that speeds up the decompression process. It facilitates the diffusion of gas from their tissues. Second, we take our divers up to 200 atmospheres pressure in the chamber and submersible *before* we send them down. They live for weeks at 200 atmospheres on the bottom. When their work is finished, we bring them up and transfer them to the decompression chambers. We begin decompression before they leave the bottom, and I monitor the process until they are released. The process is efficient and safe."

"So they don't stop at different waypoints as they surface?"

"Not exactly. The waypoints are measured in atmospheres of pressure, regardless of depth. There is always fine-tuning to be done. I have the men take blood samples at intervals on the way to the surface. The gases are excreted at different rates under different conditions. That means the time the divers spend at each waypoint must be varied."

Voss steps to the control panel. "Another week and they'll be able to come out."

"Is Sam Pruitt in there?"

"Yes. Do you know him?"

"I've been asked to say hello."

Voss strides to the center chamber. "Come on, I'll introduce you."

We leave Thorval standing next to the control panel. I follow Voss past a wide wooden table piled high with diving equipment. Helmets, weight belts, shark knives. Some knives are sheathed, others are naked. The bare blades show signs of heavy use. There are two other tables, loaded with similar equipment, next to the other decompression chambers.

The chamber itself is equipped with a sealed hatch. There is a rectangular window with a cheap tin phone box mounted next to it. Voss opens the cover of the phone box. Inside is an old-fashioned Bakelite handset and a green button. The handset hangs from a single cradle inside the box. The button is set in a recess directly below.

Voss picks up the handset and presses the button. There's a buzz, and a man's face appears in the window. "What's up, Dr Voss?"

"Pruitt's got a visitor."

The face disappears, replaced by another. This man's about thirty-five, with craggy features and movie star looks. His sandy hair is tousled as though he had been sleeping. He's wearing a plain white T-shirt. "Hi, Dr Voss."

"You have a visitor, Sam." The doctor passes me the handset. "Take your time. I must have a word with Thorval."

I settle in the chair, meet Sam Pruitt's eyes through the glass. "I'm Breed," I tell him. "Stein sent me to find out what happened to Aron."

"Stein doesn't waste time," Pruitt says. "I can't help you, Breed. I've been sitting in this chamber the whole time Aron went missing."

"There's a Russian frigate out there. Cloaked in the storm, heading our way."

"The Russians don't know we're here for the *Marshal Zhukov.*"

"Aron was murdered. Whoever killed him is probably working for the Russians. Salvaging the *Zhukov* is an act of war."

"Shit. You know, whoever killed Aron will be gunning for you."

"And you," I tell him. "Any idea who it might be?"

"No, and we've got a ship full of characters." Pruitt's forehead furrows. "The Blue Team arrived *after* Aron disappeared. That could narrow your list of suspects."

I shake my head. "That doesn't clear the Blue Team. One or more Russian operatives could have joined the killer."

"True. But why did they kill Aron?"

"Phase II is complete. We're moving the Kestrels."

"You think they're planning to move on us with that frigate?"

"What else? You're stuck in this tank. Aron was running around loose, so he was a threat."

"We can't move the Kestrels till after the storm passes." Pruitt strokes his five-day stubble. "For the same reason, the frigate can't board us."

"They can fire on us," I say.

"They'll fire on us only if they fail to board us."

"So we have time. How much?"

"Depends on the storm. Dawn."

"Let's hope the killer tips his hand." I run my hand through my hair. "What's the scoop on Thorval? He isn't at all what I'd expect from the general manager of a hard-ass rig."

"He's an odd duck, alright. Project manager. Norsk Exploration hired him because he makes things happen. He's snooty, but he's good. Lots of energy, sharp as a tack. Doesn't suffer fools."

I recall Thorval's patronizing attitude. Do I dislike him because he was right? Shit. Something about the little magician makes my skin crawl.

"What about the captain?"

"Angers? He's an old salt, as good as they come. Retired Norwegian Navy. He served on submarines, then transitioned to surface combatants. Captained a destroyer, played cat and mouse with Russian subs in the Barents. Retired, went to work in the North Sea oil fields."

"Did you know Knauss from the SEAL community?"

"No, Knauss was in the West Coast community, I was East Coast. He started out driving the SEAL Delivery Vehicle."

"The job SEALs hate."

"*Most* SEALS," Pruitt corrects me. "Some of us *like* being frogmen. Guys like Knauss couldn't wait to get into combat so they could shoot people in the face."

"Robo-SEAL."

"He built a rep, sure. The guys he killed needed killing."

"Until Burkina Faso."

"The community is split on that, nobody talks about it. Breed, people tell stories about *you* too. I don't know what I didn't see. I will tell you the Knauss I see on the *Spider* is a competent professional. He's done good work on this project."

Yeah, they tell stories about me. About the sniper who shot two American POWs being flayed alive by Afghan women. *After* he shot the women. The stories only grow from there. I've always done what I thought was right. I have no trouble looking at myself in the mirror when I wake up. It's the dreams that are hell.

"Any trouble on board before now?"

"No. Aron was aboard from the beginning. I joined at Phase II and he briefed me. Nothing untoward. I spent most of my time underwater bagging those missiles."

"When was the last time you saw Aron?"

"The day we brought up the Kestrels. Aron stowed the Kestrels, Knauss and Nygard stowed the submersibles. Thorval supervised. Didn't get a spot of grease on his coveralls."

"Where was Angers?"

"On the bridge. His job was to keep the *Spider* stable during the recovery process."

"And Voss?"

"Voss was transferring my team from the submersibles to these chambers."

"That process took a while. When was the very last time you saw Aron?"

Pruitt furrows his brow. "Voss and Knauss were still mating the airlocks between the submersibles and the decompression chambers. The Kestrels were stowed on their cradles. Aron and Thorval spoke and left the Star Pool together."

I've probably learned as much I'm going to learn from Pruitt. "I think it's time I check out some Kestrels."

"If anything else comes to mind, I'll let you know."

An afterthought occurs to me. "Hey, Pruitt. You know those stories they tell about me?"

"What about them?"

I lean close to the glass. "*They're all true.*"

11

My words to Pruitt made a good punch line, but they leave me feeling bitter and hollow. Breed the killer. Breed the machine. That's how they see me. Stein, Noa, everyone I've ever met who might want to get close.

Voss returns to her office, professing a need to return to her technical journals. She gives me a wink. We both know her taste in casual reading. Thorval leads me down another passageway. "Come," he says. "It is time I showed you the Star Pool."

We pass the elevator. The door sucks open and we are faced with Hansen and Noa.

I'm glad to see her, but feel sad at the same time.

"Magnus." Hansen greets Thorval. "I was showing Ms Larson around the ship. We're going to the gym."

"Ah." Thorval doesn't disguise his lack of interest. Hansen is smitten by Noa's beauty, and Thorval doesn't give a shit. "We are visiting the operational space. Breed might as well see the exercise facilities."

Thorval leads us at his customary brisk pace. The gym must be on the way to the Star Pool. Brightly lit, the passageway echoes with the sound of metal on metal. The compartment to the left is devoted to a weight room and circuit training course. The air is warm, humid, and smells of sweat.

Thorval pauses at the door. A group of men are working out with Nautilus equipment and free weights. Divers and crew. The crewmen are a mixed bunch. Some are rough-necks who work on the rig, others operate the vessel. I don't see research techs represented in the gym.

It's easy to tell the difference. The divers stand out. They're big, strong men in their late twenties or early thir-ties. Low body fat, lots of muscle mass. Selected for their ability to perform physically demanding work for extended periods at great depths.

Thorval's attention is fixed on a powerfully built man at the squat rack. He's balancing a bar across his shoulders. The bar is loaded with so many iron plates that it droops at both ends. Two other men stand on either side, spotting for him.

The man lowers himself, bends his knees ninety degrees. The spotters call out encouragement. The man's features flush with the strain, and purple veins on his neck swell to the point of bursting. He grits his teeth and groans harshly. Muscles quivering, he straightens his legs and sets the bar down on the rack.

"Martin," Thorval calls.

The man thanks his spotters. They bump fists and he tears off his lifting gloves. Jerks his chin toward Thorval. "Magnus. What's up?"

Dripping sweat, the man approaches. His long dark hair

and beard are matted. Boyish features lie under the beard. He's not as big as Knauss, but totally ripped. He treats us to an open, friendly smile.

"This is Martin Nygard," Thorval says. "He leads the Advance Team. Martin, this is Breed. He's taking over for Frank Aron. Miss Larson is a sedimentology analyst. She will be working in Hansen's department."

"Breed." Nygard gives my hand a perfunctory shake. There's strength in his grip, but he drops my hand quickly. He's more interested in Noa. Takes her hand and turns on the charm. "Ms Larson. Don't let Bert hide you away in that lab. He'd have the research staff working 24/7 if he could."

Noa lowers her eyes. I've never seen such a display of demure femininity. She isn't remotely like the hot chick I met in the Djevelkafé last night.

Nygard stirs my resentment.

"Are the Blue Team settled?" Thorval asks.

"Yes, everything is on track to commence operations when the storm clears." Nygard jerks his chin toward the men working out. "They're enjoying the space. It won't be long before we're cooped up in the subs."

So these are Blue Team divers. Hard-looking bunch, ex-military. Royal Navy, US Navy, Royal Norwegian Navy. Probably SEALs and Special Boat Service veterans. Corded muscles, lots of tattoos. They look like they spend six hours a day driving iron.

"Very good." Thorval gives Nygard a curt nod. "Breed and I shall leave you here. Ms Larson, enjoy your tour."

Thorval turns on his heel. Without a backward glance, he marches to the door.

The little magician is starting to annoy me.

. . .

HANSEN TAKES Noa to see the library. As they walk in the other direction, I hear him tell her about the *Spider's* internet and satellite phone facilities. Located on the library deck, they allow the crew to communicate with family and friends at home.

Thorval leads me to a bulkhead that separates the living space of the ship from the Star Pool. There is a heavy door that resembles a bank vault. A black security sensor plate is mounted on the bulkhead.

"Looks like Fort Knox," I say.

"I'm sure you've noticed there are two kinds of doors on board," Thorval tells me. "There are convenience doors, like the ones to our offices and cabins. Those are not watertight. The other kind are watertight doors. The convenience doors have normal handles and latches. Watertight doors like these are dogged shut by turning that wheel, which expands a set of levers, called dogs. Those seal the gasket on the door against the flat edge on the door frame. That makes the compartment watertight. The locking mechanism prevents the wheel from releasing the dogs."

I wave my pass over the sensor plate, and steel bolts slide aside. I spin the locking wheel, release the dogs, and swing the hatch open. Damp, frigid air envelops me as I step through the opening. Thorval follows me and shuts the door.

"Cold," I say.

"With the clam shell cover closed, the Star Pool is sheltered from the elements." Thorval zips his coveralls up to his chin. "It is not, however, climate-controlled."

He isn't joking. I'm glad I'm wearing my watch jacket. It's a couple of degrees above freezing. Exposed to the wind chill, it would feel colder.

I take a breath of dank air. The atmosphere smells of salt water and wet steel. Wet steel has a smell distinct from dry steel. When I was growing up in Montana, we washed out fifty gallon fuel drums and kept them behind the cabin to catch rainwater. That's what this metal cavern smells like.

We stand on the steel deck that surrounds a rectangular pool a hundred and twenty yards long by thirty yards wide. The overhead above the pool is three decks high. A lower deck houses hydraulics and gimbals to keep the upper deck —the operations deck—stable against the rolling, pitching and heaving of the ship. The operations deck is ringed by a safety catwalk from which workers tend the lifting equipment. Chest high, a steel safety barrier protects roughnecks from a three-story fall. The topmost deck supports the clamshell cover and houses the shutters when open to the sky. Closed, the shutters have a circular opening in the middle two meters in diameter. The derrick lowers the pipe stream through that oculus.

Powerful floodlights ring the operations deck and shine onto the waters of the pool. The reflections of the floodlights ripple softly in the black water. I'm staring into an ocean of stars. It's beautiful.

"The ship's hollow," I breathe.

"Yes." Thorval smiles. "The clamshell cover prevents aircraft and satellites from spying on our work. The Star Pool is six decks deep, from the level of the main deck to the bottom of the ship. There are hydraulic gates that can be opened or closed. When open, the water rises halfway up the pool, as high as the third deck. When closed, the water can be pumped out, and the space becomes a floating dry dock. The pool will accommodate the *Marshal Zhukov*."

To our right, on the port side of the ship, three yellow

miniature submarines sit, stowed in cradles on the deck. They are identified by black letters and numerals stenciled on their stubby conning towers. Two yellow cranes have been fixed in rotating mounts on either side. Their arms have been folded flat against the high bulkhead. The cranes are used to lower the mini-subs into the pool and hoist them onto the deck. The mini-subs are big, twenty-five percent larger than the decompression chambers.

"Mini-subs?" I ask.

"Submersibles," Thorval says. "Our divers live in them for extended periods on the bottom."

My eyes are drawn to three cigar-shaped objects resting on steel cradles. They sit on the deck next to the pool, nose-to-tail. Their skin is enamel white. Perfect cylinders, twenty-five feet long, their nose cones shine bright red.

There are two thin slits in the side of each tube. One halfway its length, and one at the back. The missiles are tube-launched. Their stabilization fins deploy from the slits as soon as the cigars clear the tubes.

"Kestrels," I say.

"Indeed." Thorval walks to the missiles with a slow, measured step. "Come see."

The magician leads me to the Kestrels as though showing off his stage equipment. He walks as though he owns the *Spider* and everything in it. Again, I'm struck by the man's air of superiority.

Thorval reaches out and caresses a Kestrel's smooth enamel surface. It's a sensuous touch. The magician's fingers, long and sensitive, taper to the tips. "How beautiful," he says. Not to me. To himself.

The deck is slick, with little puddles of standing water. Watertight doors have been evenly spaced around the pool.

They allow access from other areas of the ship. Thick wooden beams have been lashed to the side of the pool next to the missiles. Four deep, they extend into the Star Pool like a makeshift dock. A mountain of spare beams has been stacked against the bulkhead of the chamber, lashed securely with metal bands.

"What are the beams for?" I ask.

Thorval takes his hand from the Kestrel. Once again, he is all business. "Objects appear distorted underwater. We did not know the dimensions of the *Zhukov*. We designed the Star Pool with an error factor. The beams provide a dock."

The beams look slick. "Anybody ever fall in?"

"It has happened," Thorval says. "Anyone so careless learns his lesson quickly."

I circle the first Kestrel, examine the missile carefully. Reach out to touch it, withdraw my hand.

"Radiation?" I ask.

"No," Thorval says. "The reactor containment held. Radioactive coolant was diluted and flushed by two years of ocean currents."

Of course. Thorval was comfortable touching the missile, so he knew it was clean.

"They look brand new."

"Pruitt's team extracted the Kestrels directly from the missile launch tubes. The tubes protected the missiles during the sinking and after."

That means the missiles are armed with conventional warheads. Stein told me the nuclear warheads were stored in a special armory.

I walk along the deck, examine the other two missiles. All three look like they are in perfect condition.

"Have you seen enough?" Thorval asks. "I'm rather cold."

"Yes, let's go back."

"Isn't man's ingenuity astonishing," Thorval says. "Imagine building destructive devices of such advanced technology."

"Technology worth killing for."

I UNPACK my duffel and lay my clothing on the bed. Thorval wasn't kidding. Compared to the austere passageways and work compartments of the *Spider*, the officers' and scientists' cabins are like hotel rooms. Carpet, wide beds, closets. A small writing desk, a coffee table and a set of chairs complete the picture.

A glossy folder on the desk bears the Norsk Exploration logo. I flip open the cover. Inside is a brochure describing the Norsk Exploration *Spider*, the world's most advanced marine research drill ship. There are full color cutaway views of the *Spider* constructed with a series of acetate overlays. Each overlay shows the structure of one of the decks. The Star Pool is not labeled. Indeed, it is represented by an opaque black box beneath the derrick.

Stein's survival radio is waterproof. The device can't be a phone—there are no mobile towers in the Arctic Ocean. No, it must be an advanced satellite device.

Okay, let's unlock the screen. I trace Stein's security pattern among the dots. The security screen dissolves and the home screen appears.

There are four green dots that indicate a full battery, and four green dots that indicate a strong signal. Where's that signal coming from? Normally, a satphone requires exposure to the sky. How am I picking up a signal this deep inside the guts of the *Spider*? I don't know, but it's probably the same technology that makes the device effective in a storm, or under triple canopy jungle.

There are no phone numbers. A menu tree leads me to a directory of contacts. At the top of the list is an entry labeled *Pressley Bannon*. My thumb hovers over the selection. I hold my breath and tap the key.

With a soft buzz, the device vibrates in my hand. The display lights up and a woman's voice issues from a tiny speaker. I thumb the speakerphone symbol and adjust the volume.

"This is a US Navy channel," the voice says. "Who is this?"

"Commander Palomas, this is Breed."

"Breed. I wondered when we would hear from you."

"I'm on the *Spider*. Is Captain Cruik available?"

"Yes, I'll call him."

A moment of silence, and Cruik's voice comes on. "Breed, wait one. We're bringing Stein online."

Stein must be back in New York or Washington. She's never idle. What does she have? I put the radio on speakerphone. Stretch out with my back to the bulkhead.

"Breed." Stein's voice sounds like she's sitting right next to me.

"Stein, I hope you had a nice flight. I've been for a swim."

"I have intel for you. That helo crash was no accident."

My stomach clenches. "Tell me."

"The fuel drogue on the Hercules was sabotaged. The wing connector was loosened enough that it was bound to come loose."

"Are you certain?"

"No question. The right wing connector was also sabotaged. The crew went over the assembly at Evenes. The mechanics tell me most refueling accidents result from loose drogues. It was meant to look like an accident."

"We have to find the saboteur."

"I have a CID team on the way. The Norwegians aren't happy, but sabotage and espionage are great persuaders. The Norwegians are paranoid about the Russians."

"Stein, it was premeditated murder."

"We'll get him, Breed."

I address the captain. "Captain Cruik, have you advised Stein of the *Lenin's* presence?"

"She's aware. And there's more."

"Of course."

Cruik takes a breath. "We've intercepted a transmission from the *Spider*. Encrypted, directed to the *Lenin*."

"Can you decrypt it?"

"We've recorded the transmission," Stein says. "I have the NSA working on it. If we get lucky, we can track it to within a square meter. A specific compartment on a specific deck on the *Spider*."

"How does that work?"

"On land, two cell phone towers are all you need to triangulate a position. The Russian has a device like yours. It works on sophisticated satellite technology. The signals are passed from one satellite to another depending on your relative position. If the switch happens while you are transmitting, we can triangulate."

"To the deck level."

"Triangulation in the vertical plane provides depth perception. We use the same technology to target our tactical missiles. The Russians have the same capability."

"The point is," Cruik says, "this proves there is a Russian operative aboard the *Spider*. He's got a radio like yours. The sabotage means you were never meant to arrive. The Russians know we have Kestrels. They know we intend to salvage the *Marshal Zhukov*."

Stein cuts in. "It's worse than that."

"How so?"

"It means our operation was compromised from the beginning."

12

FRIDAY, 1900 HOURS – THE SPIDER - DINNER

Frank Aron's survival radio must have been on him when the killer pitched him over the side. If he left it in his cabin, the killer took it. Stein's changed our communication channels on the chance the killer got past its security.

I take off my US Navy coveralls and change into casual clothes. The *Pressley Bannon's* laundry folded my pants and shirt. I put on the US Navy watch jacket—it's heavier and warmer than my own. I slip the radio into a pocket and zip it shut.

The pocket will do for the moment, but I don't want to walk around with the radio on me. There's always a chance someone will see it and remark on its unconventional appearance. Even the sight of its outline in a pocket is unusual. I can't explain it away as a mobile phone, because mobile phones don't work out here. On the other hand, I don't want to leave it in my cabin for Frank Aron's killer to find.

Fortunately, the *Spider* is a big ship. There are six thousand people on an aircraft carrier, two hundred on the *Spider*. There's a lot of space for two hundred marbles to roll around.

I studied the schematics of the *Spider* in the Norsk Exploration brochure. A couple of ideas came to mind. I step into the passageway and close the cabin door behind me. Two research techs walk past and get in the elevator. I wait for them to leave, then go to the door that opens into the fo'c'sle. There's no security panel, no one has thought to enforce security in the ship's dead spaces.

I spin the locking wheel, retract the dogs, and unseal the gasket. Step into the fo'c'sle, secure the door behind me.

The dead space of the fo'c'sle is lit by dim, low-wattage bulbs. With three power plants and a vast supply of fuel, the crew of the *Spider* don't mind keeping the ship lighted. That extravagance doesn't extend to heating—the air is cold. Thorval said temperatures in the dead space ranged from 37 to 42 degrees Fahrenheit. The climate-controlled shoebox is this steel cavern's only heater. The bulkheads are dank with condensation. Thousands of rivulets trickle onto the deck. I advance cautiously through the dead space.

On either side of the bow are two huge chain lockers several decks high. They store the coils of anchor chains. Thick Spurling pipes lead from the chain lockers to windlasses on the fo'c'sle deck above. From there, the chains connect to anchors that sit in hawse pipes. The arrangement allows the anchors to be raised and lowered.

Similar arrangements are used for the *Spider's* eight arachnid mooring legs, but those use metal cables rather than chains. The bottom line is—the traditional anchors are not in use. I pick my way over various obstacles until I reach the starboard chain locker.

The chain locker is a massive steel box protruding ten feet from the surface of the deck. I'm sure there's more sitting in the deck below. There is a flat steel shelf between the top of the locker and the base of the Spurling pipe. I stand on tiptoe, place the survival radio on the shelf. No one will think to look there, and I can retrieve it at will.

I turn around, make my way back to the door. From the fo'c'sle, it's easy to see the construction of the *Spider*. The big shoebox of living and work space is exactly that. A big steel building set in the hull, six decks high. The sides of the shoebox are flat, and the space between them and the hull are occupied by fuel, fresh water, and trim tanks. The original VLCC was a double-hull design to guard against oil spills. The double-hull was preserved when the keel under the Star Pool was removed and the hydraulic shutters installed.

The passageway is deserted. I step inside and close the door behind me. Go to the elevator and look for the officers' mess.

I find it occupies half the forward superstructure above the boat deck. It's meant to be airy, with rectangular windows that look out on the bow and the sea. Tonight, the glass is black where the blinds have not been shut.

The storm is upon us, and the thick windowpanes shudder under sixty-mile-an-hour winds. Force 10, and the arctic cyclone promises more violence before the night is through. Blowing snow melts against the panes and the water is blasted off the surface in stilettos of ice.

Somewhere out there, the *Pressley Bannon* is standing off. The destroyer will sail a rectangular box until morning. Cruik, Palomas and their crew will not enjoy much sleep. The ship will pitch through the short sides of the box, through alternating bow and stern seas. As the vessel traverses the long sides, the beam seas will smash its sides with forty and fifty-foot waves. The ship will roll as much as forty degrees.

While the *Pressley Bannon* might roll sixty and still recover, the experience will leave the crew exhausted by morning. Exhausted from lack of sleep. Exhausted from mind-numbing anxiety. She'll come back from sixty, but what if she doesn't? What if there is enough ice on the deck to raise the vessel's center of gravity that extra bit? Enough to prevent it from recovering?

The *Pressley Bannon* seems a world away as I survey the *Spider's* peaceful, blessedly stable, officers' mess. The compartment is much larger than I expected. There are sets of long tables and bench seats bolted to the deck. At one end of the room is a raised stage. Like most environments where men are away from their families for long periods of time, skits are a staple of entertainment. We did them all the time when I was in the army. Anything to break the monotony between engagements, to have a laugh and relieve boredom. A drill ship in the Arctic is no exception.

At the foot of the stage is a round table, also bolted to the floor. Meant for Captain Angers and senior officers, it's covered with a white tablecloth. The rest of the room is comfortable, with sofas, easy chairs, and a wall-mounted television screen. I see Dr Voss folded into an easy chair, reading a paperback romance.

One long table is occupied by two rows of divers. I count nineteen, including Knauss and Nygard. Twelve in the Blue Team, six in Nygard's Advance Team, and Knauss in overall command. The other tables are occupied by research staff.

They're a young group. Almost all are in their twenties or early thirties. I look for Hansen, but don't see him.

Noa is sitting by herself at the end of one of the tables, picking at a meal.

One look at her makes me swallow hard. She's dressed in the tight Levi's she wore on the helo, and a skintight black halter top. Her golden hair is in two braided pigtails. The thin halter straps show off her broad shoulders and smooth skin. On the helicopter, she must have worn it under her shirt and jacket.

There's a buffet arranged against one bulkhead. I take a tray and help myself to some roast beef and mashed potatoes. Carry it to Noa's table. "May I join you?"

Noa looks up. Our eyes meet, and she hesitates. "It is not a good idea," she says.

She's not being rude. There's none of the in-your-face attitude we gave each other last night. If anything, there's a soft yearning between us. She looks thoughtful, like she's considered the matter and decided we shouldn't associate with each other.

Heat rushes to my scalp.

"Alright," I say. "Let me know if you change your mind."

Knauss says something to Nygard and the group of divers laugh.

There's a coffee table near Dr Voss's easy chair. I carry my tray to it and give her a questioning look.

"Breed," the little lady says. "Sit down. Make yourself comfortable."

I set the tray down and attack my meal with gusto.

"She's a beautiful girl," Voss says.

"I hadn't noticed."

The doctor laughs. "The pair of you would make a handsome couple on the cover of one of my thrillers. Do you know each other?"

I smile. "Only a little."

"Ah." Voss nods with understanding. "She's a young thing, Breed. Can't be long out of school. Her first job? She can't afford mistakes."

I finish my roast beef and set the tray aside. Lean back in the sofa. "How do you know so much?"

Voss winks. "I'm the ship's doctor. It's my job."

Noa finishes her meal, stands up slowly, and rises to her full height. Her hair shines like gold, her cheeks glow with the blush of youth. She's taller than some of the divers. There are women among the research staff, but there's no one as striking as Noa on this ship. The divers go silent.

With studied nonchalance, Noa carries her tray to a disposal rack. She sets it down and leaves the mess. I don't know whether to look at the perfect skin on her shoulders, her breasts, or her tight buttocks. They twitch rhythmically with every step of her long legs. As she walks, her pigtails swish from side to side, in counterpoint to her hips. The eyes of every man in the mess follow her like those of slavering wolves.

Oxygen rushes back into the compartment.

I turn to Dr Voss. "What were you saying about mistakes?"

Voss clucks. "My, my," she says, "that girl is trouble."

The girl is a distraction. I focus my attention on Voss. "Tell me about Aron," I say.

"What do you want to know?"

"The kind of man he was, how he spent his time."

"He was a competent man." Voss folds her novel face-down on her knee, pages spread. The kind of position guaranteed to crack the volume's spine. "Very conscientious, very detail-oriented. He never slept. He was always poking around. In that respect, a great deal like you."

I ignore the remark. "*Where* did he poke around?"

"I didn't follow him. As far as I could tell, he was always on the operations deck, the operations bridge, the navigation bridge. I sometimes saw him prowling the passageways."

"There are miles of passageways."

"Indeed there are." Voss stares at her reflection in the black mirror of a window. The wind moans and the glass rattles. "I once saw him stepping out of the dead space."

I shiver. "Where?"

"The end of the sickbay passageway. Every deck has a number of doors leading into the dead space. One at the fo'c'sle end, one at the stern, several in between. I think he explored the dead space on every deck."

"Why?"

Voss shrugs. "Who knows. Perhaps he had nothing better to do."

"You don't believe that."

"No. But it's none of my business."

Like me, Aron was drawn to the dead space. If you want to hide something on the *Spider*, you go to the dead space.

"Who did he spend his time with?"

"Before Sam Pruitt dove on the wreck, he and Aron spent a lot of time together. Otherwise, Aron kept to himself. Of course, he spent a lot of time with Captain Angers and Magnus Thorval. That's natural, isn't it?"

"Yes, it is. What are the captain and Thorval like?"

"Can't you tell? Captain Angers is honest and straightforward. What you see is what you get. A cantankerous old salt. Thorval is a dedicated professional, a perfectionist. Like

Aron, he is detail-oriented. Technically, Aron reported to him. Aron was the surface manager, Knauss the dive manager, Thorval the general manager. I think the three made a good team."

Voss's description of the men align with my perceptions. Knauss is a rough customer, but he knows his work.

"Was there anything unusual about the day Aron went missing?"

"There was a lot of activity," the doctor says. "We brought up the last Kestrel. I was with Sam Pruitt and his divers. Decompression chambers were rolled onto the Star Pool deck through a special gate. Their airlocks were mated with the submersibles, the divers transferred, and the chambers rolled back to their compartment. I recorded the divers' physiological data. They took samples and passed them through the airlocks."

"So you weren't in the Star Pool the whole time?"

"I was. Transferring the divers took longer than securing the Kestrels. Aron and Knauss were in the Star Pool. Aron stowed the missiles while Knauss and Nygard secured the submersibles. I don't remember seeing Captain Angers."

"Anything unusual?"

"No, it was busy. We knew a storm was brewing to the east, so we moved heaven and earth to prepare the Kestrels for transfer."

I stand and pick up my tray. "Thanks for your company, Dr Voss. I reckon I'll be on my way."

What did I tell Cruik? *Great minds think alike.*

I know one place Aron visited the day he died.

13

FRIDAY, 2000 HOURS – THE SPIDER - DEAD SPACE

Great minds think alike.

Frank Aron was a practical man. He wasn't sure there were bad guys on board, but he suspected. So he assumed they knew he was Stein's man. He wouldn't keep his survival radio in his cabin. He'd hide it where I thought to hide mine. In the dead space.

I take the elevator down to the sickbay deck and go straight to the door at the end of the passageway. This is where Voss saw Aron emerge from the dead space. I spin the wheel and jerk the door open. Enter the dead space, close the door behind me.

This is the fo'c'sle. My eyes adjust to the dim light. There, I see the Spurling pipes that lead from the chain lockers below. I sweep the chamber, which looks empty. There are no obvious hiding places.

I turn around and scan the gloomy space between the shoebox bulkheads and the hull. The long, cylindrical trim and ballast tanks, the valves and pumps used to fill and empty them. I'm looking down the port side of the ship. There is a similar space starboard.

Slow is fast. I'm not going to find anything by rushing around in a panic. I need to conduct a systematic search, a full circuit from port to starboard and back.

Deliberately, I walk across the space. Steel bulkhead to my left, pipes and tanks to my right. Some tanks are twelve feet in diameter and a hundred feet long. Capped and bound with steel bands.

The space is cavernous. The overhead is fifteen feet high. I'm surprised to find companionways between the tanks. There aren't many, one or two per compartment. They lead up to a closed watertight hatch set in the overhead. Of course, they allow maintenance crews to pass between decks.

All the watertight doors and hatches on the ship have colored "condition labels" fixed to both sides. A red label indicates the door or hatch should be kept dogged shut. Green labels indicate the door or hatch may be kept open and shut only in emergencies.

The hatches, which open vertically rather than horizontally, all sport red condition labels. Should the deck be holed and opened to the sea, the integrity of the decks above and below must not be compromised.

Sure enough, I find a hatch in the deck. I prop it open with a hinged metal hockey stick attached to the back. The hockey stick is a safety feature that prevents the hatch from falling shut on a man climbing through from below. I see a companionway descending to the dead space. I unlatch the hockey stick and lower the hatch. Spin the locking wheel to secure it, move on.

Wish I had a flashlight. The bulkhead and overhead

lights are enough to find my way, but I have a hard time making out detail. I'm astonished by the amount of clutter in the dead space. It's an obstacle course.

Thorval said they had searched the ship twice. Did they search the dead space? The dead space is so vast, it appears to be a whole other ship.

A hundred yards further along the side of the ship, I find myself face-to-face with a transverse door and bulkhead. I'm amidships now. I step through the doorway. The Star Pool is on the other side of the bulkhead on the left. On the right, a shadowy mass stretches several decks high.

There's no overhead. I'm staring at a cavernous space that stretches to what has to be the bottom of the lower operations deck. To my right is a mountain of narrow-gauge pipes, each thirty-five yards long. I reach out and examine one by touch. The end is threaded. The pipes are designed to fit one on top of the other. The lengths are screwed together and lowered into the ocean. This is the female end of a pipe segment.

The mountain of pipes stretches almost to the base of the operations deck. They're stored in gated metal cages. The gates each consist of three segmented metal bars, arranged a hundred feet apart along the length of the hull. They extend vertically toward the operations deck and are hinged at fifteen-foot intervals. The hinges are locked in place by horizontal steel rods connected to mechanical levers. Pulling on the levers shoots the rods aside and releases the gates, leaving them free to swing flat. As the pipes are loaded aboard, the mountains grow higher and the gates are progressively shut.

There are three such cages, evenly spaced along the hundred and fifty yards of compartment. Between the cages are more companionways and watertight hatches leading to the decks above and below. At similar intervals, doors open into the Star Pool. The doors that lead to the Star Pool have security sensors mounted to the bulkhead next to them.

The derrick and cranes on the operations deck are maneuvered over these mountains of steel. Roughnecks connect a section of pipe to the hoist so the derrick can raise the pipe. The roughnecks guide the male screw of one pipe onto the female end of the topmost one on the pipe stream. There are miles of pipe stored in these cages, on both sides of the ship. Pipe streams used to drill cores for research staff to analyze. Pipe streams to guide the lifting device for the *Marshal Zhukov*.

The engineering that went into building the *Spider* boggles the mind. Nathan Conrad might not have designed everything himself, but he conceived it. Stein told him about the *Marshal Zhukov*, and Conrad had the vision to see what could be done.

I continue to cross the compartment. To my left is one of the doors that provide access to the Star Pool. I wave my pass at the sensor plate and hear the bolts slide back. I open the door a crack and find myself looking into the Star Pool. Close the door, walk the rest of the way to the next transverse bulkhead. I go through another door and find myself in the dead space at the stern of the *Spider*.

The space smells like the Star Pool. Dank metal. I pass the aft peak trim tank, turn the corner, and start to make my way back along the starboard side of the ship. On my right are a cluster of fifty gallon metal drums. Two colors. Gray and light green. I stare at the labels. Paint and solvent.

Some lucky son of a bitch gets to hang off the side and

paint the hull from one end to the other. Then back the other side. I wonder when they last used this stuff.

The lids on all the drums are sealed and painted over. The dry paint covers the lid and the body of the drum. The paint is intact on all the drums, save one. A light green drum of solvent. It wears scratches along six inches of the circumference of its lid.

Our radios are waterproof. Aron wouldn't think twice about immersing his in solvent.

I push on the lid, try to lift it open. It won't budge, and I have no tools. I look around for anything like a crowbar. Nothing.

Further forward are tanks and pipes like the ones on the port side. The pipes and valves need to be maintained. In fact, most are controlled by hydraulics from the bridge. They enable the crew to adjust the attitude of the ship in the water.

There's a toolbox pressed up against the bulkhead under a Christmas tree of pipes. Left there by an engineer working on the tanks. Heavy wrenches lie next to it, too big to fit inside. I flip the lid open, rummage around. No crowbar. Lots of smaller wrenches, hammers, screwdrivers.

I select a big, flathead screwdriver and a hammer. Go back to the drum and push the edge of the screwdriver against the seam between the lid and the drum. Take the hammer, bang against the handle of the screwdriver. Each blow echoes through the dead space with a deafening clang. Half a dozen blows, and the screwdriver's sharp edge splits the seam. I twist the tool so the flathead points upward. Bang on it some more.

The lid of the drum pops off and I'm assaulted by the sharp smell of turpentine. This isn't the sweet, piney, gum

turpentine marketed for home use. It's industrial quality
wood turpentine, and it smells like benzene. I reel backward,
blink against the assault on my senses.

I rub my eyes, force myself to stare into the black liquid.
The surface sloshes around, two inches from the top of the
drum.

A pale, bulbous object the size of a volleyball swims into
view. It's smooth and white, like the snout of a porpoise or
baby whale. Can't make out what it is. I look closer, force my
eyes to follow the contours of the object. When I see what it
is, I choke and take a step back.

"*Fuck.*"

It's a face. Not of a baby whale, but a man. Hair matted to
his crushed skull, bleached white. His eyes are open—ivory
pupils set in glass marbles. The albino features have been
completely bled of color. The head is set on the shoulders of
a dark jacket. I can't discern the dead man's facial expression.
The corpse has been submerged for sixty hours and it's
bloating.

I've found Frank Aron.

I TAKE off my watch jacket and shirt. Hold my nose against
the chemical stench, force myself to search the dead man's
pockets. No radio. If Aron was carrying his radio, the killer
took it. I push the corpse back into the drum and pound the
lid shut.

The solvent wicks quickly from my arm. I put my shirt
and jacket back on. Step back, stare at the drum. Aron hid
his radio down here. The killer followed him.

I saw a glint of metal at the bottom of the drum. A heavy
steel wrench, undoubtedly the murder weapon. Rather than

take the time to clean the wrench, the killer tossed it into the drum.

The killer would not have wanted to attack Aron until Aron had recovered whatever he had hidden. Then the killer would have hit Aron from behind, on the right side of his head.

Aron's skull was crushed on the left side.

That means Aron heard the killer approach, turned, and got his head knocked off. That means Aron hadn't recovered his radio before he was attacked.

The radio is still down here.

I try to think. Look at the deck underneath the drums. The metal surface is clean. Except for a crescent of rust under the drum that has become Frank Aron's coffin. I put my shoulder to the drum and tip it sideways to reveal the deck underneath.

Jackpot. A flat survival radio exactly like mine. Next to it is a device equipped with a USB cable—Aron's wireless charger. With my foot, I sweep the radio out from under the drum. Rock the drum back into place. Satisfied, I pick up the radio and push the "ON" button. The device comes to life.

Did Aron change Stein's security pattern on his radio? I didn't change it on mine. Let's hope he was lazy too. I swipe Stein's pattern over the dots. Breathe a sigh of relief when the phone lets me in. I'm greeted by the home screen and comforting green dots that indicate I have a signal and a quarter of a full charge.

Stein changed our channels on the chance the killer had Aron's radio and security pattern. She needn't have bothered. I call up the channel directory. There it is, top of the list. *Pressley Bannon.* But now it's the wrong channel. I think back to the settings on my radio and reprogram Aron's.

"This is a US Navy channel," Palomas says. "Identify yourself."

"Commander Palomas, this is Breed. There have been developments."

"Our side as well. Wait one."

Cruik's voice comes on the radio. "Breed. What have you found?"

"I've found Frank Aron's corpse, pickled in a fifty gallon drum of turpentine. It's sitting in the dead space of the *Spider*. His radio was hidden under the drum."

The Captain doesn't miss a beat. "There has been another transmission from the Russian agent to the *Lenin*. Stein's team triangulated it to the officers' cabins on the *Spider*, but that's all we got. The operator was not on the call long enough to pinpoint his location."

"Upper cabin deck or lower cabin deck?"

"Upper."

"That's a start."

"Any idea who did Aron?"

"Negative. Aron didn't want to carry his radio, and he didn't want to hide it in his cabin. He hid it in the dead space. I think he learned something and wanted to report. The killer followed him. The killer wasn't quiet enough. Aron heard him, turned around, and got smashed on the side of his head. *Before* he recovered his radio, *before* he had a chance to report."

"What do you think he learned?"

"All we know is that it probably had something to do with the transfer of the Kestrels. Everything is coming together around that. Where's the *Lenin*?"

"Still in the middle of the storm, skirting the ice pack.

He's working his way toward us. With a following sea, he's making good time."

"Alright, Captain. I'd better go. I'll let you know if I learn more."

I sign off, tip the drum sideways, and slide the survival radio back under it. As I set the drum back in place, I feel the corpse shift inside—like pickled fruit bobbing in a jar.

14

FRIDAY, 2200 HOURS – THE SPIDER - WORKOUT

I return to my cabin with a lot of information to process. Hard physical exercise always clears my head. My gym clothes lie at the bottom of the Greenland Sea, so I improvise. I take my shirt off, go for a jog in my pants.

The passageway that runs the length of the officers' cabin deck is just under a hundred yards long. At the aft transverse bulkhead, it turns at a right angle into a passageway that runs fifty yards along the beam of the ship. Another right-angled turn and it leads forward to the next transverse bulkhead and the passageway where one finds the elevator and companionways.

Altogether, a serviceable three-hundred-yard track.

I jog the circuit. Slowly at first, warming up and loosening my muscles. Three laps of the deck, and I've covered half a mile. The next circuit, I hit the companionway and climb to the next deck. Keep running. Do three laps of that deck, hit the companionway and climb one more. Do three laps, head back down.

Working up a sweat. Lungs working like bellows. It's the

middle of the night and there are few people about. In the forward section of the *Spider*, most of the people are research techs. I don't know what they do for exercise, but they stare at me like I'm crazy.

They probably use the gym. Free weights, Nautilus, treadmills. Maybe I'll stop by later and do some lifting.

Infantry is an athletic event. People don't realize that an operator has to work out at least twice a day to remain fit for combat. Aerobic fitness from swimming and running. Anaerobic strength from weight training routines. Combatives and martial arts. Skills have to be honed, then maintained. Get to a level, you feel your capability degrade when you don't keep up the exercises.

I keep up the exercises.

Two circuits of three decks and I figure I've done three miles. I push the pace hard for three more decks and stop. Four-and-a-half miles. My mind is clear. Not once during the workout did Noa or the murder of Frank Aron cross my mind.

I smile to myself, walk one circuit of the deck, and make my way to the gym.

The clank of metal on metal greets me as I enter. Like most gyms, the place is like a foundry. The air is hot and humid. The compartment reeks of sweat and metal.

I step inside to check out the equipment. There are half a dozen men working out. Big bruisers, every one of them. Most are bare-chested. A couple are wearing T-shirts. One ratty shirt has what looks like a Fairbairn-Sykes commando knife embroidered over the left tit.

Lots of beards, lots of tattoos. Multi-colored sleeves, anchors, and yes—a couple of tridents.

Knauss's divers. I recognize most of them… They were

sitting at Knauss's table at dinner. Neither Knauss nor
Nygard are among the group. One or two are working out on
the machines. The others are working with free weights.
One guy is benching a barbell and a massive load of iron
plates. The dude spotting for him looks part gorilla.

A guy doing leg presses swings off the machine and gets
up to face me. "You're Breed," he says.

The room falls silent. The other divers stop their workouts, turn to check me out.

I've learned to smile whenever I enter a room. It puts
people at ease. "That's me," I say. "I'm here to take over for
Frank Aron."

The man who addressed me puts his hands on his hips
and steps closer. Blond hair, shaggy beard. He's bare-chested,
an anchor tattooed on his chest. The Viking's wearing
workout shorts and Nike trainers.

"You broke Knauss's arm," he says.

"That's right. He pointed a rifle at me."

The Viking shakes his head. "I heard you sucker
punched him."

Now, that's downright unfair. When the other guy is
drawing down on you, you do what you have to do. The
other divers look up from their workouts. They get to their
feet and form a loose semi-circle behind the blond Viking.

"Tell you what," I say. "You boys finish up and I'll come
back later."

I turn to leave, but one of the divers has circled around
behind me. "Karma's a bitch, dude. You walked into the
wrong room."

The guy wearing the T-shirt, with the commando knife
embroidered over his tit shambles forward. Jerks a four-foot
steel shaft from a rack and holds it like a billy club. One-inch

diameter, weighs about twenty-five pounds. "That's the truth, mate. This isn't your day."

An English accent. Probably ex-Special Boat Service. Drawn from the Royal Marine Commandos.

As a rule, I stay away from bar fights and street fights. The other guy usually has a fantasy in his mind about how he beats you up and leaves you broken and bleeding. In modern society, he doesn't think past the injury stage. He doesn't think of killing you.

But it's easy to kill in a bar fight. It's easy to die. A friend of mine was knocked down, hit his head on the sidewalk and died. The other man wasn't even trying to kill him. I don't know how many of these men have killed. Special Forces can spend years on deployment and never get a chance to test themselves. Men who spent their careers becoming professional divers are unlikely to have taken part in Direct Action.

Six-on-one makes it impossible for me to calibrate my use of force. I know I'm going to get fucked up. No matter how well trained, *nobody* takes on six guys without getting hurt. *Period.* This isn't a Hollywood fantasy. All they have to do is dog-pile me.

That narrows my options.

The Viking's dead. I'm sure he doesn't expect to die today. Sorry about that, but it can't be helped. Then the guy behind me. Can't leave *him* free to work mischief back there. I can do them in fifteen seconds. After that, there will be four left. From that point on, I have a fight I can win.

A throaty voice growls, "Stand down, boys."

It's Knauss. I can tell from the direction of his growl that he's standing at the door. I'm not taking my eyes off the Viking. Not until he's on the ground.

"Knauss, how many men do you need to raise that sub?"
I ask.

"Horvath," Knauss says, "I can raise that sub with twelve
men. I can't do it with six."

"Bull-shit, Knauss," the Viking says.

"Breed here, he don't take prisoners. Do you, Breed."

I say nothing.

Knauss walks into the room. Circles around to a position
on my right where he can watch all of us. "Stand down,
Horvath. That's an order."

The commando holds his club at high port, turns to face
Knauss. "C'mon, Knauss. This guy's a bleeding puff."

Knauss steps forward and grabs the middle of the steel
shaft with his left hand. The muscles in his forearm bunch
and his tattoos ripple. Robo-SEAL jerks the commando
close. With the flat of his right hand, he slaps the man four
times across the face. Forehand, backhand, forehand, backhand. So fast, Knauss's hand blurs. Such force, the
commando lets go of the club and reels. Loses his balance,
barely keeps his feet. "Who do you think you're talking to,
boy?"

There's motion behind me and to my right. The man at
my back is stepping forward. I half-turn, ready to defend
myself. Knauss shifts his grip on the metal rod. Two-handed,
he jabs the end of the shaft into the man's face. There's a
crack as the blunt weapon makes contact, and the man's
front teeth give way. With a cry, he falls to the floor, hands to
his mouth.

The commando recovers from the slaps. Humiliated, he
lunges for Knauss, who reverses his stance and spears the
commando in the chest. The breath explodes from the man's

lungs with an agonized grunt. His eyes bug, and he collapses. Red-faced, curled into a fetal position, tears pour from his eyes as he struggles for breath.

Staff in hand, Knauss faces the Viking. Robo-SEAL carries the four foot, twenty-five-pound steel rod as easily as a baseball bat. "What about it, Horvath?" Knauss snarls. "You want to run this bunch?"

The Viking glares at Knauss. Says nothing.

"Speak up, boy!" Murder gleams in Knauss's eyes. When he is sure Horvath has been cowed, Knauss locks eyes with each of the other men in turn. "Anybody else want to run this bunch? Step up right now."

Four pairs of eyes slide uneasily around the room. They're looking everywhere but at Knauss. "Either I run this bunch or you throw me overboard," Knauss says. "Now pick this man up and take him to Voss. I want him on his feet in an hour."

The man rolling on the deck has covered his mouth with his hands, but blood is seeping between his fingers. A handful of little bloody pebbles litter the deck. Knauss has knocked out all his front teeth. "Get up," Knauss's voice is devoid of sympathy. "You're not hurt. I could have killed you if I wanted. Now take him to Voss."

Two of the divers help the man with the broken face to his feet. Lead him from the room. Knauss turns to me.

"Get lost, Breed. Your time ain't come."

Heart pounding, I turn and walk out the door. Knauss calls after me.

"Soon, Breed. *Real* soon."

· · ·

I RETURN TO MY CABIN. Shower, towel off, change my clothes. Collapse into an easy chair and stare at the bulkhead.

Knauss runs a pirate crew. Rules it with an iron fist. With every minute that passes, I grow more uneasy. I shrug on my jacket and go back outside. Something is going on, and I don't like not knowing what it is.

15

Timelines are crucial. I don't have a timeline of Aron's last day.

What did Angers say? *I don't know who saw him last. The three of us were speaking here on the bridge.*

Captain Angers was speaking with Thorval and Aron on the bridge. I should have asked what time. I don't know if that conversation happened before or after Thorval and Aron supervised the recovery of the Kestrels.

I walk to the elevator and punch the button for the bridge.

As soon as the storm passes, *Lenin* will move on the *Spider*. There is no way Captain Cruik will allow Russians to board us. The Russians, however, have an ace in the hole. Operatives aboard the *Spider*. The Russians don't have to blow us out of the water if their operatives can tilt the battle in their favor.

I have to find their operatives and stop them.

The elevator door sucks open. I step into the passageway that leads to the bridge and walk toward the companionway at the far end. I hear the radio operator's voice coming from the radio room.

"Affirmative, Tiger One-five. *Spider* out."

I climb the companionway two steps at a time. My eyes sweep the bridge, looking for Angers. The captain is sitting in his leather chair, contemplating the storm. The wind howls around the bridge. I look through the back windows. The masthead light at the top of the derrick is barely visible through the driving snow.

The two lookouts stand at the wings of the bridge, staring into the night. I'm sure they can't see a thing. They remain awake, alert, and they do their job under the eye of their captain. Years at sea have taught him the human eye is not subject to power failures, electronic jamming, or faults. The eye can, however, be blinded by darkness, rain and blowing snow. Far more reliable in this environment are the men standing at the radar and sonar scopes.

I look down at one of the radar scopes. There is one strong contact five miles south. Another contact lies north-by-east. The latter contact is intermittent. One moment it is there. The next, it disappears until the restless sweep of the radar signal picks it up again.

"We're not alone." I step to Angers's side.

"No," the captain says. "The signal to the south is the *USS Pressley Bannon*. They are standing off until dawn."

"And the other?" I watch Angers carefully.

"We don't know, but we are keeping it under observation. If it gets too close, we'll hail it."

I walk up and down the bridge. Feel Angers's eyes following me.

The compartment is climate-controlled. The control tower windows are shatterproof. Still, the wind howls like a banshee. It attacks the glass with gusts that strike like hammer blows. Lancets of ice shatter against the glass or fly past like volleys of arrows.

"Force 12," Angers says, "and the barometer is still falling. I've seen worse, but this one is up there."

"Will the destroyer be alright?"

"Oh, they are safe enough. The *Arleigh Burke* design will come back from sixty degrees of roll so long as they keep the deck clear of ice. I am here to make certain we do not lose our pipe stream."

"How much longer in this storm?"

"We'll have seen the worst by midnight." Angers crosses his legs and gets comfortable. "The *Spider* is riding the storm very well."

"Mr Breed. What are you doing here?"

Thorval. I recognize the clipped, precise accent. The general manager has ascended the companionway and stepped onto the bridge. He wears deck shoes, blue flannel trousers, and a black duffel coat, belted at the waist. His hands are thrust into his pockets. It's a relaxed pose, yet his eyes are sharp with intelligence.

"It's too early for bed, Thorval. Besides, I'm still troubled by Aron's disappearance. Aren't you?"

"Of course. However, there are other pressing matters. Should the storm clear tomorrow, we will offload the Kestrels."

I look out the front windows. Stare at my reflection in the black mirror. My features are distorted by snow melting against the glass. It quivers with the beat of wind.

"Captain Angers, you said you and Thorval spoke with Aron on the bridge. When was that?"

"Does it matter?"

"Everything matters."

"Mr Breed is right," Thorval says. "A butterfly flapping its wings in South America might have caused this storm."

Angers sighs and shifts in his chair. "Late afternoon, early evening."

"After the Kestrels were squared away."

"Yes."

"Very well. Aron and Thorval came up to see you. What did you discuss?"

"I don't recall, specifically. We conferred about the status of the operation. Concluded we could report that Phase II was complete."

I look to Thorval for confirmation. The general manager says nothing, nods.

"You decided to radio Stein with that big, powerful HF set."

The captain sits rigid in his chair. "We radioed the destroyer."

"Who did?"

"The three of us went into the radio room."

"What then?"

"Then, nothing." Angers drums his fingers on his chair's leather armrest. "Aron went below."

I turn to Thorval. "Is that your recollection?"

Thorval raises an eyebrow. "Yes. How does this help?"

"I want to understand how Aron spent that day. How did you learn he was missing?"

"He was expected on the operations deck the following morning." Angers stretches his legs. "When he did not appear, he was reported missing. We went to his cabin. He was not there."

The Captain looks tense. Thorval, on the other hand,

looks calm. Hands in his pockets, he wanders to the rear windows. Gazes at the masthead light. "Breed, we have much to do tomorrow. This can keep."

On the radar screens, the blinking contacts draw me. I step to the side of the crewman on watch and stare at the *Pressley Bannon* and the *Lenin*. The two warships carry enough destructive power to wipe each other and the *Spider* off the face of the earth.

"You're right, Thorval." I look up from the screens. "Let's pick it up after the transfer."

I feel Angers's and Thorval's eyes on me as I walk to the companionway. Descend to the radio and navigation compartments. Look in on the crewmen manning the consoles. The radio operator is sitting at the Extremely Low Frequency set. Its dials glow with blue-green light.

I'm sure of one thing.

Apart from the killer, Angers and Thorval were the last men to see Aron alive.

16

FRIDAY, 2400 HOURS – THE SPIDER - SLEEP

Like a vampire, I prowl the passageways of the *Spider*. From deck to deck, fore to aft and back again. I have a crayon impression of Aron's last day. It was a big day, the day the Kestrels were raised, the day Phase II closed. He got up, went to work, and supervised the stowage of the missiles. The Gold Team were transferred to the decompression chambers, and the submersibles were stowed.

That much was normal. Aron and Thorval went to the navigation bridge to speak with Captain Angers. The three men conferred, and went to the radio room to notify the *Pressley Bannon* that the Kestrels were ready for transfer.

Aron left the others. It was early evening. He went to the sickbay deck, entered the dead space, and sought to retrieve his radio. The killer followed and killed him. Stuffed his body into a drum of solvent.

Something doesn't sit well with me.

When I first came aboard, I asked Thorval if they had

searched the entire ship. He said they had—twice. There were only so many places an injured man could fall.

Thorval patronized me with his intellect. *If, indeed, Aron was murdered, the best place to conceal the body is the ocean.*

Which sounds true, but isn't. If you murder a man in the dead space, it can be hell getting the body to the main deck without being seen. *The best place to hide anything on the Spider is the dead space.*

I make my way to the chain lockers and retrieve my radio. Sit with my back to the forepeak and thumb the button for the *Pressley Bannon.* I find Commander Palomas's voice familiar.

"Breed, don't you sleep?"

"I could ask *you* the same question, Commander."

"Between watches, naval officers sleep when they can."

"Soldiers too," I tell her. "We catch power naps all the time."

Active military bond over simple things like that. The average civilian can't understand what it's like. Power-napping because you don't know when your next chance to sleep will come.

I hear Palomas smile. "How can I help, soldier? Want to speak to the captain?"

"Any new developments on your side?"

"Our Russian friend sent another transmission to the *Lenin.* We couldn't pin it down—the triangulation base was too narrow."

When the signal bounces from one satellite to another, the two have to be far enough apart to provide an accurate triangulation. When Stein told me she would try it, I feared this would happen.

"Let's not bother the captain," I say.

"Okay, what's new from your side?"

"Thorval, the general manager, lied to me."

"What about?"

"It was a quibble. He said they searched the ship twice. I think their search of the dead space left a lot to be desired. *Then* he said the best place to hide a body was the ocean. Initially, I accepted the statement without question. Only upon reflection did I realize it was a false premise—misdirection."

Among military officers, "quibbling" is worse than lying. It's a severe violation of the honor code.

"Thorval's a suspect, then."

"Yes, but I'm sure there are at least two Russian operators aboard. We have no idea what they're planning."

"The storm is clearing from the northeast, and *Lenin* continues to close." Palomas hesitates. "They could decide to blow us all out of the water."

"They'll try to board us first. That's where their Trojan horse comes in."

"One way or another, we'll find ourselves at war," Palomas says. "The storm should clear by dawn."

"One hell of a cruise, sailor."

Katie Palomas hesitates. "Better get some sleep, soldier."

Wiser words were never spoken. "Goodnight, Commander."

"Goodnight, Breed."

17

SATURDAY, 0100 HOURS – THE SPIDER -
MURDER

The pounding on my cabin door startles me awake. I'm sitting in bed with my back against the bulkhead. I'd closed my eyes to think and fallen asleep.

"Breed," the voice calls.

"Just a minute." I swing my legs out of bed and put my shoes on. "Who's there?"

"Angers."

I open the door.

Features grim, the captain stands in the passageway. "It's bad, Breed."

He tilts his head toward the aft transverse bulkhead. Thirty feet away, Thorval and Dr Voss are standing on opposite sides of the passageway, outside one of the cabins. Thorval is dressed exactly as he had been on the bridge. Dr Voss's hair is more disheveled than usual, like she has been roused from sleep.

Hands in the pockets of his duffel coat, Thorval leans against the corridor bulkhead. He nods to Dr Voss. "Show him," he says.

Dr Voss looks shaken. She opens the door and lets me into the cabin. "Stand to the right," she says, "by the closet."

The smell of a dead man's guts rolls into the passageway. I've smelled more than my share of men with their guts opened up. Bullets, knives, shrapnel, animal horns, car crashes—you name it. The smell is nuanced by the environment, but the source is always unmistakable.

The cabin is a devastated piece of territory. The bed's been slept in... The sheets and blanket are in disarray. The abattoir doesn't bother me, but I'm shocked because I recognize the victim.

Martin Nygard lies facedown on the floor, buck naked. He's stretched between the bed and the door. There's a bloody knife wound in the lower right side of his back. It's a ragged gash over his right kidney. Like the knife went in, scraped bone, and the killer twisted it this way and that. To find a clear path into the victim's vitals. Killing is clean in the movies. In the real world, butchery is an ugly business.

I step sideways and give the others as much space as possible to come inside. The floor by the closet may be the only patch that hasn't been soaked in blood. Thorval stands next to me. Voss joins us, closes the door behind her. Angers remains outside.

I had no idea Nygard's cabin was only a few doors away from my own.

A thick crimson pool is congealing on the carpet beneath the diver. Like a slug trail, it stretches around the foot of the bed to the other side of the cabin. The furniture on that side of the bed has been disturbed. The night table has tipped over, and one of the easy chairs has been overturned. Not easy to do—it has a low center of gravity.

Nygard's diving watch and wallet lie on the floor. They

must have been on the night table. His clothing—jeans and
T-shirt—lies tangled with the feet of the easy chair. They
were hung across its back before it was knocked over. A stack
of motorcycle magazines have fallen off the coffee table.
They're scattered on the floor along with a shark knife's
sheath. The knife is missing.

"How long?" I ask.

"Rigor has not set in," Voss says. "Not more than two
hours. Perhaps significantly less."

"That's the smell of a stomach wound," I tell her.

"Yes it is," Voss agrees. "He was stabbed in the stomach
on the far side of the room. He and the killer fought while he
bled. Nygard weakened. Tried to make it to the door. The
killer followed. I would say the killer threw his left arm
around Nygard's throat. Stabbed him in the back with a knife
held in the right hand. Destroyed the kidney, severed the
renal artery. Held Nygard down with a knee in the back,
muffled his cries with a hand over his mouth. Nygard lost
consciousness shortly after that."

Thorval is staring at me.

"Where were you an hour ago, Breed?"

The question shocks me. Surely the general manager
doesn't think I killed Nygard. "Asleep in my cabin."

Thorval says nothing.

"Nygard was strong," Voss says. "A magnificent specimen
of a man. The killer had to be strong and fit."

"Where's the murder weapon?" I ask Voss.

The doctor tilts her head toward the toilet. I see a shark
knife lying on the deck. There's blood on the tiles, in the
sink, in the shower stall. The killer tried to wash himself.
The fight was an unholy mess. The killer would have been
covered in blood.

"Nygard's knife?"

"I assume so," Voss says. "There is a sheath on the table. However, we are neither trained nor equipped to conduct a proper investigation."

"I assume you turned the body over."

"Yes, to examine the stomach wound. It caused a great deal of damage, but did not kill him outright."

I study the scene, make mental notes. The bed is a disaster area. Two men fighting wouldn't have torn the blankets off. That means he was sleeping when the killer attacked. The fight started on the far side of the cabin, between the bed and the bulkhead. The furniture was knocked over in the scuffle.

"Anything taken?"

"No idea."

"I'm going to look at that wallet," I say. "If necessary, the police can take exclusionary prints when the time comes."

"Assuming they choose to exclude you." Thorval's voice is cold. "Touching that wallet will confuse the issue."

Thorval's right, but there's no time to quibble. I stare at him and say, "Why don't you stop me?"

Without waiting for an answer, I step around the blood smears and cross to the other side of the bed. Check the watch—it's still running. Open the billfold. There's cash in it. A full set of credit cards, driver's license, and—Nygard's security pass.

No blood on the billfold. "I don't think there's anything missing."

I replace the items on the floor.

"Who found him?" I ask.

Thorval's pissed off, but he retains his composure. "A

passing research tech noticed the door was ajar. Looked inside, called the bridge. Angers took the call."

"Where's the tech now?"

"In his quarters. He will speak to no one."

"We need to preserve the crime scene," I say.

"After you have fondled the evidence." Thorval's voice drips sarcasm. "Very well. A research tech will photograph everything. He will be sworn to silence. Dr Voss will write a preliminary report. The body will be frozen until we contact the proper authorities."

"We need to report to Stein," I tell him. "It's not yet midnight on the east coast."

"Yes." Thorval looks thoughtful. "Come to the radio room in half an hour."

I turn to Voss. The doctor is operating on autopilot. It's like combat. No soldier rises to the occasion under the stress of battle. They fall to the level of their training. Voss's mind hasn't found a way to cope with the reality of murder. She's relying on her professional training.

"Do it by the numbers," I tell her.

Voss nods.

Thorval's not happy with me, but I don't give a shit. I open the door, push past him. Angers is standing outside, arms folded. "We have to confer with Stein," I tell him. "We're meeting in the radio room in half an hour."

I stride down the passageway to my cabin. I wave my card over the security panel, push the cabin door open. Go inside, close my eyes and try to think. My mind is whirling. Why kill Nygard? The diver's death is unexpected, the murder scene disturbing. Not because of the violence, I'm used to that.

No. The murder scene is disturbing because of its disorganized nature. At the Provost Marshal's office, CID investi-gators classify murder scenes as organized or disorganized. Professional killers leave behind organized crime scenes. Crimes of passion result in disorganized crime scenes.

Nygard's murder has a disorganized quality to it. A professional would never have let the diver out of bed. Would have killed him in his sleep. The fight was chaotic. The killer was amateurish.

There is a kaleidoscope of questions.

Did Nygard let the killer into the cabin? He would have had to walk naked to the door, open it, then walk naked back to the far side of the bed. Possible, but unlikely. Nygard would have covered himself. The diver's pass was in his wallet. Cabin doors lock automatically. That means the killer might have a skeleton pass. Access is granted by ticking off boxes on a pass holder's profile. Such a pass would have every box ticked.

Who would have a skeleton pass? Angers and ship's offi-cers might. I doubt Thorval would be entitled to such a pass.

But why kill Nygard? What are the motives for murder? Financial gain, jealousy, revenge, concealment of a crime.

Two killings in as many days. Nygard's murder must have something to do with the transfer of the Kestrels. Dawn is a few hours away. For the first time, I feel events are running away from me. I decide to retrieve my radio.

I leave my cabin, look left and right. The passageway is empty, so I go to the doorway leading to the fo'c'sle. Step into the dead space, close the door. I stand still for a minute, allow my eyes to adjust to the dim light.

The two solid masses of the chain lockers loom ahead. By now, I'm familiar with the layout of the ship. I pick my way toward the starboard chain locker. Place my palm flat against its cold metal face. Shift my weight to step around it. My radio is on the far side.

My face explodes with a flash of pain. Tears flood my eyes and hot blood fills my nose. I stagger from the palm strike, fall backward, break my fall. A giant steps from behind the chain locker. I hook his ankle and try to trip him. He dodges the move, kicks me in the groin.

A groin strike produces agony beyond imagination, but you can fight through the pain. I grab my attacker's collar as he drops down on his knees. The light catches his face— Knauss. He straddles me, holds me down by the shoulders, and butts me in the face. Once, twice. So fast, it's like he's rapping on a door. He rears up, crown slick with my blood. His face, framed by the massive red beard, is demonic.

Knauss draws his fist back and clubs me.

The world goes black.

18

SATURDAY, 0200 HOURS – THE SPIDER - SICKBAY

A face swims into view. Blurred, haloed in white light, it looks like Frank Aron. Bloated, colorless, dead marbles for eyes. I want to scream, but the pain paralyzes me.

"What's your name?"

I know that voice. My eyes focus and Frank Aron's face morphs into that of Dr Lena Voss. She's staring down at me, wiping my face with a wet towel.

"Breed."

"Where are you?"

"I was on the *Spider*. Right now, I'm not sure."

"What day is it?"

"Friday night. No, Saturday morning... I think. How long?"

"Since you first lost consciousness, perhaps half an hour. You have certainly been in and out of consciousness in that time. What happened?"

I recognize the pattern of questions. Voss is testing me, evaluating my condition. I force myself to think. Images come back to me. The dim light in the fo'c'sle, the chain locker, Knauss coming around the corner.

"Knauss sucker punched me," I say. "One good turn deserves another."

Voss tries to hold me down, but I struggle to a sitting position. I'm on an examination table in her sickbay. Naked, swathed in heavy blankets. "I'm okay, Doctor. Alert and oriented. Times four."

That's an expression used to express the condition of a person with a head injury. It is the highest level of alertness.

"I'm impressed you remember who hit you," Voss says. "The first thing people in your condition lose is short term memory."

The world swims and I feel an overwhelming need to vomit. I steady myself with a hand on the table. Wait for the nausea to pass.

"You are concussed and hypothermic," Voss says. She adjusts the blankets around my shoulders.

I straighten. "Knauss knocked me out. Now tell me why I'm alive. I should be dead."

"The second officer found you in the forward superstructure, just inside the boat deck. You were wet with melted snow and looked like you'd taken a fall. He and a lookout carried you to sickbay."

"What do you think happened?"

"You did not sustain your injuries in a fall. You were beaten unconscious, then dragged outside onto the boat deck. Your attacker expected you to freeze to death. Instead, someone carried you indoors, where the second officer found you. Had you not been brought inside, you'd have died from exposure."

"Knauss should have tossed me overboard."

"Indeed. I don't know why he did not."

"Son of a bitch couldn't bring himself to end it quickly."

"What will you do?"

"What I should have done seven years ago." A thought comes to me. "Who else knows about this?"

"I reported your condition to Captain Angers. I am sure the second officer would have done so as well."

I push myself off the examination table, find my footing on the deck. "Damn, I'm buck naked under here. Where are my clothes?"

Voss hands me the US Navy coveralls in which I boarded the *Spider*. Underwear, a T-shirt. The US Navy watch jacket. "You are a fine specimen, Breed. Scars are so attractive on a man. Your shoes are still wet."

"Give them to me. Where are the pants and shirt I was wearing?"

"Soaking wet, I'm afraid. I had these brought from your cabin."

"How'd you get in?" Shivering with cold, I climb into the coveralls. Pull the watch jacket on, zip it to my chin.

Voss holds up my pass and hands it to me. "This was in your pocket."

I take the card from her.

"Knauss is going to come after me." I grasp the doctor's shoulders. "They will try to kill me. Get your jacket on. Whatever happens, do exactly as I say."

"This is about the Kestrels?"

"It has to be."

A bell sounds three times from the *Spider's* public address system. Thorval's voice issues from speakers in the overhead. "Attention all hands, this is Magnus Thorval. We are facing an emergency situation. There is no cause for alarm. Will all crew please make your way to the nearest mess. Research staff forward and crew aft. If you encounter security staff, follow their instructions to the letter. Thank you."

"Security staff," I say.

"I didn't know we had any."

Running footsteps in the passageway. Can't tell how many men.

"We're about to meet them."

THE DOOR to the sickbay is hinged and opens inward to our left. I step to the right cut. Motion for Voss to hide in the left. Flatten myself against the bulkhead.

The door bursts open. The first man comes in, leading with a SIG P226 held in a Weaver grip. It's Horvath, the blond Viking from the weight room.

Mistake number one.

Horvath may have been a SEAL, but he has not served in a Direct Action unit. Most people do not understand that becoming a SEAL or a Green Beret does not make a soldier a Tier One operator. You have to be *selected* and *trained* for a Tier One unit like Delta Force or SEAL Team Six. Horvath is *not* practiced in Direct Action skills.

If you're going to use a sidearm for CQB, you carry it close to your chest at retracted high ready. When you see your target, you punch your weapon system forward, fire, then retract. Identify the next target. Extend, fire, retract. If you lead with your weapon extended, you are dangerously exposed.

Which I demonstrate. I step forward, grab Horvath's wrists with both hands, push his weapon down and to the right. Break his face with my right elbow, pull him forward, off-balance. Twist the pistol from his hands.

I use Horvath's body for cover. Throw my right arm around his throat, grab his collar and pull him close. The number two man hesitates. Doesn't want to light up his friend. I raise the SIG in my left hand and point-shoot Number Two three times in the chest. *Pop, pop, pop*. He falls, drops his M4. He's on the floor, face up. I shoot him again, in the face. A cone of blood sprays the floor and the far bulkhead of the passageway.

Horvath struggles in my grip. With all that weight training, he should be stronger. I press the muzzle of the SIG against his jaw, angle it toward the bottom of his brain pan, pull the trigger. *Pop*. The bullet enters, blows through mouth, palate and brain tissue. A little fountain of blood, bone and brains spurts from the top of his head. Splatters the top of his skull against the overhead. Little drops of something fall on the side of my face.

Cries from outside. A dark object sails through the air, falls on the sickbay deck with a metallic thump. Fragmentation grenade. Three to five second fuse. Closer to three than five, but you can't be sure. No way to know how long it's cooked. I throw Horvath's dead body on the grenade, fling myself on top of the corpse. There's a *crump* and Horvath is blown an inch off the deck, carrying me with him. A body blow drives the breath from my body.

Grenades are a lot less dramatic than people think. In the movies, they always go off and unleash a blast of flames and carnage. In practice, they explode with a puff of dust and scatter shrapnel through a fifty-foot circle. That's *if* they're standing upright when they explode, and they never are. Lying on their *side*, half the blast effect is directed *down-*

ward into the ground. Or the deck, in this case. The other half is directed upward. Into my once-human sandbag.

Someone in the passageway shouts, "Eat *this*, motherfucker."

Another grenade clatters on the floor. I roll off Horvath's corpse, stretch and catch the grenade in my right hand. Wing it back into the passageway.

Cries of terror. The grenade bounces off the passageway's bulkhead and explodes in the air. Scatters a spherical burst of shrapnel in all directions. The sound is a deafening *clang* in the closed space. The cries turn into screams of agony.

I get to my feet, carry the SIG retracted high ready. Step into the passageway over the body of Horvath's number two. Check right and left.

The passageway is an abattoir. On the right, one man lies motionless on his side. On the left, another sits on the deck, propped against the bulkhead. His belly's been ripped open by shrapnel and he's trying to hold his guts inside. A third man has his back to me. His leg's been cut to pieces and he's trying to run, dragging the wounded limb behind him.

I extend the SIG in an isosceles and shoot the runner twice in the back. He pitches forward, sprawls facedown. I shift my aim to the man with the stomach wound, shoot him twice in the face. Turn back to the man who tried to run, pop him in the back of the head.

Turn to the man lying on his side. Step to the body, shoot the corpse in the ear.

I survey the five men and their weapons. Four M4 carbines and a SIG P226. Horvath was their leader. He carried a sidearm. I take one man's M4 and strip him of his load bearing vest. No plates, but the chest rig carries six 30-round magazines Velcroed in two vertical columns.

Each of the four riflemen carried a single hand grenade. I relieve the corpses of the two remaining grenades, stuff them into pouches in my ammo vest. The men wore the vests over jackets. I slip mine on and zip the front.

No suppressors. The idiots knew they'd be working inside a ship. Why wouldn't they run suppressed? No ear pro either. I lift the load bearing vest off another corpse. Now I have twelve magazines plus the one in the rifle.

I walk back into the sickbay. Voss stares at me.

Horvath is wearing a bloodstained pistol belt. It has a holster, four spare magazines, and a squad radio in a half-holster. The radio crackles.

Horvath and his friends were all working out in the weight room a few hours ago. The entire Blue Team must be involved. Ditto the six men of Nygard's Advance Team. With Nygard dead, that makes eighteen men, including Knauss. The Blue Team brought weapons aboard in their helo.

"Horvath. Respond."

I know that voice. Take the radio from the belt, key the mike. "He's dead, Knauss. They all are."

"Breed. I should have pitched you over the side."

"Nah, too easy. You wanted to see me coated with ice like a human popsicle."

Knauss says nothing—I guessed right. Freezing was a common method of torture and execution in places with harsh winters. The victim is stripped, bound, and exposed to the elements. Cold running water was run over the wretch until death supervened. The film of water on the corpse froze and formed progressive layers until the victim's body was sheathed in ice.

"Reckon I took out a quarter of your force in thirty

seconds, Knauss." I smile. "Tell you what—I'll save you for last."

I click off and stuff the radio back in its half-holster. Take Horvath's pistol belt and strap it on. I've spent eleven out of fifteen rounds. I drop the mag, rack the slide, and let the chambered round fly. Do a three-point check, slap a fresh magazine into the pistol. Charge and decock the weapon.

Stare down at Horvath. The Viking wanted a crack at me. He was happy when Knauss turned him loose. There he lies, top of his skull blown off. Got what he wanted, got what he deserved.

"What now?" Voss asks.

"They're coming for us." I hand the doctor the second load bearing vest and its six magazines of five-five-six. "We have to go."

Voss shrugs on the ammo vest. She shortens an inch under its weight. "What do we need *this* for?"

"Killing people."

19

SATURDAY, 0230 HOURS – THE SPIDER - FLIGHT

The muffled sound of gunfire echoes through the ship. The sound of the second grenade going off must have been noticed. Crew and research staff may be questioning the orders of Thorval's "security force."

"Your attention, please." Thorval's clipped voice issues from the public address system. "There has been an accident that resulted in an explosion below decks. Do not panic. Please move to the mess compartments fore and aft. Follow the instructions of our security staff."

Voss is wearing her load bearing vest over a jacket. The oversized vest hangs off her tiny frame. She looks like a comic dwarf.

"That story will not be credible for long," Voss says.

"It's not credible now," I tell her. "They're meeting resistance."

I'm carrying the M4 at my right side on a two-point sling. The SIG is in both my hands, high ready.

Got to get to a radio and contact the *Pressley Bannon*. Apart from the *Spider's* big sets, there are three I know about. Mine, Frank Aron's and that of the Russian operative.

How did Knauss know to ambush me in the fo'c'sle? My face is a mass of pain, but I'm thinking clearly. Knauss and Thorval are in this business together. I assume Captain Angers is involved, until proven otherwise. After all, Voss reported to Angers that I'd been attacked and was in the sickbay.

None of those men knew I'd found Aron's body. But they had to assume I had a radio, some means of communication with the outside. They would have searched my cabin and found nothing. They could see I was not carrying a radio on my person, so they had to conclude I hid it.

They would have reached the same conclusion about Frank Aron. They would have searched Aron's cabin. That was why they assumed he had a radio hidden somewhere on board. When he learned whatever it was he learned, Knauss followed him. Aron's killer had to be Knauss, the SEAL who beat a Taliban commander to death with a brick. The wrench to Aron's skull was the kind of thing Knauss liked to do.

Knauss *followed* Aron. He *ambushed* me.

Lucky guess? If Aron hid his radio in the dead space, it was logical I would too. The door to the fo'c'sle is close to my cabin. Knauss knew I went back to my cabin. He guessed I would go to my radio—somewhere in the dead space—and waited for me.

Knauss hid behind the chain locker because it had a view of the hatch. Didn't know that was where I hid the radio. He was going to follow me when I headed toward the stern. Instead, I came directly toward him. He could wait for me to blunder into him, or he could sucker punch me.

Speed, surprise, violence of action.

Knauss took me out.

No mystery there. The real question is something more subtle. Knauss dragged me outside so I'd freeze to death. He wanted to come back in an hour and find me coated in ice. A favorite method of execution in Eastern Europe and Russia.

Who dragged me back inside?

THERE'S a good chance my radio is right where I left it.

I descend the companionway toward the cabin decks. Knauss's men are all over the place, but they're spread thin. Thirteen men to cover a ship the size of an aircraft carrier. Let's say there are six men forward and seven men aft. That's why they have to confine the crew as quickly as possible.

There's a flicker of movement below me. Navy watch jacket, jeans, long blond hair. I raise the SIG.

Noa's eyes meet mine over the iron sights. Her jaw drops open and she turns to run. I lower the pistol and grab her by the collar. "Wait, Goddamn it."

She brushes my arm away, tries to dodge past. Climbs the companionway, runs into Voss. "Let me go," Noa gasps. "We have to get out of here."

"Where?"

"The boat deck," she says. "We'll steal a lifeboat, get off the ship."

"In the middle of a storm?"

"The lifeboats are watertight."

They're also small. In this storm, they'll be bounced around so much, whoever is inside will die of motion sickness.

"Those men will be watching the boat deck," I tell her. "They'll cover it from the bridge."

Noa's flushed, sweating. Her eyes are panicked. "No. We *have* to get off."

"That's not the way."

I take Noa's hand in mine, drag her behind me as I descend the companionway. Stop at the landing for the upper cabin deck, turn the switchback and keep going. Noa's boxed in between me and Voss. I hope my grip on her hand reassures her.

At the entrance to the lower cabin deck, I stop. Raise the SIG one-handed. Not the best CQB technique, but I'm not about to let Noa go.

My heart is a jackhammer in my chest. I move forward carefully. Listen hard for the sound of divers. Squeeze Noa's hand.

She squeezes back—there's something there.

I step into the empty passageway. Turn right, head for the door that leads to the fo'c'sle.

"Where are you going?" Noa asks.

"I'm going to call for help."

I reach the corner where the passageway turns toward my cabin. There are two bodies on the deck. Shot in the back. Dressed like seamen, they must be Angers's officers. They tried to run and were cut down.

There's nothing for me in the cabin. I open the door to the fo'c'sle, lead Noa and Voss into the dead space.

Noa has settled down. She's following me. Together with Voss, we pick our way to the chain lockers. I let go of Noa's hand, approach the locker with the SIG at retracted high ready. Part of me expects Knauss to spring from the shadows like a jack-in-the-box.

There's no one there. I lower the pistol. Reach to the shelf atop the chain locker, feel around with my fingertips. I retrieve the radio, thumb the power switch and trace the security pattern. It's working.

"Down," I say. "Get down."

We huddle together next to the chain locker.

"This is a US Navy channel." Palomas knows who's calling. "Identify yourself."

"This is Breed, Commander Palomas. I have Noa Larson with me, and Dr Lena Voss from the *Spider*. The Russians aboard have made their move."

"Wait one, Breed."

Cruik comes on. "What's going on, Breed?"

"The dive team that came aboard day before yesterday are hijackers. The men of the Advance Team as well. An ex-SEAL named Stefan Knauss is leading them. Thorval is in overall command. Captain Angers is probably involved."

"Any resistance?"

"They have the ship. They tried to kill me, I killed five. There are fifteen left, including Thorval and Angers."

"Disposition?"

"They have the crew locked in the two mess compartments, fore and aft. They need one guard each. The remainder will concentrate fore and aft of the operations deck. They have a hit squad out to get me."

"They're going to hand the *Spider* over to the Russians."

"Yes, as soon as the storm clears."

For a moment, Cruik remains silent. "Breed, we need more intel regarding the disposition of the hijackers. I'm going to send a SEAL team to take back the *Spider*."

I don't know if Cruik's being stupid or audacious. "How are you going to do that in a storm?"

"We carry an Advanced Dry Combat Submersible. It will operate at a depth well beneath the storm action. They'll surface in the Star Pool and neutralize the hijackers."

I won't argue. Maritime special operations are the SEALs' business. I know they have used a "wet" Seal Delivery Vehicle for years. They have developed a pressurized submersible to carry commandos further and deeper than the SDV.

"I'll do what I can," I tell him. "But I have to keep myself and two civilians alive to do it."

"Understood, Breed. Stay in touch."

I squeeze the radio into my pocket.

Noa grips my shoulder. "Breed, we have to escape. If we get away in a lifeboat, the destroyer can pick us up. The storm will clear in a few hours."

"No. This is a big ship. Thorval and Knauss will have trouble finding us. In fact, there's a good chance I can whittle them down further. Come on, I need to see how they have deployed around the Star Pool."

There's one thing I don't tell her.

I'm not leaving Knauss alive.

I LEAN CLOSE TO VOSS, speak in a low voice. "Can Pruitt and his men be released from the decompression chambers?"

Pruitt is an ex-SEAL. There must be other SEAL vets among the Gold Team. Special Boat Service divers. If they can be released from the chambers, we might be able to mount resistance.

Voss shakes her head. "Not for another week. You can't imagine how difficult it is to bring someone back from six thousand feet."

"No, but I can appreciate it." I cast a glance at the hatch. Part of me expects Knauss's hit squad to come through at any minute. "You pass them food from outside the chamber, don't you?"

"Yes, through the air lock."

"Let's go," I say. "I want to stop by Pruitt before we go to the Star Pool."

I'm sure Pruitt isn't in on the hijacking, and the Gold Team are probably clear too. I want to speak with him, and leave him a weapon.

The decompression chambers are on the sickbay deck. I lead Noa and Voss across the dead space on the port side. I'm looking for the watertight hatches I know allow passage from one deck's dead space to the next.

They're not hard to find. The hatches come in pairs, one leading to the deck below, the other to the deck above. With overheads fifteen feet high, there is a companionway beneath the one opening upward. I look for the companionway, find it a hundred feet further along the dead space.

I open the hatch that leads upward. Ascend the companionway with Noa and Voss in tow. Secure the hatch behind us, keep climbing. When we reach the sickbay deck, I prop the hatch open using the hockey stick latch.

"Give me your hairband," I say to Noa.

"Why?"

"You'll see. Hurry."

Noa hands me a thin, braided cord she wears around her left wrist. Another holds her hair back in a ponytail. She wears two more bands around her right wrist.

I test the cord she handed me. It's not very elastic. Doubled, it should work well. I climb the companionway, turn the locking wheel, and push the hatch open. When I am on the deck above, I prop the hatch open and secure it with the hockey stick latch. I kneel next to the hatch. Take Noa's hairband, double it, and bind one of the grenades to the underside of the hockey stick. It's tight, and with the heavy hatch propped open, the weight of the hatch and the band hold the corpus of the grenade firmly in place.

I reach around and pull the pin. When the hockey stick is released, the spoon will fly. Three seconds later, *kaboom*. I drop back through the hatch, descend the companionway, and rejoin Noa and Voss on the sickbay deck. With a snap of my fingers, I flick the pin into the darkness.

"What were you doing?" Noa asks.

"There's a hit squad on our trail," I tell her, "but I haven't heard them. If they come this way, they'll notice the open hatch above. All the watertight hatches are supposed to be closed. They'll think they are following us, climb one deck higher. When they release the hatch, I'll know."

I look for the door that leads back into the living and working space. It'll be on the left. I find it, holster the SIG and turn the wheel. When the dogs have been released, I draw the SIG and step through the opening. Blink in the bright light of the interior.

"Come on." I help Noa and Voss over the knee knocker. Voss jerks her chin in the direction of the decompression chamber.

The chamber is locked. I raise my pistol and Voss waves her pass at the security panel. I nod to her and she opens the door. I check the left cut first, then the right. The compartment is empty.

There's a muffled explosion. It reverberates through the ship with a metallic *clang*. The effects of hand grenade explosions are magnified in the confined metal spaces of ships. Shrapnel bounces off steel overheads and bulkheads before slicing open human flesh. The concussion of the blast effect searches for victims around corners.

"You got them," Noa whispers.

"I can't know that for sure," I say. "All this tells me is that someone is on our tail."

I approach the center decompression chamber. The compartment once greeted me with the white noise of pumps and air flow. Now it is eerily silent. Voss goes to the control panel.

"Breed."

The doctor doesn't need to say anything. There's blood smeared over the inside of the viewing window. My stomach hollows with the certainty that whatever lies on the other side of that glass will be appalling beyond measure.

I force myself to look. I've seen bloated men lying dead for days on battlefields. Corpses burst from gasses produced by decomposition. I press my face against the glass. Look left and right. This is the same effect, produced by the vacuum created by pumps sucking the atmosphere from the chamber. This is what explosive decompression in space would look like.

Sick to my stomach, I holster the SIG and go to the airlock. Turn the wheel and try to wrench the door open.

"Breed," Voss says, "don't waste your time."

"Someone could still be alive."

"Breed, there's no way. And you can't open the door until the chamber has been repressurized."

"We've got to try."

"Don't you understand? There is a vacuum inside. Atmospheric pressure is holding that door shut at two thousand pounds per square foot."

"*Fuck!*"

Frustrated, I kick the steel door. Turn away from the deathtrap and stalk toward Voss. Noa's holding her fists over her mouth.

A door to my right swings open and a hijacker steps into the compartment. One of the divers. Ammo vest, jeans, boots. He's carrying an M4. Raises it toward his shoulder.

My own M4 is slung and the SIG is holstered. I snatch a shark knife from the table. Take a breath, hurl the blade with all my strength. It pinwheels through the air and buries itself in the gunman's throat. The man's eyes bug and he drops the rifle. Raises his hands to clutch the handle, draws the knife free.

Not smart. A crimson gout spurts from the hole. The man chokes on blood as it pours down his trachea. Falls to his knees, then slumps to one side. His backup bursts into the room. Rifle raised, he opens fire. I dive under the table, draw the SIG as I fall. Noa and Voss throw themselves on the floor behind the control panel.

These divers can't *all* be ex-SEALs or commandos. They have skills, but they haven't practiced CQB together. When two men go into a compartment, they should go in nut-to-butt. One man left, the other right. Get *two* guns into the compartment at the same time, dig the corners. When you delay like this, it's no better than having only one man. They made the same mistake in the sickbay.

Recruitment for this hijacking can't have been easy. The most important qualification had to be deep-sea diving experience. The next requirement was greed, and a willingness to commit a crime. CQB proficiency had to come third. Finding eighteen men with *all* those qualifications would have been next to impossible. The vast majority of vets wouldn't have considered the job. Recruiters would be happy with two out of three.

The gunman blazes away at me, shoots up the gear on the table. Lying on my side, I extend the SIG and fire from six inches above the deck. Decocked, the SIG trigger has a long first pull. The subsequent pulls are single-action, much faster. I unload the weapon.

I shoot the first man in the face and chest. Kneecap his number two. I put rounds in both his knees, shins and thighs. He screams and falls to the deck, firing the M4 into the overhead. I cringe from the ricochets. There's no telling where they'll fly. I keep firing, pounding rounds into his face and chest. He slumps over his friend.

Weapon empty, the SIG's slide locks back.

Get up, drop the mag. Pistol in my right hand, I tilt the weapon, draw a fresh magazine from my pistol belt. Hold my first finger over the feed, guide it into the mag well. Seat it with the palm of my hand, charge the weapon.

Step over to the two men. I put so many head shots into these two, any more would be overkill. I decock the SIG, holster it, transition to my primary. Raise the M4 and flick off the safety. Rifle to my shoulder, I approach the door the gunmen used to enter.

Check the left cut, then the right. The passageway is empty.

For now.

20

SATURDAY, 0330 HOURS – THE SPIDER - THE CAGE

The squad radio on my belt crackles with Thorval's voice. "Hello, Mr Breed."

I lead Noa and Dr Voss back into the dead space. Find a companionway, descend to the cabin decks. The *Spider* is a maze. This is terrain that can be used to our advantage. If we keep moving from compartment to compartment, and deck to deck, the hijackers will have a tough time finding us.

"Breed, don't be tiresome. I know you can hear me."

I ignore Thorval, press on across the dead space. It's safer than the passageways of the climate-controlled shoebox, but harder work. All kinds of trash and work materials left over from building the ship are scattered in the space. It's like an obstacle course.

A companionway leads to the lower cabin deck. I open the hatch and allow Noa and Dr Voss to descend. Secure the hatch behind me, continue toward the forepeak and my cabin on the port side.

Noa's muttering under her breath. She's fit, but it's not easy going. My eyes search the gloomy space behind her.

Damn. Where's Voss?

I stop, put my hand on Noa's shoulder. "Where's Dr Voss?"

Noa shakes her head. "I don't know. She was behind me a minute ago."

"Wait here."

I retrace our steps across the dead space. It isn't long before I find the little doctor sitting on a wooden crate, not far from the companionway.

"What's wrong, Dr Voss?"

"I turned my ankle," she says. "It's not broken, I'll be fine."

"Are you sure?"

"Yes. But why do I need to carry all this?"

The little doctor has taken off the ammo vest I gave her. No plates, but six thirty round magazines are a heavy load. I should have relieved her of the vest when we ran into Noa.

"There's thirteen of them and one of me," I tell her. "A little extra ammo can't hurt."

I take the vest from Voss and she gets to her feet.

"Can you walk?"

We take a few steps together. "Yes," she says. "Let's go."

I throw the spare vest over my shoulder and lead the way. This time, I look back from time to time to make sure Voss is with me. Relieved of the extra weight, the little doctor is doing better.

When we reach Noa, I hand her the ammo vest. "Put this on," I tell her.

Noa shrugs on the vest and zips it up the front. She's not happy, but there are probably a lot of things she's not happy about. Wearing a heavy ammo vest isn't top of the list. I swap her position in the file with Voss. Noa brings up the rear without complaint.

The two dead ship's officers lie crumpled a few feet from my cabin door. I step around the pools of blood that surround the riddled bodies. Unlock the door, wave Noa and the doctor inside.

Voss and Noa collapse onto the bed. I rest my M4 against the closet door. Go to the bathroom, run the tap and take a long drink of water.

Thorval's disembodied voice issues from the squad radio. "Don't be childish, Breed."

I pull the radio from its half-holster. "I'm listening."

"You've done well, Breed. Give yourself up, join the crew in the mess."

"If I'm doing well, why should I?"

"Probability and statistics, Breed. Play a game long enough, you're bound to lose."

"I think I'll play a while longer."

Thorval allows his voice to betray impatience. "Mr Knauss is determined to kill you. It is difficult for me to control him when he gets like this. I give you my word. You will not be harmed."

"Why are you feeling so generous?"

"As you Americans like to say, I have bigger fish to fry. Remain with the crew and research staff. We will complete our business by dawn. Leave you and the others alive."

"Why do you care?"

"I don't like loose ends."

Of course you don't. Especially those that cost you a third of your force.

"I don't think so, Thorval. I'm having too much fun."

A deep voice cuts in. "Fuck this shit, Thorval."

"Knauss," I say. "It's been a while."

Noa and Voss stare at the radio in my hand. It's like Knauss is standing in the cabin, big as life. Red-bearded, tattooed, muscled and sweaty. I can smell him.

"Thorval wants to give you a chance, Breed. I want to kill you. I'm going to squeeze your head until my hands meet in the middle. I'm going to give you this chance because I know you won't take it."

"You're right, Knauss. I'm not going to take it."

"Think again. I got your pilots here. You know, the ones you almost went with to Davy Jones's locker."

McMaster and his copilot.

"Tell him," Knauss says to the pilots. "Tell him I'll kill you if he doesn't come in."

McMaster's voice is calm and collected. The same voice with which he announced he was ditching the King Stallion. "Breed, I reckon you heard him."

"Knauss, I'm not coming in."

There's the crack of a pistol. It's a metallic echo that comes through the radio.

"That's the copilot. Breed, I'm not fucking around."

I say nothing.

"Mr Knauss," Thorval says, "is a force of nature. Like the storm outside, he does what he wants. He has just gotten some... *stuff*... on me. Spare us this distressing business."

"Count of three, Breed." Knauss's voice is a low growl.

Noa gets to her feet. Stares at me like she expects me to do something. Like what? I'm not going to give myself over to a man who kills for fun.

"One." Knauss counts deliberately. "Two. Three."

Another crack. Noa clutches me tight, buries her face in my shoulder. My eyes meet those of Voss. Noa, McMaster and I survived the helo crash. Now McMaster's dead. The girl's shoulders shake with sobs. I hold her close and stroke her back.

"Think what I'll do to *you*," Knauss says.

I shut the radio off, gently disengage from Noa. "I'm going to recon the Star Pool," I say. "Wait here. I'll come back."

Voss frowns. "Breed, none of this is wise. We're outnumbered."

"Doctor, there's no time to argue."

Noa looks like a hunted animal. "Breed, how long will you be?"

"Not long, maybe half an hour. Don't worry, I won't forget you."

THE PASSAGEWAY OUTSIDE IS QUIET. I step over the bodies and reenter the dead space. Climb back to the sickbay deck, make my way toward the Star Pool. I use my ears. If pursuers are careless, they might make noise that will echo through the hull, Knauss's team of tough guys aren't so tough.

Something doesn't make sense. The murder of Pruitt and the Gold Team was extravagant. Voss told me they couldn't be let out of the chambers for another week. Given the hijackers would achieve their objectives by dawn, the Gold Team was no factor.

Why kill them?

Knauss and Thorval both want me out of play. Knauss's reasons are personal. Thorval doesn't want me running around armed. Already, I've taken out at least seven of their team. I don't know how many the booby-trap killed or wounded.

Thorval and Angers are not foot soldiers. With Nygard and seven others dead, that leaves Knauss and eleven men to do wet work. With two men guarding the crew, they're down to Knauss and nine. They'll probably form two roving hit teams. Four men working in pairs to find me.

I pick my way through the dead space, heading for the Star Pool. It's a big ship, 330 yards long and 65 yards wide at the beam. The Star Pool itself is 30 yards wide, leaving 35 yards of dead space amidships.

Spider's a lot of ship for four men to cover.

They have to narrow the search down. Their core force will be on the navigation bridge and operations bridge. That's where the *Spider's* command and control is located. I'm sure Thorval and Angers have suborned a small number of the crew to perform essential duties. There will be a pair of lookouts on the navigation bridge and operations bridge. Two or three men operating the radios, radar and sonar. These men aren't fighters. They won't be armed, but they are needed at their posts.

The living space has watertight doors that open to the Star Pool. Thorval took me through one. There are others along the sides of the pool that open to the dead space. The Kestrels are lashed in their cradles along the starboard side. I'll go through the port side where the submersibles are stowed.

I make my way toward the transverse bulkhead that separates the forward space from the Star Pool. The trim tanks crowd me on the right, cast long shadows on the floor. I carry the M4 at high ready.

There's a noise behind me. Nothing too loud. A shoe bumping a piece of metal on the floor, a metallic sound that echoes more loudly than one would expect. I sprint ten feet, dodge into a niche between two sets of trim tanks. Bark my shin against the companionway.

A crash of gunfire reverberates in the closed space. None of these weapons is suppressed. There's the supersonic crack of the bullets, followed by sharp metallic echoes. Bullets whine off the steel sides of the trim tanks, strike the opposite bulkhead, strike the transverse bulkhead. Sparks fly in all directions.

I look back. M4s raised to their shoulders, two hijackers stand fifty yards away. I raise the rifle to my shoulder and fire three rounds in quick succession. The banging against my ears is so painful I stop shooting.

"Mr Breed."

Fucking Thorval. The gunmen must have reported contact. They return fire. I pull the squad radio from my pistol belt. "I'm busy, Thorval."

"So I'm told. I warned you Mr Knauss can become unruly. Why don't you make it easy for everyone. In a few hours, we'll be gone and you can sit down to breakfast with the lovely Noa Larson."

Son of a bitch brings Noa into it. I lift the radio into the air and point the mike in the direction of the gunmen. They let fly with another burst. "Hear *that*, Thorval?"

"It sounds exciting."

"Is Knauss still with you?"

"That would be telling, Mr Breed."

The little magician, with his clipped accent and precise diction. Did he study in the United Kingdom? Stein must have chapter and verse on his background. If that's his real identity.

"Ask him why he didn't bring suppressors. None of us is leaving with our hearing intact."

"I trust my subordinates to know their business."

Thorval wouldn't talk that way in front of Knauss. Robo-SEAL never expected me to surrender. That charade was an excuse he gave himself to kill two innocent men. This is a crack in their force structure. Thorval obviously considers himself the brains behind the plot. Knauss is muscle... a blunt instrument.

I stuff the radio back in the half-holster. Measure the distance to the stern transverse bulkhead and the closed door. Twenty-five or thirty yards. I can make that in five seconds. Turn the wheel, open the door. Easy peasy.

"Give yourself up, Breed."

Thorval's pissing me off. I ignore him, take the last grenade from its pouch. Hold the lever down, pull the pin. I wait for the gunmen to open fire again. With a ping, I release the spoon. Hurl the metal lump at the muzzle flashes.

Grenades are heavy. It's hard to throw them very far. Guys have fragged themselves with grenades that bounced back because they couldn't make the distance. The lump of steel sails thirty yards through the air and lands in front of the gunmen. They shout with panic and run. Dive behind trim tanks, throw themselves to the deck. I sprint for the transverse bulkhead.

Slam into the door, scrabble for the locking wheel. I'm sucking wind as I release the dogs. I jerk the door open and throw myself into the opening. The explosion sounds like it's slammed a gigantic gong. The concussion bangs the door shut behind me.

To my left is the long bulkhead separating the dead space from the Star Pool. To my right, the mountains of pipes in their steel cages, rising to the height of the operations deck.

I dash across the pipe store. Crouch and flatten myself behind a cage.

"What are you doing, Breed?" Thorval's voice sounds tense. He's received a report from his shooters. I watch the door, raise my M4. The locking wheel spins, the door swings open. I fire at the man stepping through. He breaks right and ducks behind the pipes.

The gunman opens fire. I break cover, dash the length of the pipe stream. Throw myself on the deck and crawl into a niche behind the center cage. The second man comes through, firing his weapon. He holds the forestock with his left hand in a C-clamp grip. Moves the muzzle in tight little circles, hosing the dead space with a cone of fire.

Perfect CQB doctrine. This man has had combat experience. He knows that kind of fire will force me to keep my head down.

"This is not necessary, Breed."

"Of course it is."

The gunmen open up, advance under the cover of a torrent of fire. They're daring me to stick my head out. They'll walk right up and pop me in the face.

I *could* stick the M4 around the corner and hose them down without sticking my head out. Throw enough lead across the space, I'm bound to hit something. But the noise would hurt. There's got to be a better way.

A retaining rod holds the lowermost gate of the cage in place. I remember it from my earlier exploration of the dead space. The rod is controlled by a mechanism connected to a three-foot steel lever.

The men are halfway across the length of the compartment. They are right beneath the center cage. I let my rifle hang by its sling. Reach up, grab the lever with both hands. Pray it works, yank the lever. There's a sharp clang as the retaining rod shoots aside. The metal gate, a large frame with three vertical posts, swings free.

With a crash, the gate slams flat on the deck. The two gunmen are advancing across the dead space, separated by ten feet. The topmost bar of the gate's frame crushes the shoulder of the man closest to the bulkhead. He screams.

The second man looks up at the mountain of steel pipes. He's never been in the dead space. Didn't know they were there.

"Breed, why don't you make this easy on everyone."

I pick up the radio. "Things are about to get interesting, Thorval."

With a rumble, the pipes roll from the cage and spill into the dead space. The gunman screams as the first pipes sweep his legs out from under him, and he finds himself on the deck next to his friend. He scrambles to his feet and tries to run, but more pipes fall from above. He's injured, he can barely stand. He drops his rifle and tries to stay above the mountain of pipes rapidly filling the dead space.

The man with the smashed shoulder has been buried. The other gunman has managed to climb above much of the pipe, but his ankle's been crushed. He goes down under the weight of the rolling stack. He throws his head back and howls. The scream echoes from the vaulted overhead.

Thorval is on the bridge and men are shouting in the

background. Their voices are so loud I can make out their words.

"We're listing!"

The weight of pipe, shifting toward the center of the ship, is a redistribution of trim. In this stormy sea, even a small list can overwhelm the ability of the gimbals to compensate for the ship's roll.

"The pipe stream will break!"

"Flood port trim one quarter," Angers shouts. "Open the clamshell!"

The port trim tanks will compensate for the redistribution of weight. Opening the clamshell shutters will prevent the pipe stream from breaking against the edge of the oculus. With a loud thrum, machinery on both sides of the Star Pool comes to life.

I sense movement above. Stare at the overhead. The base of the operations deck hides the movement of the clamshell shutters from view. The operations deck is another story above us, and the clamshell cover is a further two stories above that.

With a roar, tons of seawater flood the trim tanks.

"It's working," Thorval says. He's forgotten the radio is on.

I turn my attention back to the hijackers. The stack of pipes has rolled to a stop. It fills the dead space to a height of about fifteen feet. There's a further twenty feet of pipe held back by the upper sections of the cage.

The first gunman is gone, buried under the mountain. The second gunman is moaning. His head, chest, and one arm are visible. I pick my way up the side of the pipe mountain. My feet slip on wet metal. Seems everything inside the *Spider* is damp.

I approach the gunman with the radio in one hand and SIG in the other. The man's rifle is nowhere to be seen. It's buried in pipe. He stares at me.

Click the radio. "You there, Thorval?"

"What are you doing, Breed?"

I raise the SIG and shoot the hijacker between the eyes. "That's nine, Thorval."

21

SATURDAY, 0400 HOURS – THE SPIDER - RECON

I turn the locking wheel and ease the door open a crack. I'm in the dead space on the starboard side. The crash of pipes I unleashed on the port side would have drawn too much attention. In fact, Thorval and Knauss have probably sent a hit squad to find out what happened. They may even have sent two hit squads, one port and another starboard. It's a chance I have to take.

Mounted on their shiny steel cradles, white enamel cigars with bright red nose cones greet me. I'm a yard away from the three Kestrels.

The Star Pool has been transformed into a magical Christmas scene. The clamshell shutters have been opened wide. Legs mounted astride the operations deck, the derrick straddles the open space. The masthead light shines through the slurry of driving snow and sleet. A sparkling funnel of white whirls about the pipe stream. The snowflakes pour through the opening and chase each other round and round like spinning coils of DNA. The *Spider's* submersibles, stowed portside, are barely visible through the white veil.

Powerful floodlights mounted on the operations deck shine into the Star Pool. Their reflections shine from the black water. The wood beams lashed to the side of the deck glisten with snow that's starting to stick.

I'm looking for threats. The deck around the pool and the catwalk above are deserted. The hijackers are confident enough not to leave a sentry in the Star Pool.

I ease the door shut, turn the locking wheel, and make my way back into the forward dead space. Every step, I'm afraid I'll run into a roving patrol. I settle in one of the niches next to a companionway. Take out Stein's survival radio, draw the security pattern on the screen.

"This is a US Navy channel," Palomas says. "Identify yourself."

"Commander Palomas, this is Breed."

"Good to hear from you, Breed. Wait one, the Captain and Ms Stein wish to speak with you."

Palomas patches in Stein and Cruik. "Mr Breed," Cruik says, "have you anything to report?"

"I've killed nine hijackers. Excluding Angers and Thorval, that leaves ten. Knauss, two men to guard the crew, and six unknowns. They could be on roving patrol. The clamshell cover is open, the pool deck is exposed to the elements."

"Why did they open the clamshell?"

"Long story. They had to address a trim problem. Has our Russian operator had further contact with the *Lenin*?"

Cruik takes a deep breath. "I have news on that front. *Thorval isn't working for the Russians*."

That's a surprise. "Who for, then?"

"I'll let Stein tell you."

Stein speaks in a terse, matter-of-fact tone. "Breed,

Thorval is a private operator. He's demanding a ransom. Says he'll sell the Kestrels and the *Marshal Zhukov* to whoever pays him fifteen billion dollars by dawn."

"How are we supposed to get Thorval the money? Even more important from his perspective, how is *he* supposed to get away?"

"If we agree, he wants us to deposit the money in a series of accounts. From there, he'll shift the funds around. He has told us nothing about his plans to escape. Told us not to worry."

"You spoke to him?"

"Charming fellow. We had him on speaker. He told us he was also making the offer to the Russians."

"What's the deal with the Russians?"

"Same money. He'll either hand over the Kestrels or sink them. Knauss and the Advance Team wired the *Marshal Zhukov* with explosives. Upon payment, he'll blow it up or leave it intact. Whatever they want."

"That implies he has a way off the *Spider*."

"It would seem so, but that's the least of our problems."

"What's the plan?"

"I'm seeking approval to pay the money," Stein says. "Captain Cruik has other options."

Cruik takes a breath. "Based on the intel you have provided, our SEAL team will board the *Spider*. When they take the ship, Thorval becomes no factor. However, the Russians remain a problem."

I grunt. "You think they'll blow us out of the water."

"Consider the following, Mr Breed. If we agree to pay the ransom, they will try to destroy us. If they don't want to spend fifteen billion, they will try to destroy us. Either way, we are looking at a fight."

"What if they pay the ransom?"

"I will not allow them to board the *Spider*."

Stein cuts in. "COMSURFLANT has ordered the *USS Nimitz* strike group to sail north. It will not arrive in time."

We fall silent with the weight of the implications.

Cruik speaks with his Marlboro Man drawl. "I would like to make one minor observation."

"Go ahead, Captain," Stein says.

"Thorval contacted us with the *Spider's* HF radio, in the clear. He did the same with the Russians."

Chest hollow, I suck a breath. *My God, why didn't I see it?*

"Thorval and Knauss are private operators. To the best of our knowledge, the ransom call was their first contact with the Russians. That means there remain unidentified Russian operators aboard the *Spider*."

"My team," Stein says, "is reviewing backgrounds on everyone aboard."

"I can't believe eighteen divers slipped through."

"I'm not happy about it," Stein says, "but a lot depends on what red flags you're looking for. Let's take your friend Knauss. He might be a psychopath, but otherwise, he's Mr Red, White and Blue. He came aboard with top security clearance. Ditto those divers who are ex-military. The corporate divers probably showed no strong political affiliation."

"Has the Russian operator been in touch with the *Lenin* since Thorval made his move?"

"No," Cruik says. "It's possible the Russian operators are locked up with the crew. They wouldn't be aware of the ransom request."

"I never suspected Thorval was a third-party operation. He's got a big team, with saboteurs at Evenes and top-notch intel."

"Mr Breed, we're staging our SEAL team in the next half hour."

"I have Noa Larson and Dr Voss with me. I'd like to link up with the SEALs when the Star Pool is clear."

"I see no problem with that. Until then, stay out of their way."

"Yes, sir. I'm wearing a US Navy watch jacket. Make sure they know there's an armed friendly about."

22

SATURDAY, 0430 HOURS – THE SPIDER - SEAL
REVEAL

I unlock my cabin door and step inside.

Voss is sitting in a chair at the far side of the room. Noa's sitting on the bed, wringing her hands. "Breed, where have you been?"

"Sightseeing," I say. "Come on, I'll show you the Star Pool. It's beautiful."

We reenter the dead space and climb back to the sickbay deck. I lead them through the dead space on the port side toward the Star Pool. We come to the transverse bulkhead leading amidships, and I motion for them to wait. Pistol in hand, I open the door a crack and peer inside.

The mountain of pipes I rolled covers the deck. Because it rolled from the center cage, it leaves the two companionways clear on either side. Ditto the doors leading into the Star Pool.

"What happened?" Noa asks.

"Something massive."

I'm sure Thorval and Knauss would have sent a roving patrol to check the compartment. They're long gone. The hijackers don't have enough men to maintain permanent posts.

They would not have been able to dig out the man buried in pipe. The man I shot in the face is three-quarters buried at the top of the pile. His head, shoulders and one arm are free. The arm is bent, hand stretched toward the overhead. They didn't bother to dig *him* out either.

"Who is that?" Voss asks.

"One of the hijackers," I say. "He's my contribution to modern art."

Noa shivers.

"Watch your step." I pick my way up the hill of pipes.

In the dim light, the corpse stirs. I raise the M4 to my shoulder. He can't be alive—a thick mass of gore hangs from the exit wound in the back of his head. Pairs of red eyes stare at me from behind the ghoulish sculpture. With squeaks, the rats scurry away into the darkness. They run over and among the pipes, wriggle inside.

Noa swears in Norwegian. "What are we doing *here*, Breed?"

She places her hand on my shoulder. I reach up and put my hand on hers. She doesn't pull away. We did the same when we arrived on the helo. Why am I acting like this after one night with the girl? She's not *that* beautiful. More to the point, why is *she* acting this way? Maybe we're both scared, looking for reassurance.

Whatever is going on between me and Noa is a dangerous distraction.

The rats peep from within the ends of the pipes. With jealous eyes, they watch us move past their feast.

"This places us on the other side of the pool from the

Kestrels," I tell her. "If there's shooting, I don't want to get between the SEALs and the hijackers."

I pick my way down the other side. Look back, wait for Noa and Voss to join me. To my right are the niche and companionway where I sought cover. Against the side of the cage is the lever I pulled to open the gate on the hijackers. To the left is the door that opens to the Star Pool.

My pass unlocks the hatch with a click. I lower myself to the deck, sit with my shoulder against the bulkhead, and open the door a crack. Noa and Voss crouch behind me.

The Star Pool compartment is deserted.

I search the catwalk for signs of sentries. There are none. The clamshell shutters remain open, and the storm continues to rage. It's not as fierce as it was a while ago, but intimidating all the same. Snow swirls into the compartment and piles up on the deck around the pool. The wood beams, lashed three deep, form a pier.

There's a dusting of snow on the Kestrels. A couple of inches on the pool deck.

"What now?" Voss asks.

"Now, we wait."

THE SEALs ARE SUPPOSED to arrive in an Advanced Dry Combat Submersible, and I have no idea what it looks like. The *Spider's* submersibles look like miniature submarines. Cigar-shaped, with short conning towers that extend verti-cally like little sails. I don't know if the SEALs' submersible will also have a conning tower.

Will the submersible's conning tower break the surface of the pool? The SEALs could then emerge dry and kill any hijackers in the compartment. I wanted to help, but Cruik made it clear the SEALs would run their own show.

No, I think the submersible will carry the SEALs to the *Spider* in a dry, pressurized environment. Submerged in the Star Pool, they'll probably flood the submersible and deploy the SEALs in diving gear. The SEALs would then surface stealthily and take out the hijackers.

Except there aren't any hijackers in sight.

"They're not coming." Noa's voice is a whisper.

"Give them time."

I strain my eyes, sweep the surface of the Star Pool. It's hard to see anything against the glare of spotlights reflecting from the black water.

There. Two slender pipes extend about eighteen inches from the surface. Periscopes, spaced three feet apart. Controlled from below, they revolve slowly. The SEALs are studying the compartment. They've already studied plans provided by Nathan Conrad. Now they are correlating those plans with what they are eyeballing on the ground.

The periscopes disappear from view. I sweep the deck of the Star Pool again. Quarter the ground. Shift my gaze to the catwalk above.

Nothing.

I don't like it. The Star Pool is the one place the hijackers should cover. It's true they're short of men, but even so, they could spare at least one sentry. Thorval is an arrogant son of a bitch. Arrogance produces overconfidence. The little magician has been silent for a long time. I keep the squad radio on low volume so I can hear him when he comes on. I'm sure I haven't missed him.

A black rubber skullcap emerges from the surface of the pool. I smile to myself. The "Seal Reveal" has become an

action thriller cliché. In the movies, SEALs always emerge
from a body of water, grim-faced and armed to the teeth.
Another SEAL joins the first, and they swim slowly to the
side of the pool.

The men haul themselves from the pool. They're dressed
in black dry suits, dive masks, and re-breathers. Re-breathers
operate on a closed circuit. They provide divers with breath-
able air while not releasing bubbles. *No bubbles, no troubles.*

Army Special Forces Combat Dive trained me on the
Dräger LAR V. One hundred percent closed-circuit oxygen,
filtered for Co_2. That was good to seventy feet. I'd made it
deeper with a Mark 16 mixed-gas rebreather. I stuck the
experience on my résumé and was happy not to dive again. It
wasn't hard for me to believe Knauss, Pruitt, and other divers
could get down to six thousand feet with special rigs and
mixed gas.

The SEALs lift their face masks and remove their mouth-
pieces. The rebreathers are worn on their chests. They carry
sidearms and suppressed HK-416s with short barrels and
red-dot sights.

Six more SEALS emerge from the pool. They join the
first two on the deck. Raise their face masks, take off their re-
breathers and unlimber their weapons. They form a circle
and crouch low to the deck. Each man covers a section of the
circle. They alternate low and high cover. That means every
other man covers the catwalk.

I take a breath. Maybe now is the time to link up with the
SEALs.

Thorval's voice issues from the squad radio. "Hello, Mr
Breed. Have you missed me?"

Damn. I say nothing, dial the volume still lower. Noa's
eyes search mine.

"I've arranged some entertainment for you," Thorval says. "I think you'll enjoy it."

My shoulders tingle and I tighten my grip on the M4.

The sound of gunfire from M4s echoes from the steel bulkheads. It is followed by the crack of suppressed 416s. "Contact high left," someone cries. "Contact high right," calls another. Hijackers have stepped onto the catwalk from all sides. From the elevated position, they fire down onto the SEALs.

Gunfights are noisy. The sound of gunfire is unbearably loud. Inside the steel cocoon of a ship, the noise is indescribable. The sound of shooting echoes from the bulkheads. Suppressors help if the person firing is standing immediately next to you. Then he doesn't blow your ears out. But there's no silencing the boom of supersonic bullets as they crack overhead. The sound of ricochets adds to the racket.

All the SEALs are hit in the first thirty seconds. They return fire, but the angles aren't working for them. The steel safety barrier on the catwalk serves as a barricade and provides cover for the hijackers. High on the catwalk, at the head of the compartment, Knauss stands with an M4 to his shoulder. He drops an empty mag, levers another into the mag well. Slaps the bolt release, resumes fire.

I raise my M4 and fire on Knauss. Double tap. He leans forward to fire, and the first round misses him by half an inch. Strikes sparks high on the bulkhead behind him. He hears the round crack past, throws himself flat on the catwalk. My second shot strikes close to the first, misses him by a mile.

Knauss spotted my muzzle flash from the corner of his eye. He pops over the safety barrier and dumps the mag on me. I throw myself to one side of the doorway. Noa and Voss dive to the other.

"Cease fire," Knauss yells.

The SEALs lie crumpled. It's a large compartment, open to the elements, but the faint odor of cordite hangs in the air. Several inches of snow cover the deck. The SEALs' blood has stained it red, but the color won't last. Already, snow whirling through the open clamshell is covering the blood with a white veil.

The whole gunfight lasted less than a minute. Speed, surprise, violence of action. Whoever gets off the first shot usually wins. If he's under cover, firing from an elevated position, that's more than enough of an advantage.

Knauss stands, changes mags a second time, slaps the bolt release. Lifts the rifle to his shoulder and covers my door. "Breed, I know that was you."

Seven men on the catwalk, plus Knauss. He snaps orders. One man stays with him and five others rush to the doorways. They're coming for us.

I look at Noa and Voss. "Run," I tell them. "Head aft. I'll stall them."

The M4s on the catwalk crack again. Strident, high-pitched. Bullets splatter against the hatch and bulkhead. I poke the muzzle of my M4 through the crack between the door and the bulkhead. Without aiming, I point the weapon in Knauss's general direction and fire as fast as my finger can pull the trigger.

Knauss and his friend light me up again. I change mags and thumb the bolt release. Watch Noa and the little doctor scramble through the door at the aft transverse bulkhead.

The five hijackers have to descend three decks to reach

me. Three decks, then maneuver across the dead space. I have time. How much of it can I give Noa and Voss?

I empty my second mag. Fire on Knauss, fire on his buddy. I have ammunition for six of these exchanges. Noa's carrying the spare ammo vest. We had to move fast, there was no time to agree a meeting location. There was no way to *know* where to meet. We have to improvise.

Knauss's men were ringing the catwalk. Two descended forward, three aft. I don't know which way Knauss and the sixth man will go. There's a good chance Noa and Voss will run into the three who went aft. I have to catch up to give them support.

I break contact with Knauss, run for the transverse bulkhead, step through the door. I shut it behind me, spin the wheel, cast about for a metal bar. Anything I can use to jam the wheel and secure my rear. Nothing leaps out. I push myself to keep moving. Where have Noa and Voss gone?

I reach the aft peak. Drop to a crouch, whip out my survival radio.

"This is a US Navy channel. Identify yourself."

"Commander Palomas, this is Breed. The SEALs were ambushed, we have eight KIA."

"What is your condition?"

"Armed and effective."

Cruik's voice comes on. "Breed, what happened?"

"The hijackers were waiting, Captain. They killed eight SEALs in the Star Pool. I don't know what's happened to your submersible. I'm on the run, separated from Noa Larson and Dr Voss."

"The crew of the submersible had orders to return as soon as the team deployed. We'll pick them up." Cruik pauses. "Here's what's important. Sonar's no good in this sea state. Our communications are secure, so someone told them the SEALs were coming."

Crouched at the aft peak, I cover both port and starboard approaches from the dead space. "Have you got a nomination?"

"Stein's background checks have produced results. Noa Larson isn't half Swedish. She's half Russian."

"Shit." Noa and Voss *both* knew the SEALs were coming. But when could Noa have communicated with Thorval? She's been with me or Voss the whole time.

Cruik reads from a report. Stein must have messaged him. "Noa Larson. Age 23. Father Norwegian, mother Nenets Russian."

"What's that?"

"Nenets are Reindeer People, Mr Breed. They are Native Russians from the arctic. Noa Larson's mother and grand-mother were politically active. Seems there was a natural gas fire in the Nenets lands in the 1950s. So fierce the Soviets had to use a tactical nuke to blow it out. The land was contami-nated for decades and the Nenets people in the region suffered. Indeed, they continue to suffer today. Noa Larson's grandmother became an activist for the Nenets people. She died of cancer, probably associated with radiation exposure."

"What about Noa Larson and her mother?"

"Before she died, the grandmother moved to St Petersburg. She married there years later and bore Noa Larson's mother. After she died, the mother took over her work. Noa's mother got in the bad books of the Soviets in the 1980s. The Berlin Wall came down. The Soviet Union disintegrated and the Russian Federation opened up for Western business. In 1998, the mother married Bengt Larson, a Norwegian oil and gas engineer. In 1999, she bore him a daughter, Noa. Bengt is quite senior in his company. He wanted to take the family to Stavanger. The mother refused to go, but allowed him to take Noa."

"Broken home?"

"We don't know what their relationships were like. It is significant that the mother allowed Noa to go. Noa grew up in Stavanger, went to university in Trondheim, studied sedimentology. One of the best petroleum engineering programs in Europe. Bright girl, near the top of her graduating class. Before graduation, she was offered her pick of internships. Accepted a job with Royal Dutch Shell."

"I can guess what's next."

"Maybe not everything. Noa Larson's mother died earlier this year. A long, painful battle with cancer."

"Noa's mother must have been born long after the gas fire."

"Yes, she was. But we don't know how these conditions are inherited. Noa Larson reneged on her offer with Shell. Instead, she accepted an internship with Norsk Exploration. An internship that put her on the *Spider*."

"Jesus."

"Noa Larson is our Russian operator, Mr Breed. She's the one who has been trading signals with the *Lenin* since you both came aboard. It all fits."

"That's not a reason for her to warn Thorval the SEALs were coming."

"It is if the Russians have decided to pay the ransom. There are three parties involved here. Ourselves, the Russians, and Thorval. Allegiances are complicated, but it makes sense for Thorval to swing toward whoever pays him.

For that matter, it makes sense for whoever decides to pay him to swing to Thorval."

Cruik's right, but I don't want to believe Noa betrayed eight good men. "What have we learned about Thorval?"

"Nothing that wasn't on his résumé. Stein's team is digging deep, but it's unlikely Thorval is his real name. They have his fingerprints and biometrics, but he has no prior record."

I'm sure Thorval has a criminal history. The little magician has made his past disappear. "He has a way about him, Captain. A man like that is distinctive."

"Breed, events are running with a momentum of their own. Stein is close to obtaining approval to pay the ransom. The storm is clearing from the northeast, and *Lenin* is closing. Arctic dawn comes at 0900 Hours."

"If we pay the ransom, all we have to worry about are the Russians."

"And if we *don't* pay the ransom, we need to worry about *both* Thorval and the Russians."

"Can you advise me when Stein gets the green light?"

"Yes. What are *you* going to do?"

"I'm going to kill as many of Thorval's crew as I can."

23

E levators are coffins. Inside the climate-controlled shoebox, companionways are the avenue of choice between decks. Noa and Voss can take companionways within the dead space, but they'll tire of handling the heavy hatches. Hatches designed to resist the pressure of water welling up from below.

They can go up, or they can go down. If I'm going to catch them, I have to guess which. If they go down, they'll try to hide in the cavernous maze of the engine space. If they go up, they'll head toward the crew's mess, operations bridge, and the helideck.

No idea which way Voss would go.

From the moment we ran into her, Noa wanted to reach the boat deck. She was obsessed with the idea of escaping in a lifeboat. She wasn't hoping to be picked up by the *Pressley Bannon*. She was trying for the *Lenin*.

The smart move is to hide on one of the intermediate decks. Find an empty compartment and give the hijackers time to pass. There is so much empty space on the *Spider*, it's easy to lose yourself like that. If you go racing up the companionways, you'll collide with the gunmen coming the other way.

I decide to stay in the dead space and climb the aft superstructure. The boat deck is one above the main deck, one below the mess deck. The crew are confined in the mess. There will be one hijacker on guard duty, plus three from Knauss's ambush. That makes four hijackers aft of the Star Pool.

My rifle is on a sling and I allow it to hang at my right side. My sidearm is in an open holster. I go to the nearest companionway and start climbing.

"Did you like my surprise, Breed?"

I ignore Thorval. Lever myself through a hatchway. Close the hatch, keep climbing. It's three decks to the operations level, then I'll be in the aft superstructure. Five to the boat deck, six to the mess deck, seven to the operations bridge. I have a lot of climbing to do.

"Help isn't coming, Breed. In fact, Mr Knauss is on his way. He has regaled me with rather vivid descriptions of what he intends to do to you."

Mess deck. I step to the door that separates the dead space from the climate-controlled interior. Try to recall the layout from Thorval's quick tour. The crew will be sealed in the mess, the door shut and locked. One hijacker outside, unless he's been pulled away to augment Thorval's shrinking force.

"I'll be in the Star Pool, Breed. Surrender to me there."

He's getting ready to move the missiles. But how?

Never mind. Kill hijackers. Seize the high ground. I climb until I reach the operations bridge. Open the door a crack and peer into the climate-controlled living space.

The door opens into the passageway that leads from the helideck to the operations bridge. The space looks deserted. I step through the door, rifle low-ready. Check the left and right cuts of the operations bridge. It's clear.

Down the companionway to the mess deck. Step into the passageway outside the mess. The first door is locked. No sound carries from within, no sign of a sentry. Thorval may have pulled him off to join the search. It's a long passageway, with doors at the other end.

I can't afford to miss a hijacker and get attacked from behind. There are two doors at the end of the passageway. One leads into the mess. It's locked. The other leads to the head. Of course there are facilities on every deck. I advance, rifle high-ready.

The door to the head swings open. Zipping his fly, a hijacker steps into the passageway. We come face-to-face, so close neither of us has room to point his rifle. He grabs my M4 with both hands, tries to tear it from my grasp. Professional diver, ex-military, he's strong.

We're in a wall fight. The kind you get into when a Talib rushes you from a dark corner. My rifle's on a sling, I won't lose it. I let him take it, throw my weight against him and pin him to the bulkhead. Clamp my left hand over his nose and mouth to stifle his cries. Create a frame in which to work. Textbook CQB.

I transition to my secondary. Draw the SIG with my right hand, press the muzzle against the side of his chest, pull the trigger. *Thump, thump, thump.* Contact shots, all muffled by his body. The rounds punch through his ribs into the chest cavity. His eyes stare into mine, widen with pain and astonishment.

Nine mil is a small round. I change the angle of the

muzzle, fire three times more. *Thump, thump, thump.* Shred the guy's heart and lungs. Life drains from his eyes and I lower his corpse to the deck. Decock, holster the SIG, transition to the M4.

I recognize the bulge of a fragmentation grenade stuffed in his load-bearing vest. Each rifleman carries a hand grenade. I tear open his Velcro, take the grenade, put it in my pocket.

The crew inside the mess are quiet. No point letting them out now. I go back to the companionway, raise the rifle to my shoulder, descend to the boat deck. This is where I find out if I guessed right.

Icy air pours in from the boat deck. Someone's left the damn door open. Driven by the wind, daggers of sleet fly through the door and shatter against the bulkhead. I see a hijacker crossing from the top of the companionway to the door. His attention is on the snow-covered deck. By the time he sees me, it's too late. He twists at the hips, rifle raised. I fire three times—all my shots hit him in the chest. One round smacks a spare magazine. The other two drill him center mass. He lurches against a bulkhead and crumples.

I step off the companionway. Through the open door, I see Voss and Noa standing in the storm, hands raised protectively to their faces. Noa's looking for a lifeboat to steal.

There was no missing the crack of my M4. There's a rush of footfalls as the other hijackers race up the companionway. I shoot the slumped body once more in the head. It splits like a burst watermelon. I turn my attention to the companionway. They'll toss a grenade onto the landing before charging the deck.

I take the grenade from my vest, pull the pin, let the spoon fly. Staring down the companionway, I hold the grenade in my hand and let it cook. One thousand one, one thousand two. A hijacker stares at me, rifle in one hand, grenade in the other. I lob my grenade underhand down the companionway.

With a cry, the hijacker drops the spoon and throws his grenade at me. I gasp. One of us—maybe both—is going to Jesus. The frag lands on the deck and rattles in my direction. I stop it with the inner edge of my shoe. Flick it back like a soccer ball, dive to one side.

There's a deafening boom as my grenade explodes. Black smoke spurts from the companionway. The blast blows a puff of dust and rust from the bulkheads. A heartbeat later, the second grenade goes off with a metallic clang.

I raise the M4 and stand at the top of the companionway. Tendrils of smoke drift through the air. The first hijacker is lying on the metal steps. The side of his head and neck are slick with blood. Through glassy eyes, he stares at me. He's lost his M4. Doesn't know where he is, doesn't know what happened. I shoot him in the face.

Rifle to my shoulder, I step over the dead man's body. The third hijacker is lying facedown at the bottom of the companionway. The grenade I kicked had longer to go before detonating. It must have bounced past him and exploded before hitting the deck. The back of his jacket and ammo vest have been ripped to shreds. His hair is matted with blood.

I shoot the man once in the back of the head. Roll him over, relieve him of his grenade. This is the main deck. Where's Knauss? He must have heard muffled echoes of the shots and explosions. Can he localize them? I scramble over the bodies. Make my way back to the boat deck.

Eyes wide, I suck breath. Voss is standing at the top of

the companionway, holding the first man's rifle at her hip. She's pointing it at me, and her finger is on the trigger. Six pounds of pull, and her knuckle's gone bone white.

There's a crack, and the muzzle flash flares in my face. The side of my neck is cut by a burning knife. That's what getting shot feels like—a sensation of intense heat. Pain comes next. There's shock. You fight through it. If you're not hit somewhere vital, you try to control the bleeding and go on fighting. Greasy blood runs from my neck onto my shoulder. I blink, lurch against the side of the companionway.

Noa hurtles from the boat deck and body-checks Voss.

I raise the M4 and try to get a clear shot. The two women struggle for Voss's rifle. The doctor fights like a wild animal, eyes wide, teeth bared. She twists the rifle out of Noa's hands and slams the butt into the side of the girl's head.

Noa reels. I fire twice, hit the doctor center mass. She drops her rifle and falls to the deck.

I climb the companionway and keep Voss covered. She's still alive, blood bubbling from wounds in her chest. She's choking on it. I must have hit a lung. I separate her from her weapon system, set the rifle against the bulkhead a good distance from Noa.

Noa sits up. Snow and sleet are pouring through the open door. A blanket of white is rapidly covering the deck and the body of the dead hijacker. The snow is everywhere. Noa's jeans and watch jacket are dusted with it. The flakes are melting on her hair.

"Breed, you've been shot."

"Grazed. It's bleeding like a son of a bitch."

Noa unzips her ammo vest and digs in the pockets of her jacket. She produces a plastic-wrapped pad, tears it open with her teeth. Does she carry bandages? No... it's a feminine napkin. She hands me the pad. "Hold this over the wound," she says.

Snow is swirling through the air. It's like we're standing inside a snow globe. Noa lurches to the open door, shuts it.

I let the M4 hang by its sling. Draw the SIG and cover Voss with one hand while I hold the dressing over the wound.

The rage has bled from Voss's features. She struggles to speak. "Tell me, Breed."

"Tell you what?"

"Why did you kill Nygard?" Blood trickling from the corner of her mouth, Voss smiles. "You know I love thrillers. Why did you kill the boy?"

Out of the corner of my eye, I see Noa undoing her jeans. What is she doing? Her belly is pale and flat. Her navel is an innie, the way I like them. She tears at her underwear.

Noa's a distraction. I focus on Dr Voss, shake my head. "I didn't kill him."

Voss's face darkens. "Don't lie to me, Breed. I'm dying, I won't tell anybody."

"I'm not lying."

Noa buttons her jeans. She steps to me and says, "Let me bandage that."

I let go of the pad. Noa stands close, uses her torn underwear to bind the sanitary pad in place. It's not so easy. She has to bind it tightly enough to keep the pad in place without choking me. "It's stopping," she says.

A good woman.

I think back to the way Angers called me to Nygard's cabin. Thorval was suspicious of me. He was unhappy that I touched the diver's wallet. Voss was suspicious too. Nygard's death didn't make sense.

I was totally focused on Aron's murder. The death of the surface manager made sense in the context of the Kestrel transfer. He learned something the hijackers didn't want him to share with Stein.

Nygard's murder lacked a motive. Moreover, the crime scene had a disorganized quality.

A crafty gleam lights up Voss's eyes. "I'll trade with you."

"What do you have to trade?"

"I'll tell you who killed Aron and Pruitt if you tell me why you killed Nygard."

Voss coughs. Droplets of pink spittle land on her face.

"I know who killed Aron." I struggle to mask my revulsion. The doctor with the wonderful bedside manner.

"You don't know everything."

Maybe not, but I can't be far off. Uneasy, I glance toward the companionway. Strain to hear sounds of Knauss and his men coming after us. Hand to her head, Noa looks lost.

It's clear now who killed Pruitt and betrayed the SEALs. I want a confession. Voss's wounds are not survivable... She doesn't have long. "Who betrayed the SEALs?" I ask. "Who killed Pruitt?"

Voss smiles. It's a garish smile, lips and teeth painted red, cheeks stippled with pink flecks. The smile of an aged whore.

"I killed Pruitt," the doctor says. "It was all part of the plan. Before Thorval took over the ship, I went to the compartment and evacuated the atmosphere from the decompression chambers. Imagine my surprise when I returned to the sickbay and found you there."

"Pruitt and his men didn't need to die," I say. "You said yourself, they had to remain in the chambers for another week."

"Had they been willing to risk decompression sickness, they could have come out earlier. They could have caused trouble."

"And the SEALs?" I hold my breath, afraid she'll deny it.

Proud of herself, Voss cackles. "In the dead space, I hung back. I went back inside, used a deck interphone to call the bridge. Sat down, pretended I'd hurt my ankle, and waited for you to come back for me."

I let out a breath. Noa didn't betray the SEALs. "Were you involved before you came aboard, or after?"

"Thorval offered money, encouraged me to apply. He made sure I was hired."

My God. The woman is a monster. "What about Aron?"

"I told you I saw him in the dead space. He had to be in contact with the outside. We searched his cabin for a radio and found nothing. It was obvious he hid it in the dead space. I told Knauss. We never found the radio. Did you find it? Knauss assumed you hid yours in the dead space on *your* deck."

I bend closer to Voss. "What I want to know is *why* Aron was murdered."

Voss coughs. "It's your turn, Breed. Tell me why you killed Nygard, and I'll tell you why Knauss killed Aron."

I've played my string. "I *didn't* kill Nygard."

"You're lying. No one else had a reason to kill Nygard. He was a diver, a nobody. Tell me the truth."

"That *is* the truth. I had no reason to kill Nygard."

Voss's mouth froths with blood. "Liar!"

I raise the SIG and shoot Voss in the face.

24

SATURDAY, 0530 HOURS – THE SPIDER - INTO
THE STORM

I grab Noa by the arm and hustle her down the companionway. My heart pounds—we could crash into Knauss at any moment.

We reach the landing on the main deck. I open the door, and a demonic wind blasts us with snow and sleet. A million icy scalpels slash our faces and cut straight through our watch jackets. Our clothing was fine for the interior of the *Spider*. Out here, in thirty degrees of frost, we might as well be naked on another planet. We look amidships toward the raised platform that is the operations deck. The dark tower that is the *Spider's* derrick rises above it.

"What are we doing here?" Noa asks.

I remind myself she's operating for the Russians. But she's standing with me, not Thorval.

"Knauss is bringing company up those companionways. We can't let them trap us in the superstructure."

I secure the door behind us. We zip our jackets all the way to our chins, and I lead Noa to the port gunwale. The howling wind blows snow and sleet across the deck. Six inches have built up, despite the superheated steam pipes fighting to melt the snow.

Build-up of ice on the decks can become dangerous. The weight of snow and ice raises the vessel's center of gravity. A narrow-beamed ship can capsize. The *Spider's* wide beam makes it safer, but it is still good to clear snow and ice from the deck.

On the flight in, I noticed snow was already building up. McMaster told me the *Spider* was designed with a mesh of steam heating pipes stretched across its decks. Computer-controlled from the operations bridge, the heaters prevent excessive build-up of snow and ice. A destroyer like the *Pressley Bannon* does not have such heaters. Its wider beam is safer than old destroyers, but Cruik and Palomas still send crew topside to sweep snow and ice off the deck.

Noa and I battle across the main deck of the *Spider*. The temperature is near 32 degrees, but the wind chill factor is far below freezing. My throat and lungs burn with every breath. I see panic rising in Noa's features. We have to get back inside quickly.

The masthead light at the top of the derrick is more distinct than I've ever seen it. The storm is past its peak, the wind has fallen to sixty miles an hour. The light casts a pale glow on the deck, and the *Spider* is surrounded by a dim halo. The waves are black, their crests white.

Noa clutches me for warmth and support. Her cheeks are red from the wind, and her blond hair is matted with snow. We bend double against the Force 10 gale.

"My God," Noa says. "We can't make three hundred yards."

"We don't have to," I tell her. "We'll go as far as the operations deck, then go inside."

From the operations deck amidships, we can descend toward the Star Pool. Find a way to lose ourselves in the living space.

Every ten yards, I turn and pull rear security. It's too much to ask of Noa. A civilian, she's never acquired the basic skills expected of an operator. The Russians must hold some kind of *kompromat* over her.

I'm forced to take shallow breaths to keep my lungs from frosting. Every breath is agony. We're almost to the base of the operations deck. I look back toward the aft superstructure. Rows of hatch covers have been welded shut. They used to lead to oil storage tanks. When Norsk Exploration gutted the *Spider*, they shut the hatches forever. The long lines of heating pipes melt furrows in the white powder.

My eyes are drawn to a beam of light. Someone has opened the door leading into the aft superstructure. I tighten my grip on Noa's arm and freeze. A hijacker pokes his head into the storm, looks around. We're hunters, our eyes are drawn to movement. If Noa and I stand still, he could miss us.

The figure withdraws to the interior of the superstructure. Swings the door shut. The beam of light narrows, then disappears.

"Come on," I say.

We're fifteen yards from the operations deck, but the structure seems a mile away. Its base spans the gunwales of the *Spider* from port to starboard. The operations platform floats inside the base, supported by gimbals that allow it to tilt and shift with the seas. Computer controlled, the gimbals continuously adjust for pitch and roll. A massive heave compensator allows the platform to rise and fall with the waves.

The complexity of the engineering is made even more impressive by the structural strength of the arrangement. Towering above us, set in the middle of the platform, squats the derrick. Massive steel A-frames support the one-hundred-and-fifty-foot tower.

Companionways at the corners lead up to the operations deck. I glance back to make sure the door to the aft super-structure is still shut. Satisfied, I lead Noa forward. My hands and face are on fire from thousands of slashing needles—snow and sleet driven by the wind. The pain is comforting. So long as I can feel it, I'm not frostbitten.

We reach the top of the companionway and step onto a steel catwalk. Lights at the corners cast a comforting glow. This catwalk is fixed to the ship. A second catwalk, separated from this one by a foot, stretches around the gimbaled plat-form. Floodlights mounted on the inner catwalk illuminate the Star Pool, three decks below.

I guide Noa onto the gimbaled platform. This catwalk is where the roughnecks work, joining sections of pipe together. I step to the catwalk rail and look down into the Star Pool.

My breath catches in my chest. From here, I can see the expanse of the Star Pool. It's surrounded by the pool deck, gray steel covered with snow. Driven by the Coriolis Effect, a whirling white vortex spirals counterclockwise into the ship. The flakes melt on contact with the Star Pool's surface. Pile onto the deck. The cranes and submersibles squat on the port side, the Kestrels starboard. Next to the Kestrels is the stack of heavy wood beams used to construct docks.

Piled next to the stack of beams is a grisly sight—the bodies of the dead SEALs. One can see red-and-white trails in the snow over which the bodies were dragged. They were then shoved into the corner. Puddles of congealed blood have frozen around the bodies.

The surface of the Star Pool is a black mirror. It glitters with the reflections of floodlights. Except for—

—a black whale floating in the pool.

A submarine.

Sixty yards long by six wide. It's tied to the makeshift dock of timbers extending from the pool's edge. There is a tall black sail amidships, and loading hatches fore and aft. The hatches are open. Circles of warm light spill onto the deck.

Voices carry from the Star Pool. Men are working on the pool deck and on that of the submarine. Angers supervises men who are moving one of the Kestrels onto the wooden dock. It rolls on its steel cradle to a large truck equipped with a mobile crane. They are going to load the missile onto the submarine.

My eyes sweep the deck, count the men. Half a dozen are working with Angers to transfer the Kestrel. These men are dressed in heavy jackets and black watch caps. They're not divers. They must be the submarine's crew.

A slender figure watches the activity from the pool deck. Lean and handsome, he wears Norsk Exploration coveralls, a warm kapok jacket, and expensive gloves. His bearing and expression convey one hundred percent confidence.

Thorval.

No sign of Knauss or any of the divers. I've killed thirteen men. That leaves Thorval, Angers, Knauss and four others. It's a good bet Knauss and one man are aft and working their way forward. That leaves three armed divers in the vicinity of the pool.

"Let's go." I take Noa's hand and hurry along the catwalk.

Spent shell casings mark the positions from which the hijackers ambushed the SEALs.

Forward of the Star Pool, we step off the operations platform and onto the fixed catwalk. Find a door and enter the living space. Damp and shivering, we stand in a warm, brightly lit passageway. There are companionways on either end, leading to the lab deck below.

I force myself to switch on. Heft the M4, cautiously descend a companionway. When we reach the lab deck, I push a door open. I move down the passageway, checking compartments left and right. The doors aren't watertight. I find a large office and pull Noa inside.

Trembling, we examine each other for signs of frostbite —There are none. We were not exposed to the elements long enough. The pain is exquisite as we rub circulation back into our hands and faces. I take a deep breath and look around.

There's a kneehole desk with an open laptop. A comfortable recliner has been pushed against the desk. The rest of the space is occupied by filing cabinets, two easy chairs and a conference table. I offer Noa one of the easy chairs and take the other.

We stare silently at each other for what seems like a full minute. This is the first chance we've had to catch our breath. This beautiful girl I've slept with is a Russian operator. That will have to be faced. But not yet.

I sit with the M4 pointing at the door. Take the radio from my pocket and select the *Pressley Bannon*.

"This is a US Navy channel," Palomas says. "Identify yourself."

"Breed here, Commander. There have been developments."

"Here too, Breed. I'm putting you on speaker."

Cruik's voice is tense. "What do you have for us, Breed?"

"Chipping away, Captain. I have Noa Larson in the room with me. Killed four more hijackers, which leaves five. Dr Voss was working with the hijackers. She betrayed the SEALs and killed Pruitt's team."

"One woman did that?"

"She got under people's radar, Captain. Got under mine. There's something else you need to know."

"Let's have it, Breed."

"The hijackers have a submarine. I don't know much about those boats, but it looks like one of those new diesel-electrics. It's small. About sixty yards long, seven yards wide. The hull has a narrow top deck and sharply sloped sides. They're loading the Kestrels onto the sub."

"You're describing a German Type 6. Crew of fifteen. Eight thousand miles range, deep diving, runs submerged three weeks without snorkeling. It's a good choice for Thorval. From here, it can reach any number of landfalls submerged. It's *quiet*, and it has a stealthy hull. We've trained against them, and they've defeated our towed array *and* active sonar."

"That crew sounds awfully small."

"The sub is a marvel of automation. The Germans minimized crew size to maximize endurance. Is Thorval setting up for a double-cross?"

"It looks like it, but we can't be sure. It could be how he intends to escape *and* deliver the Kestrels to the winning bidder."

"If the *Spider* is going to become a battlefield, it makes sense to get off," Cruik says. "Stein has not yet obtained approval to pay the ransom. There is nothing to do but sit tight and wait for developments."

"Agreed. I'll sign off, Captain. Noa Larson and I need to have a conversation."

MY FACE HURTS. From the beating Knauss gave me, the cold, and now the return of circulation as we warm up. My neck hurts from the bullet crease, and the makeshift bandage is damp. Noa's dressing is holding, and twenty-two degrees of frost outside was enough to freeze blood solid. I won't bleed to death anytime soon.

How to handle her? An innocent, compromised by the Russians. To what end?

I stare into Noa's bright blue eyes. "Alright," I say. "Where's your radio?"

"What radio?"

"The radio you've been using to communicate with the Russian frigate. Do I have to search you?"

I don't think Noa has a pistol, but she could have a knife or some other weapon in her vest or jacket. I don't want to go in heavy. If I handle this right, she might give me what I want without trouble.

Noa takes off the ammo vest and sets it on the table. Then she unzips first the front of her jacket, then an interior pocket. She takes out a survival radio that looks much like mine. Holds it up to me.

"Put it on the table. Turn your pockets out."

She sets the radio down, shows me the contents of her pockets. From the left, she takes another feminine napkin. Her jeans are skintight. She isn't hiding weapons.

"Stand up, lift your jacket, turn around."

Noa does what she's told. There's nothing in her waistband.

I pick up her radio. Form follows function, it's remarkably like mine... a quarter of an inch thicker. I press a blister in the laminated seal, and the security screen comes to life. Mine requires the user to draw a pattern. Noa's requires an access code.

"What's the number?" I ask.

"I won't give it to you."

"Noa, give me the number."

"What will you do, beat me? I won't betray my country."

I zip the radio into my pocket. "Alright," I say, "but you won't be using it."

Noa shrugs. "You're wet. I can change your dressing while we talk."

She's decided to try the light touch. Steps forward and reaches for the makeshift bandage. I flinch, allow her to start work.

"You're Russian," I say.

Noa smiles sadly. "At Djevelkafé you thought I was Norwegian. I said you were half right."

"You didn't tell me."

"You didn't ask."

Once again, a hint of the tension we felt at the bar. Was it just two nights ago? I feel myself stir.

"What's your role in all this?"

"I'm not a professional spy, if that's what you think." Noa ties the fresh pad over my wound. "The bleeding has stopped. Now you will have a *visible* scar."

"Tell me about your mission."

25

SATURDAY, 0600 HOURS - TRONDHEIM – FELIKS

Noa tells me of a night eight months ago. She was in Trondheim, finishing her last term at NTNU, Norway's finest engineering school. She had picked the old port, now a chic university town, to gain a measure of independence from her father. The university at Stavanger was also top flight, but too close to home.

FEBRUARY NIGHTS in Trondheim aren't always black. When there's a lot of snow on the ground and mist in the air, the city lights diffuse through the atmosphere. Trondheim appears to spread under a light box.

Noa unlocked the door to her apartment building. It was one of those converted warehouses by the old wharves. The ones with the colorful facades. Bright colors in the summer, muted in the winter.

Inside, she loosened her scarf and undid her wool duffel coat. She slung her briefcase of research notes over her shoulder and checked the mail.

The wharves were one of the best addresses in Trond-heim. Her father paid to keep her comfortable. She wasn't spoiled, but he didn't want his lovely girl living in a hovel. Noa took the elevator to the third floor and let herself into her apartment.

Her rooms were dark and shadowy. Open plan, with a living room in the center, kitchen and dining room to the right, and a library and sleeping space to the left. The living room looked out onto the water through enormous picture windows. The blinds were open. Her sofa, coffee table, and side tables faced the wharves. An easy chair was placed with its back to the windows.

She set her briefcase down on the sofa. Hung her duffel coat on a wood hanger and set it on a coat tree. She turned to flick the light switch and froze.

A dark figure was sitting motionless in the easy chair. The man stared at her. Her stomach tightened.

"It's alright, Ms Larson," the man said. "We need to speak."

Noa flicked the light switch and the rooms blazed with light. Her mood was easily affected by the darkness. She would have preferred to come home to a brightly lit apart-ment, but she was careful with money. Especially her father's.

"Who are you?" Noa asked.

The man did not bother to stand. He was about forty. Close-cropped blond hair and a medium build. He looked perfectly average. He could have been a professor from her college, the Norwegian University of Science and Technology. The best school in Norway, the best program in petroleum engineering. She was about to graduate at the top of her bachelor's class.

"My name is Feliks," the man said. "Please, sit down. We have important matters to discuss."

Noa stepped around the sofa. The man's eyes registered her attractive features, her sculpted figure. He watched her sit down.

"How did you get in?"

"Surely you have more relevant questions than that."

"What do you want?"

Feliks smiled. "I knew you had it in you. First of all, understand that this conversation must remain between us. I have no need to repeat that admonishment. Agreed?"

Noa shivered. "Yes."

"I assure you, you have nothing to fear from me. I am here to help you."

"Why don't I believe you?"

"Hear me out. I work for the government of the Russian Federation."

Noa had known it from the first. But she knew of no reason her grandmother's and mother's activities should involve her.

"I know what you are thinking," Feliks said. "It is nothing to do with the subversive activities of your mother and grandmother, I assure you. It is something else entirely. The country of your mother, the country of your birth, requires your service."

"In what way?"

Felix leaned forward. Clasped his hands together and rested his elbows on his knees. "You are a very bright girl. Graduating at the top of your class, I'm told. You have numerous job offers for the spring."

"I've accepted a position with Royal Dutch Shell."

"Ah. You passed up a generous offer from Norsk Exploration."

"A year at sea does not appeal to me."

"It is a prestigious internship. You will be doing cutting-edge research and analysis. The financial impact of your findings could be immense. You will have an opportunity to learn from the finest minds in the field of petroleum engineering and sedimentology."

"I will be happier with Shell."

"Happiness is a second-rate ambition. Ms Larson, we want you to take the position with Norsk Exploration. We want you to sail on the *Spider*, the most advanced research ship ever built."

"I have already accepted the position with Shell."

"Renege."

"I value my reputation too much to do so."

"Such decisions are not unheard of, Ms Larson. You may burn one bridge, but there are many others. In the grand scheme of things, it matters little."

"Not to me."

Feliks treated Noa to a theatrical sigh. Leaned back in the easy chair and crossed his legs. "When was the last time you spoke with your mother, Ms Larson?"

Noa's throat tightened. Her whole life, her mother had discouraged contact. It was not that she felt no love for Noa. Quite the opposite. Noa's mother was politically active against the government. As Noa's grandmother had done before her, she championed the rights of the Nenets people. She sought protections and compensation for harm done in the past. The great gas fire of 1956. The catastrophe that burned for weeks. The Soviets resorted to a tactical nuclear weapon to blow it out.

It was not that the crusade meant more to Noa's mother than her family. She loved Noa and encouraged her to leave Russia to live in Norway with her father. She wanted to protect her family from the Russian government.

"A year," Noa said.

"A year and two months." Feliks corrected her with the precision of a schoolmaster. "I am sorry to say your mother is not well."

Noa's mouth went dry. She felt as though her cheeks had been stuffed with cotton. She found herself unable to swallow. "What is wrong?"

"Cancer," Feliks said. "I fear it is the same aggressive disease that took your grandmother."

"I must see her."

"She does not wish it. You know she has always been protective of you and your father. Unreasonably so."

"Yes, but surely a visit can do no harm."

"She did not want you or your father to know. It is silly, of course. Your father's status in this country affords his family considerable protection. Your mother, however, harbors many unreasonable fears. She thinks our State has not changed in eighty years."

"Is she wrong?"

"More wrong than you can imagine," Felix said. His sincere tone was halfway reassuring. "Ms Larson, do this work for us, and we will ensure your mother receives the best care possible. There can be no promises, of course, but the doctors assure me her condition will respond to treatment."

"You would not offer her such treatment if I said no?"

"Of course we would. But these treatments are expensive. Your mother will receive the best of everything, funded by the State. When you return in a year, we will arrange a reunion."

"Whether she wants one or not."

"We will persuade her she has nothing to fear."

Noa looked away, considered her options. She had none.

"What do you require from me on the ship?"

"Our country's territorial claims on the ocean floor are under dispute. The purpose of the Norsk Exploration *Spider* is to collect data to challenge those claims. The value of those claims is incalculable. We want you to evaluate the quality of their work."

"You want me to spy on them."

Feliks shrugged. "Nothing in life is free."

NOA'S STORY doesn't hold together. She strikes me as sincere, yet I see two glaring inconsistencies. I have to deal with both.

"Feliks said your mission was to assess the quality of the *Spider's* data with respect to territorial claims?"

"Yes." Noa looks puzzled.

"He didn't say anything about the missiles or where they came from?"

"No."

I lean forward and look into Noa's eyes. "You weren't surprised when you saw the Kestrels in the Star Pool. It was like you knew what they were and why they were there. In fact, you haven't expressed the slightest bit of curiosity about them. Why is that?"

Noa breaks eye contact, stares at the bulkhead behind me. "You're mistaken."

"No, I'm not. The funny thing is—you were sincere a minute ago. When you told me Feliks wanted you to assess

the *Spider's* data quality. That means you only found out
about the Kestrels once you were aboard. You've been
trading messages with the *Lenin* all night. Long before
Thorval broadcast his ransom demand. Feliks didn't find out
about the Kestrels from Thorval. He found out about them
from *you*."

Normally rosy, Noa's cheeks turn pale. "Please, Breed.
Does it matter?"

The innocence in the girl's plea touches me. I take her
hands in mine.

"Everything matters. Noa, you... *must*... tell me."

She does.

26

SATURDAY, 0630 HOURS – THE SPIDER - THE
CLOCK TICKS

Noa looks close to tears. She's leaning forward, elbows on her knees. She clasps her hands, opens them, rubs them together. I glance at my watch and the survival radio. Still no word from Stein, but dawn is approaching. Not much time remains to pay the ransom.

It doesn't matter. Noa needs to be treated gently. She's half-child, half-woman. The impression of strength she conveys is illusory. Not only is she vulnerable, she conveys a puzzling fragility. She tells me what happened after dinner, while I was exploring the dead space.

NOA SAT IN THE OFFICERS' mess, staring at her empty plate. She felt terrible brushing Breed away. She'd been attracted to him from the moment she saw him, knew he felt the same. The tension between them was electric. Too many men were intimidated by her beauty. Others fawned over her, worshiped her. They wanted to make her their girlfriend when all she wanted to do was have fun and get to know them.

Breed was different. He wanted her and didn't hide it. But he had things to do. The sex they had was fun and liberating. She wanted to get to know him, but she had much weighing on her shoulders. It was only at the helo pad that she found out they were bound for the same destination.

Noa forced Breed to the back of her mind. Got up, carried her tray to the disposal rack. She felt the divers' eyes on her, licking her body. She was used to the attention. Sometimes it felt nice, most of the time it was annoying. Noa did not consider herself particularly beautiful, though she knew men found her so.

That was another check mark in Breed's favor. He was not intimidated by attractive women. His desire wasn't a matter of life or death. She'd lost track of the number of boys she'd had to ghost to maintain her sanity.

She was happy to leave the mess. Went to her cabin, closed the door, took out her radio. It was much like Breed's. Laminated in plastic, high-tech satellite technology, wireless charging. The keys and menus were labeled in a choice of languages. Hers was set to English. It would not do to have someone notice her using a device equipped with a Cyrillic keyboard.

"This is Feliks."

Before she left for the *Spider*, Feliks told her he would be on a warship close by. She was to remain in close contact. He wanted reports at specific contact times during the day. In between, if necessary, but at the pre-specified checkpoints in any case.

"This is Noa."

"What do you have to report?"

"I have been on a tour of the vessel. I have access everywhere, except the central operations space."

"What is your sense of that space?"

"It is very large. Half the length of the ship, most of the beam. They do drilling there. Raise cores. Other samples."

"There is no way that much space is required for only cores and samples."

"How do you know?"

"The *Spider* is not the only drill ship in the world. It is only the largest."

"Perhaps they have built more capacity than they require. Americans and Europeans are extravagant."

Feliks was silent. Noa could sense his skepticism. At last, he said, "Let us make certain. I require you to enter the space and confirm its purpose."

"How am I to gain access? My job does not require me to be there. I am not even allowed inside on a tour."

"That in itself is suspicious. Use your ingenuity. I expect a report."

Feliks signed off. Miserable, Noa pocketed her radio, stood up and paced the cabin. There had to be a way into the Star Pool. She thought of going outside to the operations deck and climbing down. But the clamshell shutters were closed. Climbing through the pipe stream oculus was suicide. The doors and hatches leading into the space would be locked.

She left her cabin, walked the passageways of the vast ship. Finally, she wandered back to the officers' mess. Dinner was over, and there were few people remaining. A handful of research techs were sitting at a table, drinking beer. She didn't know any of them. Why should she? She'd only been aboard a few hours.

A pair of divers were playing pool. She recognized the man with long black hair she'd met in the weight room. He wore jeans and a black T-shirt stretched across his biceps and pectorals. He was smoking a cigarette under a "NO SMOKING" sign. He and the other diver were sharing a bottle of Scotch whisky.

Martin Nygard recognized her and took a drag of his cigarette. "Ms Larson. Join us."

Noa's mind whirled. She thought of Feliks, Breed, and her mother. She'd found Nygard charming when they met. He was a good ten years younger than Breed. More muscular. The diver worked on his body, probably had some notion of how to use it.

Not that Breed was a slouch. After the mutual violence of their first bout, he became more gentle, almost tender. She'd started the night wanting a man to give it to her. She hadn't anticipated the range of emotion and sensation Breed brought to their encounter.

She was fascinated by Breed's scarred body. The bullet wounds, front and back. The knife scars across his chest and through his side. Was he a criminal? No. A tattoo covered his right shoulder. The American flag, reversed. The field of stars on the right, facing front. The reversed flag was a sigil— it bled gallantry. Breed was a soldier.

Noa joined Nygard and his friend at the pool table. Let him pour her a glass of whisky. Listened while the divers tried to impress her with their undersea exploits. It was tiresome chatter, the kind she was used to from men who wanted to take her to bed. She didn't mind it. If the man was witty enough or sexy enough, she'd let him hit on her. She'd giggle and resist. There would be a brief wrestling match, then delicious surrender.

Breed had been different. He'd pushed all her buttons—she really *wanted* to hit him.

Until she didn't.

That's when the idea came to her. Nygard was a diver. He had access to the Star Pool. Noa began to consider the possibilities.

Nygard was attractive. Young, full of himself, a bit insecure. The kind of young man she might go to bed with had she met him in a Trondheim bar. That made it okay, didn't it? She wouldn't feel too much the whore.

She began to flirt.

Drank more. Whisky never had much of an effect on her, but it took the edge off what she was about to do.

"Play my turn for me," Nygard suggested.

Why not? Noa knocked back a shot, took the cue from Nygard, and leaned over the table. She leaned over far enough to present her buttocks to him. The research techs looked to see what was going on. Turned back to their conversation.

"Hold the cue like this," Nygard said. He leaned over the table, close enough for their hips to touch. He manipulated her fingers with one hand, rested the other on the small of her back. Noa shifted closer so they could feel the warmth of each other's bodies.

Nygard won the game and his friend left.

Forty-five minutes later, the bottle was down by three-quarters. Noa and Nygard were in his cabin. It was a young man's cabin. Dirty laundry lay piled in a stack inside the closet door. Motorcycle and fitness magazines formed a tower on the coffee table. Next to the magazines rested a shark knife in a sheath. The sheath was equipped with leg straps. A pair of dumbbells occupied one of the easy chairs.

Nygard closed the door and they stared at each other. Overcome with urgency, they began stripping off their clothes.

She fell on the bed, opened her legs. Nygard's muscular body loomed over her. His thing looked angry and alive. Throat clotted, she reached for it. Found the member thick as her wrist and hard as rock. His testicles were raisins. The young buck liked his steroids.

Noa laughed to herself that Breed's talent came *au naturel*. She wrapped her legs around Nygard and clawed his back as he went to work.

When they were finished, Nygard slept with a satisfied smile on his face. Snored lightly. Noa rolled out of bed and pulled on her jeans, shoes and halter. Nygard's diving watch and wallet were on the nightstand.

Nygard's security card was in the wallet's first acetate sleeve.

NOA LEFT Nygard's cabin and made her way to the sickbay deck. Found it deserted. She went to the transverse bulkhead that separated the living space from the Star Pool. Heart pounding, she waved Nygard's security pass over the panel next to the door.

What if Nygard woke up? What if she were caught? She'd nearly run into Breed outside Nygard's cabin.

Noa thrust aside her fears. Feliks had to be satisfied. She spun the locking wheel, heard the dogs retract. She pulled gently. The gasket separated from the edge of the bulkhead with a soft sucking noise. Like opening a refrigerator. Noa opened the door a quarter of an inch and peeped inside.

Cold air blew through the crack. The hairs on Noa's arms stood and her nipples hardened.

Presented with the Star Pool's cavernous cathedral, Noa gasped. She was too frightened to open the door, or step inside. She twisted this way and that, searching the corners, the heights of the overhead, the rippling black water.

There, against the starboard bulkhead, were the three Kestrels. The white enamel cigars with their bright red nose cones. She shivered, not from the cold.

Noa closed the door. Seated the gasket firmly against the edge of the bulkhead, spun the locking wheel. When the dogs were secure, she turned, heart hammering against her chest.

She ran.

IN THE SAFETY of her cabin, Noa held the radio to her ear.

"This is Feliks."

From the moment she met him, she had thought of Feliks as the enemy. He was the man who had upset her orderly life. Brought her terrible news about her mother. Offered her a choice that was not a choice at all. Now she clung to him like she'd clung to the life raft in the Greenland Sea.

She blurted what she had found.

"Do not leave your cabin." Feliks's voice was calm and deliberate. He might have been reading from a printed document. An instruction manual prepared for exactly such an eventuality. "Do not permit anyone to enter. Do not speak to anyone. Wait for me to contact you."

Noa closed her eyes.

.　.　.

THE DISPLAY of Noa's radio lit up and its case vibrated. She lifted the device to her ear.

"This is Noa," she said.

"This is Feliks."

Feliks had spent the time communicating with Moscow. Without wasting words, he told her what she had found. That the *Spider* was floating six thousand feet above the hulk of the *Marshal Zhukov*. That the cigar-shaped objects were advanced cruise missiles the Americans were attempting to steal. That the Star Pool was designed to accommodate the *Zhukov* itself in the most audacious theft ever attempted.

Then he told her what had to be done.

Noa pulled on her jacket and pocketed the radio. With a determined stride, she returned to the Star Pool. Waved Nygard's pass at the panel and spun the locking wheel. The dogs retracted and she opened the door a crack. Peered inside. The Star Pool was deserted.

The cold air kept Noa alert. She closed the door behind herself and walked to the first Kestrel. It was the one closest to the pile of timbers. She placed her hands flat on the missile's smooth enamel skin. The material didn't look like metal at all. More like an artificially hardened plastic.

The engineer in Noa was fascinated. Feliks had told her the missile was hypersonic. That meant air friction would superheat its surface in flight. At ten times the speed of sound, its parts would expand. Such expansion had to be factored into the weapon's design. The Kestrel was a treasure trove of materials science technology. Its glossy skin was engineered specifically to reduce the superheating from hypersonic flight.

Feliks had told her exactly what to look for. She found the slits in the sides of the missile from which its stubby wings would deploy. They were a third of the distance from the tail. Starting from the portside slit, she ran her hands over the smooth skin. Worked her way forward.

Three feet from the tip of the nosecone, Noa's fingers found a shallow groove and a thin seam. She slipped a fingernail under the groove and lifted a hinged cover six inches square. The contour of the cover matched the curve of the missile's fuselage. The cover was perfectly machined. She wouldn't have known it was there had Feliks not told her what to look for.

Under the cover lay a digital panel. The labels were in Cyrillic. Russian was her first language, and she read them without difficulty. The digital numerals were still glowing after years of immersion in six thousand feet of salt water. The weapon had been designed to be proof against extremes of temperature and pressure. In fact, the missile was more vulnerable to physical damage than environmental stress.

Feliks had given Noa a six-digit code. She typed it into a pressure-actuated keypad. The display blinked, then lit up with green alphabetic characters.

Активация самоуничтожения

Below the first display were two more, side-by-side. The one on the left provided an adjusted local time. The one on the right showed a long string of 8s. Its value had not been set. Noa checked her watch against the local time displayed in the left panel. She was impressed by the precision of the automatic clock.

Noa punched six digits into the touch keypad. The 8s in the right-hand display flashed four times, then rearranged themselves into an alphanumeric pattern.

09:30:00 Часов

The display on top flashed four times, and rearranged itself.

Самоуничтожение активировано

The display flashed four times, and rearranged itself again.

Введите код для деактивации

The seconds digits in the lower left-hand display ran inexorably forward. The minutes counter incremented by one. Noa withdrew her hand from the panel as though burnt. Closed the cover and hurried from the Star Pool.

Noa had set the Kestrel to self-destruct thirty minutes after Arctic dawn.

27

SATURDAY, 0700 HOURS – THE SPIDER - NYGARD

I want to haul Noa out of her chair and shake her. "You set the Kestrel to blow up with you on the ship?"

Noa straightens. The misery on her face is replaced by determination. "I didn't want to. Feliks told me that if I refused, the State would withdraw my mother from treatment. She'd die and I'd never see her again. The storm was too strong for me to get off the ship right away. If I waited till dawn, the storm would clear, and I could escape in a lifeboat. The *Lenin* would pick me up. That's still the plan."

I check my watch, look at the radio. Stein, where *are* you?

"I didn't know Thorval was going to take over the ship. When the shooting started, I panicked. Tried to get off right away. That's when I ran into *you*. Breed, this is all wrong. I wanted to know you. I *tried* to make you leave with me."

"There are two hundred other people on this ship."

Noa's cheeks color. "Feliks promised to warn the *Spider's* captain. Give him time to abandon ship. The *Lenin* has orders to sink us if the Kestrels cannot be recovered. Russia will not allow you to steal them. Russia is not playing games. And I'm willing to die to give my mother a chance."

"Noa, did you visit your mother after speaking to Feliks? Did you speak with her?"

"No. I tried to telephone her, but there was no answer. Feliks said she was in hospital, and it was best I see her when I returned. By then her condition would have improved. She might be in remission."

"You believed him."

"I didn't trust him, but I agreed to work for him. After he left, I went to Stavanger to visit my father. I didn't tell him about Feliks, but I asked him if he had spoken to my mother recently. He said no, he had tried to telephone, but couldn't reach her. He planned a visit to St Petersburg, but Russia would not issue him a visa. They cited tension between our countries."

Feliks had put Noa in an impossible position. She had to work for him.

Uncertain of how Noa will react, I speak slowly. "Noa, your mother has passed away."

Noa stares. "I don't believe you."

"When we became aware of your transmissions to the *Lenin*, we reviewed background checks on everyone aboard. Dug deeper. Your mother passed away from cancer last year."

"Prove it."

"Sitting here, I can't. I told my friend in Washington that you came aboard with me. She ran thorough intel checks. Told me what she had learned about you. Your mother's death was a data point. It held no extraordinary significance to me at the time. At some point, my friend can share information with you."

Noa shakes her head. "Feliks would lie to me, but so would you."

"I'm not. You have to decide."

There's no point pursuing the matter of Noa's mother further. I want to tie up one more loose end. It's obvious what happened, but I need to hear it from her.

"Tell me how you killed Nygard."

BLOOD POUNDING IN HER TEMPLES, Noa returned to her cabin and took off her jacket. Turned on the survival radio and informed Feliks that she had done what he asked. Satisfied, he told her to wait till dawn to abandon the *Spider*. She was to contact him before taking any action.

Noa zipped the radio into her jacket pocket. Left it in her cabin. Wearing only her halter and jeans, she went to return Nygard's security card. Fished it out of her pocket and let herself in.

The cabin was dimly lit. She closed the door softly behind her and stepped to the far side of the bed. The blanket and sheets were in disarray from their lovemaking. Nygard was sleeping soundly.

Noa stepped around the chair on which he had draped his jeans and T-shirt. Picked up his wallet and opened it to the sheaf of acetate sleeves that protected his identification. She slipped his security pass into place. Flipped it back so she could look at his Royal Norwegian Navy ID. The familiar flag with a navy blue cross on a red field. He was close-shaven in the photograph. A handsome man.

Time to leave, as she had left Breed and so many other men. No attachments. With luck, Nygard would remember her only as a woman he'd bedded. He was not exceptional, but he wasn't a bad fellow.

She closed Nygard's wallet. Her gaze, once focused on the ID card, refocused on the figure of the man on the bed. He was awake and staring at her. Eyes cold and alert, he knew what she was doing.

Noa gasped and dropped the wallet. Turned to run. In a flash, Nygard leaped from bed. Grabbed her by the wrist and jerked her toward him. She clenched her fist and twisted towards his thumb. Broke free, grabbed the easy chair and overturned it between them.

With a roar, Nygard scrambled over the chair to get to her. He tripped and threw out a hand to steady himself. Knocked over the pile of bike magazines. The stack slid off the table, knocked the knife to the floor. From the other chair, Noa grabbed a ten-pound dumbbell. Holding it like a fist weight, she punched it into the naked man's stomach.

Nygard grunted. The man had a six-pack of steel. He tore the dumbbell from her hand and tossed it aside. Grabbed her by the shoulders and threw her facedown on the deck. Her nose inches from the scattered magazines, Noa inhaled the musty odor of paper. She felt something hard beneath her stomach.

The shark knife. She jerked the blade from its sheath. Nygard stooped to grab her. His fingers dug into the bare skin of her shoulders. As he rolled her over, she thrust the point of the blade into his belly. Both hands on the haft, she shoved it straight in. His eyes bugged and he cried out.

Flat on the deck, Noa had no leverage. She did not know enough to thrust with the knife's blade facing up. The drop point guided the blade into Nygards's guts, not up toward his chest cavity. The cutting edge severed fascia, muscle and bowels. Released the foul stench of a belly wound.

Nygard fell back on the deck. He pulled the knife from his stomach and dropped it. The wound opened. He clutched at the bedclothes for support. Planted one hand on the bed, the other on the overturned armchair. He levered himself to his feet and staggered toward the door.

Teeth gritted, Noa snatched the knife from the deck. She caught Nygard just past the bed. Tackled him, brought him down. He raised himself on all fours. From the open wound, his guts slid like eels. A big, strong girl, she wrapped an arm around his throat. Like a limpet, she clung to his back.

Noa never thought blood would be so slippery. The handle of the knife felt like a greasy bar of soap. She thrust the blade into his lower back and hit bone. Her hand slipped on the haft. Were it not for the guard, she would have cut herself. She withdrew the cutting edge a few inches, changed the angle of entry, stabbed him again. Her palm slipped on the haft a second time. She pressed against the guard for leverage, thrust deep. This time she got around the bone and sank the knife into soft tissue.

Nygard struggled to shake her off. She clung to him with all her strength. Weighted him with her body, twisted the knife this way and that in his back. A half inch to the left and the edge ground against bone. A half inch to the right and the blade slid right in. She slashed internal structures she couldn't see. Doing, not thinking, tears flooded her eyes. Her mind screamed for Nygard to die.

She must have severed an artery. When Nygard collapsed on the deck, the blade left his body. A crimson jet spurted from the triangular wound. Splashed Noa's arm to the elbow and reached as far as the bed. Successive spurts lost their force as he bled out.

Noa grabbed Nygard's hair with her left hand and twisted his face sideways. His sightless eyes stared at the closet. She planted her palm on his face and struggled to her feet. Staggered to the head, dropped the knife, vomited.

She knelt and emptied her stomach. Retched some more. When she finally sat with her back against the bulkhead, she found herself shaking. She sat and stared at Nygard's body until the shaking stopped.

Then she washed herself.

I EVALUATE Noa's story for signs of mendacity. There are none. She's given me the raw truth. Probably found the telling therapeutic.

It takes balls to kill with a knife. Even seasoned hunters have trouble. Killing a man is not like skinning and gutting game. We're taught the science of killing, but it's hard to do. You're sweating and scared, heart going like a jackhammer. Your target's moving, fighting back. Not a joke, not easy.

Noa's description of the blood clinched it. Men who've killed with knives always talk about how slippery the work becomes. The knife is a tool, but I will never reach for it first. Every time you get close enough to cut or put hands on the enemy, things get sporty.

"You did good," I tell her.

Noa blinks.

"You did what you had to do," I say. "It's alright."

"He didn't deserve to die."

"If you didn't kill him, I'd have to."

"How can *you* do it?"

I say nothing.

How *can* I do it? I kill for my country. It's a talent. The Army trained me, but I was never top of the class. A lot of guys from the top of the class are dead, and I'm still here. I was born with the skill that counts most.

My survival radio comes to life. The screen glows with a dim light and the case vibrates.

Stein.

28

"This is Breed."

"This is Captain Cruik. I have Stein on the call. You are on speaker."

"I'm here with Noa Larson. There have been developments."

Stein's voice sounds crisp and clear. "Breed, we've twisted the budget into knots. We are going to pay the ransom."

"That's great, Stein. Unfortunately, Ms Larson has complicated matters. The Russians suborned her to operate for them on the *Spider*. She has set one of the Kestrels to self-destruct at dawn."

Stein is unsurprised. Thorval and Knauss came aboard with a pirate crew. What could the Russians hope to accomplish with a single operator? A lot, but only *if* that operator could destroy the *Spider* and everything in it.

"No factor," Stein says. "If we pay the ransom, the Russians will try to destroy the *Spider*, one way or the other."

"The Russians might try to outbid us," I say.

"I doubt Thorval will let them," Stein says. "Delays could jeopardize his escape."

Cruik is speaking from the *Pressley Bannon's* Combat Information Center. Palomas's voice cuts in. "*Lenin* closing at twenty-eight knots, range thirty nautical miles."

"Warn him off, Commander," Cruik says.

"Attention *Lenin*," Palomas says. "You are approaching a US Navy warship. Stand off."

"Ms Larson can disarm the Kestrel." I lock eyes with Noa and address Stein. "I think she can be convinced."

"What will it take?" Stein asks.

"Ms Larson's handler told her that her mother was dying from cancer. I have told her that her mother passed away last year. Stein, tell her *how* you know."

Noa leans forward, cocks her ear.

The voice of a man, speaking with a Russian accent, is audible over the CIC's speakers. "Attention, US warship. The *Spider* is carrying property of the Russian Federation. Stand off or you will be destroyed. Attention, *Spider*. Prepare to be boarded."

Palomas's voice carries from the *Pressley Bannon's* CIC. "Attention *Lenin*. This is US warship. I repeat, stand off or we *will* engage."

"Ms Larson," Stein says, "your mother passed away from cancer last year. She was under treatment at the Moscow Oncology Center. We have a copy of her death certificate and I had a brief conversation with our Moscow Chief of Station. At the time of her death, he made brief contact with a number of her associates. She was respected and is badly missed. Her loss was a blow to their movement. I learned this several hours ago. I'm sorry, but that is all I can tell you."

Noa's face is white.

Palomas's voice is tense. "*Lenin* still closing."

Cruik's voice is level and perfectly modulated. "Arm Harpoons. We will engage at twenty nautical miles."

I lay my hand on Noa's shoulder. "Feliks lied to you. Noa, you must help us."

Palomas cuts in a second time. "Captain, unidentified aircraft. Six bogeys approaching from the east, eight hundred sixty knots closure. Estimated time of arrival forty-five minutes."

"Run their signatures," Cruik says.

Palomas says, "*Lenin* is painting us with fire control radar."

Cruik doesn't miss a beat. "Lock him. Arm Standard 2, Activate CIWS."

"He's locked. Harpoons armed. Standard 2 armed. CIWS active in Standby." Palomas hesitates, checking her readings. "Aircraft confirmed bandits. Six MIG-31s, probably out of Kola. They carry KH-101 cruise missiles."

"Arm Standard 6," Cruik says.

"Standard 6 armed, aye. Captain, *Lenin* is turning away at twenty-five miles. He still has lock on us."

"That's his minimum firing distance. Maintain lock. Call *Nimitz* for air support."

"*Nimitz* launching alert fighters. COMSURFLANT advises—engage at your discretion."

Cruik's tone remains flat. "Warn me when the MIGs break two hundred miles."

It's a Mexican standoff. The *Lenin* is holding at twenty-five miles. Any closer, and its missiles will not have time to arm and descend to attack altitude. The *Pressley Bannon* has Harpoons cocked and locked.

The MIGs might be the game changer. There was no

need to run their signatures. No civilian aircraft flies at eight hundred sixty knots. Together, the *Lenin* and the MIGs could overwhelm the *Pressley Bannon's* air defenses. The *Nimitz's* alert fighters will not arrive in time.

We can't seem to get a break. The Russians are Cruik's problem. Noa and the Kestrels are mine.

Stein says, "Ms Larson? I understand these are the worst possible circumstances under which to receive this news. Please, we did not create this situation for you."

"I believe you," Noa says, "but what can we do?"

Stein's voice conveys only the slightest hint of relief. "I'm going to contact Thorval and advise him of the situation. We'll pay his ransom, grant him safe passage to escape in his submarine. He has to let you guys disarm the Kestrel."

"What about the Kestrels he's already loaded on the sub?"

"I'll demand he unload them. The Russians won't pay him to get one back. They want to make sure we don't get *any*."

"That's a plan," I say. "We're heading to the Star Pool."

"Contact us when you get there," Stein says. "I have a call to make."

I sign off and pocket the radio. Get to my feet. The wear and tear of the last twenty-four hours is catching up with me. There isn't one square inch of my body that isn't hurting. Noa stands, looking like a lost child. She throws her arms around me, and we hold each other close.

"I trust you Breed," she says.

"Let's not let each other down."

29

SATURDAY, 0800 HOURS – THE SPIDER - ENGAGEMENT

Noa and I follow the lab deck's central passageway forward. The bright lights in the *Spider's* living space are disorienting. We've grown used to the dim lights and deep shadows of the dead space.

I check behind us constantly. Passageways creep me out —they are death traps. One man with a rifle can wipe out a squad trapped in such a narrow space. All he has to do is dump a mag, move the muzzle of his weapon in a little circle. He can't miss. Noa's upset by the news of her mother and it shows in her movements. She's sluggish and a bit clumsy.

There's a vibration in my pocket. One of the radios. Left pocket—it's Noa's.

I unzip my ammo vest and take the radio out. The security screen has come alive. I hand the radio to Noa. "Find out what Feliks wants. Don't give anything away."

Noa taps in her code. "This is Noa."

"This is Feliks. Have you anything to report?"

"No, but it is almost dawn."

"Go to the Star Pool. You are to remain aboard *Spider*

until I instruct you to leave."

Noa swallows hard. "I should go to the boat deck now."

"No. You may be required to disarm the Kestrel."

"Why? What has happened?"

"There is no time for questions. Do as you are told."

Noa is left staring at a silent radio. Before she can hand it to me, I activate my own and contact the *Presley Bannon*.

"What's the situation, Breed?" Cruik's voice is as calm as ever.

"Captain, the *Lenin* is preparing to attack."

"How do you know that?"

"Ms Larson's handler wants her to stay close to the Star Pool. She might be required to disarm the Kestrel. That can only mean the Russians are submitting a bid."

"Stein is speaking with Thorval," Cruik says. "It's going down to the wire."

"Yes, sir. I'll sign off now. We still have some distance to cover."

I squeeze the radio into a pouch on my ammo vest. I have to decide how to approach the Star Pool. The Kestrels are on the starboard side, where the Type 6 is moored. To get there, we'll have to descend to the sickbay deck.

We descend the companionways. At the sickbay deck, I step into the passageway and see a hijacker come around the corner from the starboard side. I've got the M4 in a C-clamp, look down the barrel over my thumb. I point my thumb at the hijacker and open fire before he can bring his rifle up. My rounds hit him in the throat and chest—blood and sparks fly. Crimson gouts spurt from his throat and face. Fireflies twinkle from the magazines Velcroed on his vest.

Another gunman leans around the corner and opens fire. The sound of running footsteps signals the arrival of reinforcements. I grab Noa by the arm, push her toward the door that leads to the dead space. She grasps the wheel, spins it to release the dogs. I fire back along the length of the passageway.

The man I shot is writhing on the deck, hands to his throat. He's out of action. A third man has joined the first two. He and his friend ignore the wounded man. Instead, they dump their mags on me.

Noa wrenches the door open and dives through.

I follow Noa into the dead space, slam the door behind us. We're in the fo'c'sle. The Kestrels and the Type 6 are starboard. If we run that way, we could get caught in a crossfire between our pursuers and gunmen coming from the Star Pool. I push Noa toward the port side.

"Run."

Noa needs no urging. She tears along the dead space, stumbling and dodging obstacles in the dim light. There's something primal about running from a threat. It's easy to give in to panic, surrender to the mindless need to flee. It's like your mind shuts down and adrenaline takes over.

Training forces you not to give in. You switch your mind on. As you run, you force yourself to register your surroundings. The availability of cover and concealment. The location of threats.

The hijackers approach from the fo'c'sle. Turn the corner and open fire. I stop, turn, and fire from a kneeling position. They dive behind ballast tanks and my rounds strike sparks. The passageway flickers, three sparks for every round fired. One from the initial impact, two from ricochets.

Noa reaches the transverse bulkhead, slams into the door. I run toward her, turn and look back.

One of the hijackers steps into the middle of the dead

space and throws a grenade at us.

Noa is struggling with the locking wheel. I grab her by the collar and yank her behind the ballast tanks. The grenade doesn't have the distance. There's a clang as it lands on the deck, thirty yards away. It bounces, lands a second time and rolls on steel.

I shove Noa hard against the bulkhead, cover her with my body, and cringe behind the ballast tank. The grenade goes off with a deafening bang. Shrapnel bounces off the ballast tanks.

Prone, I fire along the length of the dead space. A thin veil of smoke drifts in the air. In the low wattage lights, the tendrils shine a luminous gray. The sharp smell of cordite overwhelms the metallic dank. Under my covering fire, Noa yanks the door open and steps through. Still firing, I back through the doorway and close it behind us. Noa is already running past the pipe cages. I turn and run after her.

I'm forming a plan.

Wherever you might find yourself, the principles of combat remain the same. Tactics need to be adapted to circumstances, but the game doesn't change. One rule is, *always fight from an elevated position.*

Looming ahead of us is the mountain of pipes I rolled onto the two hapless hijackers. On the other side of the bulkhead to our left lies the Star Pool.

"Climb," I say. "Get over the top."

Noa reaches the pipe mountain and clambers toward the dead hijacker's stump of a body. I remember rats feasting on the corpse, wonder what they've left. Stop at the foot of the mountain, drop to a kneeling position. I train my M4 on the transverse bulkhead, the door the hijackers have to come through.

I check over my shoulder in time to see Noa reach the top.

The locking wheel spins. Its mate is being turned by a hijacker on the other side. I take aim. A gunman pushes the door open, dives into the compartment. I squeeze off a round. The brass flies from the ejection port, tinkles against the deck.

Miss.

The hijacker cowers in a niche behind the first pipe cage, sticks his rifle around the corner, dumps a mag. I scramble up the pipes. Bullets clang around me. Apart from human bodies, there's nothing but metal in this steel cocoon to hit.

I roll over the top, lie next to Noa and the corpse. Ignore the mass of black tar hanging out the back of its head. I dig in and point the M4 back along the dead space. I have cover, and the high ground is mine. I can hold this hill.

The second hijacker comes through the door. Fires in our direction. Blinding muzzle flashes, banging ricochets. Another man comes through the door, weapon raised. That makes three.

I've drawn the last of Thorval's reserves. Only Knauss remains.

Two of the gunmen unload on us. I hold my ground, trusting the pipes to cover me. They're bounding. If I turn away, the first hijacker will get a free shot. He steps away from cover, runs forward, cocks his arm.

He's throwing another grenade. I lay the front post on him and squeeze the trigger.

Hit.

The gunman crumples. The grenade falls from his hand and rolls onto the deck.

The other two hijackers dive behind the cage. There's a

clang as the grenade explodes. The dead space lights up with shrapnel like a roomful of sparklers on the Fourth of July.

"Mr Breed."

It's the squad radio, sitting in the half-holster on my belt. Thorval calling. I keep my rifle pointed into the kill zone. Hand the radio to Noa. "See what he wants."

The two remaining gunmen dodge behind the cage. One kneeling, one standing, they dump their mags in our general direction. They're intimidated by the accuracy of my aimed fire.

"Who is this?" Noa asks.

"This is Magnus Thorval. Ms Larson, let me speak with Breed."

I squeeze off single aimed rounds at the gunmen. Force them behind the cage.

"He's busy killing people," Noa says.

"Give me that." I snatch the radio from Noa's hand. "Nice submarine, Thorval."

"I'm glad you like it. It provides me with a means of escape."

"It also explains why Knauss killed Aron."

"Must you have an answer for everything? *Yes*, Aron stumbled on us speaking with the submarine by ELF."

The motive for Aron's murder had to be something like that. Thorval and Knauss could not allow Aron to report the presence of a submarine.

The last two hijackers have stopped shooting. An eerie quiet descends on the dead space.

"That's why your radioman was at the ELF even though the submersibles were stowed in the Star Pool." Another dig comes to mind. "By the way, I killed your poison dwarf.

What do you want, Thorval?"

"Come to the Star Pool. The United States has won the bid. Stein says Ms Larson has armed a self-destruct device on a Kestrel. I want her to disarm it. Now that monies have been paid, you and I are no longer antagonists. I have ordered my men to leave you alone."

"Order your men to withdraw across the bulkhead and seal the door."

"One moment."

Thorval goes silent. He must be giving instructions to Knauss. The gunmen back their way through the door and close it behind them.

"Is that satisfactory, Mr Breed?"

"Yes. Give us a few minutes."

"Very well, let us get on with it. The clock is ticking."

"Hold your water."

I sign off, take my survival radio from its pouch and raise the *Pressley Bannon*.

"You're on speaker, Breed." Palomas sounds tense. "We're patching Stein through."

"Breed," Stein says, "we've paid the ransom, Thorval is going to allow Ms Larson to disarm the Kestrel. You're to come out and put your weapons down."

"What if I don't?"

"Then it's no deal. He's afraid of you. Can't imagine why."

"Did he agree to unload the Kestrels that are on the submarine?"

"Yes. There are two loaded. It's up to you to confirm."

Noa and I climb down from the pile of pipes. I spin the locking wheel and open the door a crack. We peer into the Star Pool.

The fairytale scene is breathtaking. Snow and sleet

continue to spiral into the compartment. The clamshell shutters remain open. Six inches of snow cover the pool deck except for the space between the missiles and the dock. The crew swept that area clear to push the cradles to the submarine.

Two Kestrels are gone from the deck. Large rectangular areas, clear of snow, mark where their cradles sat. The cradles themselves have been rolled onto the wooden pier. A large mobile crane on the pier has been used to raise them over the sub and lower them through the forward missile loading hatch.

One Kestrel remains on deck. It sits in its cradle next to the pile of timber and the dead SEALs.

"That's the one," Noa says.

"The Kestrel we want is still on the deck," I tell Stein.

"Alright, it's in your hands."

Palomas's voice is audible in the background. "*Lenin's* firing. Kalibrs in the air."

Cruik has been brooding over this eventuality all day and night. "Left full rudder. Salvo Standard 2, four-round engagement. Release CIWS."

A throaty whoosh pours from the speaker as the *Pressley Bannon's* Standard 2 air defense missiles take flight. The sound of the missile launch pervades every compartment of the destroyer. Audible in the CIC, it announces the *Pressley Bannon* is going to war.

"Standard 2 away," Palomas calls. "CIWS on auto, free to fire."

There's fear in the Commander's voice. Fear checked by rigid discipline. She knows that if the Standard 2s miss, a single Kalibr can blow the *Pressley Bannon* out of the water.

In the Star Pool, all eyes turn to the heavens above the

open clamshell. I watch the reactions of Thorval, Knauss and Angers. Thorval's jaw drops. He never expected the Russians to fire.

Two golden orbs of light arc over the *Spider*, trailing long, rapidly expanding plumes of rocket exhaust. The Kalibrs look alive with a mad light of their own. They follow a northeast to southwest trajectory.

The first Kalibrs have been aimed at the *Pressley Bannon*. If the *Lenin* can take out the US destroyer, it will be free to board the *Spider* at will.

Four more brilliant lights arc to meet the Kalibrs. The *Pressley Bannon's* Standard 2s fly interception tracks. Cruik is firing two Standard 2s for each Kalibr. Statistically, one Standard 2 is not enough to take down an incoming Kalibr. They have to intercept the Kalibrs before the Russian missiles drop their boosters and descend to wavetop altitude.

There's a flash of light as one of the Standards finds it mark. A blazing flare lights up the sky, silhouettes the derrick in stark relief. From the center of the flare, burning orange fragments scatter in a beautiful starburst. Each fragment leaves its own plume of fire and smoke as at arcs through the sky.

Seconds later, the boom of the explosion rocks the *Spider*. Angers and Knauss, both military men, are not surprised. It takes time for sound to travel. Thorval's body jerks.

"Splash one," Palomas says. "We missed the second Kalibr."

"1-MC." Does Cruik *ever* raise his voice? He's calling for the Main Circuit, the *Pressley Bannon's* public address system.

"1-MC, aye."

"All hands, this is the Captain," Cruik says. "Missile inbound port side. Sound collision."

There is the strident buzzing of an alarm bell. Five short bursts alert the crew to danger. It is followed a second later by the sound of hail. The noise of gravel thrown against a metal wall.

"Splash two," Palomas says. "CIWS got it. What the fuck is that?"

"Debris, Commander." Cruik sounds pensive. "Stand by to salvo Harpoons, two-round engagement. What's he doing?"

"*Lenin* standing off twenty-five miles. Enemy aircraft, six hundred miles. Eight hundred sixty knots closure."

"Lock bandits. Hold Harpoon. Hold Standard 6. Fire on my command."

When the MIGs are in position, the *Lenin* and the strike aircraft will fire simultaneously. They will launch a swarm of missiles in an effort to overwhelm the *Pressley Bannon's* air defense. We are running out of time.

Noa stares at me, wide-eyed. Feliks expects her to disarm the Kestrel only if the Russians destroy the *Pressley Bannon*. To that end, he is willing to sacrifice her.

"Wish us luck, Stein."

I squeeze the survival radio back into its pouch. Take Noa by the arm.

"Breed."

Noa puts her free hand on my shoulder. Leans forward and kisses me. I close my eyes, absorb the sensation. When we pull away from each other, Noa licks her lips.

If only we had met another time.

"Let's go."

30

I step through the door on the Star Pool's snow-covered deck. Across the pool, Angers orders the crew of the submarine to make ready for departure. He strides onto the pier, waving his arms. Directs the crane to be moved out of the way.

Knauss's eyes are fixed on me.

Noa and I approach from the port side, picking our way over the fresh snow. We stop a few feet away from Knauss and Thorval.

"Put down your weapon, Mr Breed," Thorval says. "This affair will be over shortly."

I bend at my knees and set the M4 on the snowy deck.

Thorval clasps his gloved hands behind his back. "The pistol also."

I set the SIG down next to the carbine.

Angers joins us. "All the crew is aboard except for those required to shift missiles," he says. The captain's eyes flicker over me and Noa. They settle on the guns I've set on the deck. "What shall we do?"

Thorval's feeling in control.

"Indeed, what shall we do. Ms Larson, there were three Kestrels arranged in a row." The magician raises his left arm to indicate the rectangular spaces on the deck bare of snow. "Which Kestrel did you set to self-destruct? Was it this one, or one of those we've transferred to the submarine?"

I glance at Noa, nod my encouragement.

"That one." Noa indicates the Kestrel on the deck.

Thorval smiles. "Thank you. Captain Angers, prepare for departure."

"What about the third missile?"

"Sadly, the Russians may not allow us time to load it."

I turn to Noa. "Disarm the Kestrel."

"No." Thorval raises one long index finger, gestures for Noa to remain where she stands. A cunning smile flickers across his features. "I don't think so."

"What are you talking about, man?" Angers's voice is harsh with outrage.

I know exactly what Thorval's talking about. He's going to leave with two Kestrels and leave the *Spider* to blow up at dawn. Neither the Russians nor the Americans will know he escaped. He'll make safe harbor in the Type 6, reopen negotiations for more money.

The magician will treat everyone to his closing act. He will make a pair of Kestrels disappear.

Knauss raises his M4. I step between Angers and Thorval. The move puts Thorval between me and Knauss. I grab the startled magician by his jacket to control his body. Thrust him into Robo-SEAL. Knauss swears, brushes Thorval aside, and tries to bring his rifle to bear.

This is a SOC fight—Special Operations Combatives—martial arts for Close Quarters Battle. Dirty fighting for assaulters. I close with Knauss and grab the forestock of his M4 with my left hand. Push it aside as he pulls the trigger. Bullets skid off the snowy deck. One of the ricochets hits a crewman in the stomach. His buddies dive for cover. Other rounds strike sparks from the submarine's sail.

Seven years ago, we started this fight. Now I'm going to finish it. I thrust four fingers into the side of his neck. He's ready for me. Twists away from the spear hand so I miss the kill spot. His rifle's on a two-point sling and he drops it, transitions to his secondary. Draws the SIG with his right hand. Grabs my collar with his left.

Knauss is a head taller than I am, and thirty pounds heavier. I let go of his rifle and bump chests with him, pinning the weapon between us. I mustn't allow him to create a frame. Grab the wrist of his pistol hand with my left, grip his collar with my right. Stamp on his right instep and twist. Wheel him over the pivot and throw him on the deck.

The giant still has a grip on my jacket, and he drags me with him. We fall into two inches of snow covering solid steel. The impact rattles our teeth. With a fist of stone, Knauss punches me in the ribs. I feel my intercostals separate, cry out. Slam his pistol hand against the deck. I dig my thumb into a pressure point on his wrist. Stab the median nerve. The move sends electric bolts straight to his elbow, and he drops the SIG. He tries to butt me in the face, but I dodge. His head glances off the side of mine. There's a crack, and a blinding shock flashes through my skull.

Knauss wraps his legs around my abdomen and locks his ankles. A brutal leg scissors. He squeezes my abdomen so hard my diaphragm can't expand to fill my lungs. If I let him, he'll crush the life out of me. I jab my thumb into his eye and he jerks his head. My hand slips off and my thumbnail gouges a bloody furrow in his temple.

"Fucker." Knauss grunts, reaches down and draws a shark knife from a leg sheath. Releases the scissors, tries to stab me in the side. I grab for his wrist but the force of his thrust breaks my grip. All I can do is deflect the blade. The knife rips into my thigh. You never stab a guy once, you stab him full of holes. Twenty-five, thirty times, you stab him to death. Knauss tries again. I grab his wrist—hard. He tries to break my grip but I hang on.

We roll on the deck, slippery with melted snow. The roll carries us to the edge of the pool, those thick timbers that form a makeshift dock.

The clock is ticking. Noa rushes to the Kestrel.

Thorval picks up my M4. Raises it, flicks the selector to full auto, shoots Noa in the back. The crackle of automatic fire echoes from the bulkheads of the Star Pool. Crimson flowers blossom across the back of Noa's jacket, and she is slammed against the side of the Kestrel.

I bite Knauss's cheek and rip off a chunk. Tear all I can off the apple. Spit meat and gristle of beard onto the snow. Slam his knife hand on the deck. Bite his nose. Knauss shrieks, drops the knife and grabs me by the shoulder. I spit torn flesh in his face and butt him. Once, twice, three times. My crown smashes his face and the back of his head bounces off steel.

Noa struggles to one knee. Her fingers claw at the Kestrel's nose cone. Thorval takes careful aim, shoots her again. Noa collapses on the deck, arm outstretched.

Angers picks up my SIG. Raises it and fires one round into the side of Thorval's head. The magician's handsome features deform from the pressure of the bullet's cavitation.

His face ripples like a rubber mask, hollowing here, bulging there. The slug passes straight through his skull. A gory plug of bone and tissue explodes from his left temple. Thorval crumples.

Knauss screams in my face. *"Goddamn you, Breed!"*

He tries to throw me off but I hang on tight. Together, we roll into the pool. The shock of hitting cold water jolts my whole body. I taste brine, mixed with the copper flavor of Knauss's blood. I force my eyes open. Weighed down by our ammo vests, we grapple underwater. Knauss is tangled up in his carbine's sling. Pink tendrils stream from the open wounds in his face. Without survival suits, the pain from the ice water is excruciating. In seconds, I find my arms and legs hardening into stumps.

Jesus Christ, we're *sinking.*

Knauss is suffering as much as I am. As if by agreement, we let go of each other and splash to the dock. My hands slip on the wood beam strapped to the deck. I fall back into the pool. Knauss can't get himself over. His weight, an advantage on land, has turned into a liability.

I get my fingers into the crack between the beam and the steel deck. That's the grip I need. With a grunt, I throw a leg over the beam and haul myself out of the water.

Angers stands fifteen feet away. He stares, my SIG at his side.

Noa is a pitiful crumpled figure on the deck.

Knauss is duplicating my maneuver. Right hand on the beam, fingers wedged in the crack.

The shark knife is lying on the deck. I grab it, raise it over my head. With one motion, I bring it down with all my strength. Its point pierces the back of Knauss's hand and pins it to the beam. Robo-SEAL shrieks.

I lunge. Grab Knauss's lapels in both hands, wrists crossed. Pull sideways in opposite directions. It's a choke-hold, using the fabric of his collar to constrict the carotid arteries on either side of his throat. I shove his head underwater.

With his free hand, Knauss struggles to break my grip. I hold fast. Stare into his eyes, will him to die. He's struggling to hold his breath. His free hand goes to my face. Tries to push me away. It slips on my wet skin. I pull harder on the chokehold. Push him further under the surface.

Knauss's mouth opens and air explodes from the cavity. His eyes widen. I watch bubbles pour from his mouth as his lungs fill.

I don't think drowning is a painless death. Knauss's expression alternates between terror and hate as he struggles to gulp air and finds only water. His struggles grow feeble. I enjoy the luxury of studying the giant's face as life fades from his eyes. When I'm sure he's dead, I take my arms from the freezing water and struggle to my feet. My left leg is stiff. Not from the cold, but from the knife wound.

Limping, I turn to face Angers. "Make up your mind."

"I already have," the captain says. "Who do you think dragged you indoors when Knauss left you out to die?"

"Why?"

"I signed on to hijack a cargo and make money. Not murder people. Now, unless you can disarm this missile, we have to go."

I look at the Kestrel, Noa's broken body lying next to it. I want to cry, but this isn't the time.

The Type 6 submarine waits. Two crewmen stand on the pier. Two others are carrying the wounded sailor into the submarine. I doubt he'll make it. The crew stare at us, waiting for Angers to give orders.

"Can you captain this boat?"

"That was the plan."

I claw my survival radio from its pouch. Palomas answers immediately, puts me on speaker. Stein and Cruik are waiting.

"What's the story, Breed?" Stein asks.

"Thorval double-crossed us. We were unable to disarm the Kestrel. Angers and I are leaving in the submarine with two Kestrels."

"Enemy aircraft four hundred miles," Palomas says. "Eight hundred sixty knots closure."

"Godspeed, Mr Breed," Cruik says. "This is World War III."

31

SATURDAY, 0900 HOURS – THE TYPE 6 -
ARCTIC DAWN

Angers strides to a bulkhead-mounted interphone. "This is the Captain."

I can't hear what the man on the other end of the line says. Angers must be speaking to the men on the bridge. Crewmen suborned to play minor roles in the conspiracy. Men who steer the ship, man the HF and ELF radios, operate the *Spider's* radar and sonar arrays.

"Release the crew from the mess decks," Angers says. "Give me the 1-MC."

The bridge patches Angers into the public address system. "All hands, this is the Captain. Abandon ship."

There isn't much time. It's a race between the self-destruct mechanism in the Kestrel and the next attack by the *Lenin* and the MIG-31s. Angers and I clamber through the Type 6's forward loading hatch. I descend the ladder first. Slide most of the way with my weight supported by my arms. The adrenaline is wearing off, and the knife wound in my thigh is on fire. The captain dogs the hatch behind us, and we make our way through the torpedo room.

Two Kestrels gleam on either side, mounted on specially designed cradles. The Type 6 has been modified expressly for the transport of Kestrels. Long and sleek, the Kestrels lie with their familiar red nosecones and white enamel sides.

Compared to the *Spider*, the Type 6 is a cramped boat. The crew spaces are tighter than those I saw on the *Pressley Bannon*. Angers leads the way aft through the narrow control room and into the small CIC. We pass crewmen at the diving and maneuvering controls. One man sits at a small, compact navigation desk. The navigator has both electronic navigation equipment and a manual plotting table at his disposal.

The CIC has fewer crew than the control room. Several consoles are unmanned. Angers leads me to the center of the compartment. With practiced commands, he orders the crew to secure all the hatches and dive.

There is no stirring klaxon. No strident command. Angers gives calm, clear instructions. The crew flood the ballast tanks, and the Type 6 loses positive buoyancy. Slips beneath the surface of the Star Pool and goes straight down.

Angers and I exchange glances as the Type 6 sinks deeper. Down, past the open gates at the bottom of the *Spider*. I count seconds in my head, decide we are well out of the Star Pool. I drum my fingers against a console. Wish Angers would hurry and get us away from the blast effect.

How far do we have to go to escape the explosion? The missile's armed with a conventional warhead. Based on its size, I reckon eleven hundred pounds of high explosive. The Russian equivalent of RDX and aluminum. Depending on where it hits, enough to kill a warship. If we can put half a mile between us and the blast, we'll survive. A mile would be better.

"Three hundred feet," a crewman calls.

"Steer course two-zero-zero," Angers says. "Ahead flank."

I allow myself to breathe. A little.

"How fast does this baby move underwater?" I ask.

"In excess of twenty knots submerged," Angers says. "The oxygen-hydrogen propulsion is completely silent, and no heat signature."

A man approaches us, carrying a small canvas bag and tourniquets. He carries himself with the bearing of an officer, addresses Angers in Norwegian. Angers nods. "This is Hans, my first officer," Angers says. "He brought the submarine to the *Spider*. The American destroyer did not detect it."

The man says something to Angers in Norwegian. Angers laughs and slaps Hans's shoulder.

"Hans says the American is lucky we have no torpedoes." Angers smiles. "I reminded him we are allies."

"You are wounded," Hans tells me. "Let me see."

The officer doesn't approve of me dripping messy blood onto his clean deck. Can't say I blame him.

"I don't need a tourniquet." I don't feel lightheaded or nauseous. In combat, hastily applied tourniquets often caused more harm than good. "A bandage and dressing will be sufficient."

"Let me be the judge," Hans says. "I know what I am doing. Now sit down."

"Not until this is over." I rest one hand on a piece of equipment to steady myself. Angers eyes me critically. He's afraid I'll accidentally bump some switches and sink his submarine.

The first officer takes a pair of trauma shears and opens up my pants leg from knee to hip. He examines the knife wound critically. "You are lucky," he says. "The wound is in muscle."

Hans sets to work dressing my wound.

Minutes pass. Hans knows what he is doing. He's probably received Navy training as a corpsman. It occurs to me that the crew of this pirate submarine must have been as difficult to recruit as Knauss's divers. Ex-Navy officers and sailors willing to commit a crime for money.

Maybe not so hard to find. I remind myself of the personal problems veterans and serving military face. Family issues, alcoholism, drug use, post-traumatic stress disorder, financial problems. Many showed no evidence of those problems at work. Despite their military professionalism, these sailors are human beings.

"All stop," Angers says. "Periscope depth."

The Type 6 rises gently.

"Periscope depth."

"Up periscopes."

The Type 6 has been stripped of its torpedo tubes, but not its targeting optics. It is equipped with two periscopes, one for general viewing, another for precision targeting. Angers takes the precision scope and invites me to use the other.

I fold down the handles and lean into the rubber eyecups. Angers is more practiced than I. He rotates his periscope until he finds the view he wants.

"There they are," he says. "Still afloat."

I face in the same direction as Angers. Rotate the scope until I see what he sees.

There, a mile away, sits the *Spider*. Further south lies the *Pressley Bannon*. The storm is clearing from the northeast, and the *Spider* is silhouetted against the rising sun. We are staring at a wild and terrible dawn. Borne of the savagery of the storm, beautiful in its primal majesty. The sky has lightened... There are hints of blue on the horizon. The sun's rays shine between the drifting clouds and sparkle on the whitecaps. The decks of the *Spider* and *Pressley Bannon* are covered with films of snow and ice that glitter like fine crystal.

The clouds are drifting away from the ships. Snow and sleet continue to pour from the belly of the overcast, but the tempest is leaving the scene. Winds have fallen to fifty miles an hour. The worst of the weather is marching south toward the *Nimitz* battle group.

I glance at my watch. It is not quite 0930 Hours, the time Noa set the Kestrel to explode.

The periscope is equipped with a zoom. I increase the magnification. If I strain to look, I see little orange specks floating next to the *Spider* and powering away from the mammoth vessel.

"Some of the lifeboats have gotten away," I say.

Angers grunts. "Yes. Not as many as I'd like."

A mile to our right, I watch the *Pressley Bannon*, steaming in its box. I wonder what the *Lenin* and the MIG-31s are doing.

"I see the *Pressley Bannon*." I rotate the periscope left, then right. There is no sign of the Russian frigate. "Do you see the *Lenin*?"

"No," Angers says, "he's over the horizon. The important thing is—no smoke, no rocket plumes."

The captain's right. There hasn't been a further engagement. The MIGs haven't yet broken two hundred miles, but they must be close.

There is a vibration in my pocket. It's Noa's radio—Feliks. I don't know her pass code.

Is Feliks calling to have Noa disarm the Kestrel? Or is he ordering her off the *Spider*? It doesn't matter, because it's too late for either. I care about one thing. If the Kestrel blows up, there will be no reason for the Russians to attack the *Pressley Bannon*.

A great orange flash lights up the ocean. From amidships of the *Spider,* great gouts of black smoke and debris spurt skyward. The derrick, tall and heavy, is thrown into the air like a champagne cork. I watch it soar into the sky, pitch over, and tumble into the water.

The operations deck was located amidships. The derrick was right over the Kestrel when it exploded, and much of the force was vented up through the opening. The flames flicker out as debris rains into the ocean around the *Spider*.

For a moment, I think the great ship will survive the blast.

"There it goes," Angers says.

I press my eyes against the periscope's binoculars. Sure enough, the *Spider's* stern, disconnected from the bow, tilts forward. The helideck, with McMaster's Sea Hawk still tied down, tilts at a crazy angle, and the *Spider's* screw lifts from the surface of the water. The mooring legs hang from the sides like long outriggers. Like thin filaments, the mooring cables snap.

The *Spider's* stern stands at a sharp ninety-degree angle. With astonishing speed, it slides straight down into the depths. The bow wallows, awash in the waves. It sinks slowly. When it is gone, all that remains on the surface is a vast field of floating debris and the orange specks of lifeboats.

"Look to the northeast," I say.

A speck on the surface is growing in size.

"It's the *Lenin*," Angers says. "Law of the sea. They will help rescue the survivors."

The *Pressley Bannon* and the *Lenin* steam toward the lifeboats.

Combatants no longer. I remember yesterday's ordeal in the ocean. Tossed around at the mercy of thirty-foot waves, freezing, alone but for men and women as helpless and insignificant as I. I remember the rescue crews on the Sea Hawk and *Pressley Bannon* struggling to drag us aboard.

I like to think that, at such a moment, I'd reach for a Russian and he'd reach for me.

"Can you contact the American destroyer?" Angers asks.

"Yes, but I'm not going to. We were able to monitor Noa's communication with the *Lenin*. I'm sure they are able to monitor mine with the *Pressley Bannon*. The Russians don't know about this submarine and I don't want them to. Let's run for a while before we contact friendlies. By then we'll be hidden."

"Where?"

I meet Angers's gaze. "Can you make the Grand Banks submerged?"

"Yes. Easily within the range of this submarine."

"Let's go."

"Anything else?"

"Yes." I turn to Hans. The first officer has done a professional job on my leg. "Can I have a change of clothes? I'm freezing."

Hans shows me to a cabin aft of the CIC. It's small. No bigger than a compartment on a sleeper train, but it's private.

"Very nice," I say. "Is the rest of the sub this comfortable?"

"Only the captain and I have private cabins. This is mine. With a normal complement of twenty, the crew have to hot-bunk. This Type 6 is not equipped with torpedoes or the most sophisticated sonar equipment. For that reason, we operate at three-quarters complement and hot-bunking is not necessary."

Hans opens a small closet, hands me a folded set of coveralls. "You and I are approximately the same size. Try these."

"Thank you."

Hans has a good eye. His clothes are a decent fit. His dressing is doing its job. Blood is seeping through, but we can change it in a few hours. I'm limping but, provided infection doesn't set in, should be alright. The danger with a stab wound is skin bacteria being driven deep inside the body by the weapon. I remind myself to ask him if there are antibiotics aboard.

Noa's makeshift dressing is still tied about my neck. I push her from my mind and join Angers.

"You're a resilient character, Breed."

"I feel like I've been run over by a truck."

"Imagine how Knauss feels."

I collapse into an empty seat in front of one of the consoles. Vacant because of the reduced complement. "Where did you get this submarine? Looks like it's got all the latest bells and whistles."

"Not all," Angers says. "It was sold to Thorval in a civilian configuration."

"Thorval bought it?"

"Thorval, or one of his associates. He recruited me

because I had served as first officer on a Norwegian submarine. These boats are joint projects with Germany. We took delivery last year. They stripped it of weapons and most of its classified electronic equipment. He told me to meet him in Eckernförde."

"Where's that?"

"A Bundesmarine base in Schleswig-Holstein. In fact, the submarine was tied up in a closed pen, off-base. I waited for him outside. He arrived in an expensive black limousine. Handsome and well-dressed. A thousand euro suit and sharp trench coat. We went inside and met a representative of the manufacturer. You would know the name."

"One of the big German industrials, I bet. The kind that built U-Boats for the Austrian painter."

Angers smiles. "I am sure your friends in the CIA will learn chapter and verse. There is more I can share with them."

"Who was Thorval? And why do you think he tried to double-cross us? We paid the money."

"Thorval was always a mystery to me." Angers lowers himself into a seat next to me. "He was a man of manners, highly educated. Yet I always had the feeling he was not personally wealthy."

"Why not?"

Angers shrugs. "It's a sense you get, for which there is no direct evidence. That submarine cost at least a billion Euros. Sophisticated he might have been, but Thorval does not have a billion Euros. I think he was working for someone else. A man who planned the hijacking."

"Thorval was a hired hand who got greedy."

"You paid the money, so his sponsor was happy. Thorval

decided to collect the ransom twice and keep the rest. To do that, he had to escape with the Kestrels."

"But who was Thorval's employer?"

"I don't know," Angers says. "When Thorval met me at Eckernförde, he got out of the limousine, and it drove away."

I lift an eyebrow, wait for the captain to finish.

"There was another man sitting in the back seat." Angers smiles. "I could not see who it was."

32

MONDAY, 0900 HOURS - BRYANT PARK

Flying on her broomstick, a witch dressed all in black stares down at me from the ceiling. Del Vecchio's, a posh wine bar on 40th Street, has decked out for Halloween. There are bright orange pumpkins in the windows to greet passers-by. They smile, with their gap-toothed grins, at their cousins across the street. Those scary fellows occupy the outdoor café that sits between the New York City Library and Bryant Park.

It's a fine fall day. Bright and golden, the sun slants across the street. Low in the sky, its glare casts long shadows. The sky is blue and cloudless. There won't be many more days like this. The days are getting shorter, and next week the clocks will turn back. In the Arctic, night without end is coming to Svalbard.

Police have roped off forty feet of the street in front of the restaurant. They move the barriers aside for two glossy black Suburbans that park next to the curb. The up-armored vehicles are positioned to screen the front of the restaurant from the street.

Stein dismounts from the front passenger seat of the first Suburban. Her driver remains in the vehicle. Two corporate-looking men in dark suits dismount the second Suburban. One walks with Stein to the front and opens the door for her. Inside, he goes to the bar and finds a spot from which he can cover the room. His partner stands outside by the front door.

The men wear clothing cut to conceal weapons. The man at the bar is wearing a suit with a pistol in a hip holster. The man at the front door is wearing a coat that easily conceals Ground Branch's favorite concealed weapon, the H&K MP-7.

A waiter takes Stein's coat. She's wearing her signature black pants suit and low-heeled shoes. I get up and hold her chair for her.

She notices my limp. The cut from Knauss's knife will heal, but it's still fresh. A cloth kerchief conceals my neck wound. Noa's cotton, stained with my blood, sits at the bottom of my duffel.

"Always the gentleman," Stein observes. She accepts the gesture graciously. No feminist statements from the CIA's youngest Assistant Director. "Are you okay?"

"Nothing permanent. It's good to see you."

"And you. Breakfast?"

"No, thanks. Orange juice and coffee."

Stein signals the waiter. I notice our table has been discreetly tucked into a back corner. The restaurant is crowded, but all the tables in our immediate vicinity are empty. It looks like we've been shunned. In fact, Stein's booked all the tables within a fifteen-foot arc.

The waiter is a trim young man wearing a white dress shirt, black pants, red suspenders, and a red bow tie. He offers us menus, but Stein waves them away. She orders coffee and a pitcher of ice-cold orange juice.

When the young man has left, Stein treats me to a smile.

"You look like the cat that ate the Kestrel," I say.

"We have the missiles," she says, "and we got our money back."

"Congratulations."

"We couldn't have done it without you. You'll be very pleased with your bank account."

The waiter brings our coffees and two glasses of orange juice. Sets a massive pitcher before us. I drain my glass in one gulp, pour another.

"Reminds me of the first time we met," Stein says.

We sat in the restaurant of a hotel in El Paso. I liberated a pitcher of orange juice from the buffet. Stein had stared at me with disapproval.

"You liked her, didn't you?" Stein says.

I think of Noa. The waste of innocents. She should never have been caught up in the games of great powers. Perhaps one day I'll visit her father. What could I tell him? I'm bound by a non-disclosure agreement. All I can say is that his daughter died a hero.

"Yes. She didn't deserve to get pulled into this."

Stein's expression darkens. "This business tends to do that."

"There are loose ends."

"What do you mean?" Stein asks. "The Kestrels are safe."

Angers navigated the Type 6 to Black Cove, on the South Coast of Nova Scotia. Canada is a NATO ally, and its Atlantic provinces sport numerous harbors, coves and inlets. The best locations are occupied by hotels and marinas. There are many isolated locations, of which Black Cove is an example.

It's occupied by a small Canadian Coast Guard station with facilities for cutters and air-sea rescue helicopters.

Black Cove is connected to the Atlantic by a long, narrow inlet. Deep woods lined both shores. The Type 6 is a small boat, and it is easy to camouflage it under trees and vegetation. There it will remain undetected by satellites until plans can be made to take off the Kestrels.

Angers and the crew were taken off and held at the Coast Guard station. The Coast Guard discreetly blocked access to the inlet. I was flown to New York and debriefed.

"The Kestrels are safe," I say. "But there's a fifteen-hundred-ton whale in the inlet."

Stein stirs sugar into her coffee. I help myself to more orange juice.

"Where did Thorval get that Type 6 U-Boat?" I lean forward, rest my arms on the table. "Angers took me on a tour. It's military, but there weren't any torpedo tubes. It operated with a skeleton crew of ten men. All the space was used to load the Kestrels."

"Angers knows submarines."

"Yes, he served on a similar boat in the Norwegian Navy. An older model. That's what qualified him for Thorval's operation. Not only was he experienced in deep sea operations and salvage, he could also command a diesel-electric submarine."

"We figured as much when we reviewed his background," Stein says. "Again, there was nothing suspicious about it. Angers was an excellent retired naval officer. Twenty years in the Navy, fifteen in the North Sea."

"That submarine cost a billion dollars, as much as the *Spider*. It's a naval weapons platform. Purchase would be restricted to state actors. The contracts for the purchase of a

Type 6 would fill a small garage. Two years ago, the US coughed up a lot of money to convert a VLCC into the *White Spider*. Did we buy a submarine too?"

Stein recoils. "Doesn't anything get by you?"

"Voss and Noa got past me. A fifteen-hundred-ton whale —I notice."

"The United States did *not* buy that submarine," Stein says firmly. "You have my word."

"Neither did Thorval," I say. "You know the firm that built it. With sanctions, you can put them out of business. They've already told you who they sold it to."

Stein frowns at her coffee, refuses to meet my eyes. "You know who they sold it to."

"I can guess. Why are you so reluctant to tell me?"

"You want your pound of flesh, don't you?" Stein's tone is bitter. "Breed, you have a mean streak."

"We both do."

"*Touché.*"

Stein puts her hands flat on the table, on either side of her coffee cup. Her fingers are long and slender, like she played the violin in college.

"He was my first," she says at last.

My shoulders relax. She's going to tell me everything.

"Nathan's been a friend of my father's for years. He was an engineering wunderkind. Developed new kinds of metal, new manufacturing processes, machines. My father found financing for Conrad International. Together, they made millions. Billions. I met him at my parents' house. When I was studying at Wellesley, he came to visit me."

Stein's voice issues from a clotted throat. I say nothing, allow her to continue.

"Nathan was much older than I was, but I threw myself

at him. He wouldn't have done anything if I hadn't seduced him."

I don't believe that. Had Nathan Conrad been made of iron, he wouldn't have visited a friend's daughter at her college. But Stein believes she took the initiative, and that's what counts.

Stein looks wistful. "Imagine me, this skinny nerd, flirting with a handsome billionaire twenty years older. He was thirty-eight, athletic and handsome. He had all the women he wanted."

I give Stein my most encouraging look.

"It wasn't serious enough to call an affair," she says. "We got together a few times a semester for a year. He inspired me. Nurtured my ambition. We saw each other less when I went to Harvard Law. It became platonic. He was my mentor.

"After Harvard, I pushed hard in my career. First the FBI, then the Company. There were occasions I approached Nathan for help. Back-door financing. His offices in other countries were useful too. I had a shadow support network."

"It sounds like your relationship worked well."

"Yes. When I learned of the *Marshal Zhukov*, he was the first person I thought to approach. In fact, because he had control of Norsk Exploration, he was the only person who could help me. Together, we devised a plan. I sold it to the highest authority."

"So you got the budget to build the *Spider*, and Conrad bought the Type 6 with his own money?"

"Exactly. We built the *Spider* with the Black Budget. I knew how much was being spent because I had to account for it. Nathan had to hide the purchase of the Type 6 from me, so he found the funds elsewhere. I didn't know about the submarine until you reported it. It took a while for me to put everything together. It only made sense when the shooting was over."

"It must have been easy to figure out."

"Yes. Nathan and Thorval never meant for us to learn about the Type 6. The hijackers would escape and leave us with a mystery. The Russians might blow up the *Spider*, and there wouldn't be any evidence to recover."

"There were other reasons to be suspicious."

"Yes, but the Type 6 clinched it. Nathan used his connections to obtain approvals to buy the Type 6. He told the manufacturer and the German government he wanted to convert it to a deep-sea research vessel. The Germans approved the sale on the condition the torpedo tubes were removed. But Nathan didn't care about the torpedo tubes. The feature of the Type 6 that interested him most was the hull."

I lift an eyebrow. "What's so special about the Type 6 hull?"

A nerdy gleam lights up Stein's eyes. "If you compare its cross-section to that of our *Los Angeles* and *Virginia* class boats, you'll see it's more a fat diamond than a circle. As subs have gotten quieter, our anti-submarine tactics have shifted to active sonar. That means we don't just *listen* for noises submarines make. We actively *ping* them. The sonic pulse reveals the sub's location. The Type 6's diamond cross-section deflects active pings. That's why the *Pressley Bannon's* active sonar did not detect it."

"What about the towed array?"

"Towed arrays are less effective in storms. The *Pressley Bannon* had a towed array deployed but failed to pick up the sub."

"When you learned of the sabotage of our helo, you said we'd been compromised from the beginning."

"Yes. Imagine my horror when the realization hit. But I was focused on the Russians. I couldn't figure out how they knew what we were up to. The sabotage meant *someone* did. When Thorval made his move, it was obvious there was a *third* actor involved. It was that third actor who was responsible for the sabotage."

"But Thorval wasn't the type of player who could finance a submarine."

"No." Stein sips her coffee. "Thorval was a resourceful manager. Planning and execution were his strengths. Someone else had to finance him. That fact hovered in the back of my mind all night, but there was too much happening for the solution to click."

"So Nathan Conrad came up with the concept, and hired Thorval to execute."

"Thorval's strength was planning and organization. He recruited the entire gang. He started with the core. Angers, Knauss and Voss. Knauss recruited his two dive teams. The Advance Team under Nygard and the Blue Team. Eighteen divers plus Knauss. I selected two key men. Frank Aron to work the surface, and Sam Pruitt to lead the Gold Team. Sam recruited his own team."

"That meant Thorval and Knauss had to eliminate them."

"Yes. No one imagined Knauss's teams would be rotten to the core. They were ex-military, most had top security clearances *before* they applied. They passed all our background checks."

"Knauss found every bad apple in the bunch," I say. "You know, it's common in special operations. Whenever we're bored, we all plan bank robberies and hijackings as tactical exercises. No one ever carries them out."

"Until they meet someone as rotten as Knauss. Thorval remains a mystery. The Magnus Thorval that Nathan hired does not exist. Everything on his résumé is a fabrication."

"There is one person who can tell you who he is."

"The man who hired him, Nathan Conrad."

"Yes, but all this begs the question, *why* did Conrad do it?"

"I had my team dig up Conrad International's financials. For twenty years, Nathan grew the conglomerate. Interest rates were low, and he leveraged the capital structure to the hilt. When inflation started to rise with the price of energy, Nathan's interest costs rose. He sold assets and retired some debt, but he couldn't deleverage fast enough. He was bank-rupt. Needed that $15 billion to plug the hole in his balance sheet."

Silent, we stare at each other.

"Want to hang around New York for a few days?" Stein asks. "There are a couple of plays I'd like to see."

"Sure." It'll be good to spend time with Stein. "What now?"

Stein looks out the front window at her two Suburbans, the armed Ground Branch operators.

"I'm going to arrest Nathan."

EPILOGUE
REUTERS, MONDAY OCTOBER 18

The Norwegian research ship Spider *was lost Saturday, October 16, in the Greenland Sea, 230 miles north of Svalbard. The casualty occurred in the wake of an arctic storm. Sources speculate that a fire weakened the hull of the modified VLCC, causing it to break in half. A number of the crew were able to reach lifeboats before the ship went under.*

American, Russian, Danish, and Norwegian aircraft are criss-crossing the area in search of survivors. An American destroyer, the USS Pressley Bannon, *and a frigate of the Russian Federation, the* Lenin, *were close by and sped to the rescue. In a display of humanitarian cooperation, the two vessels are recovering survivors. Not all lifeboats have been accounted for. Missing lifeboats, if not destroyed, may have been scattered in the wake of the storm.*

Story ends

ACKNOWLEDGMENTS

I first conceived WHITE SPIDER in 2019, as a standalone novel. I had the climactic battle in mind—the USS Pressley Bannon and the Lenin exchanging missile salvos over the helpless Spider. I also had a loose plot. However, the novel seemed a little "retro" for the time, so I shelved it. Recent events have brought immediacy to the New Cold War, rendering the novel's theme more current.

WHITE SPIDER would not have been possible without the support, encouragement, and guidance of my agent, Ivan Mulcahy, of MMB Creative. I would also like to thank my publishers, Brian Lynch and Garret Ryan of Inkubator Books for seeing the novel's potential. Garret, in particular, provided a great sounding board and his editorial efforts are much appreciated.

Thanks go to Claire Milto of Inkubator Books for her support in the novel's launch. The novel also benefitted from the invaluable feedback of members of my writing group and Beta readers.

If you could spend a moment to write an honest review, no matter how short, I would be extremely grateful. They really do help readers discover my books.

Feel free to contact me at cameron.curtis545@gmail.com. I'd love to hear from you.

ALSO BY CAMERON CURTIS

Made in the USA
Columbia, SC
31 March 2024

33874544R00183